ALSO

MW00465290

The Villagers

DI Claire Falle series

Lonely Hearts

Home Help

Death Bond

The Dr Harrison Lane mysteries

Broken Angels

Beautiful Remains

Deadly Secrets

Innocent Dead

Perfect Beauties

Captive Heart

Winter Graves

Dark Whispers

PLEASE NOTE: SPELLINGS USED IN THIS BOOK
ARE BRITISH ENGLISH.

For American readers, there is a short glossary of British
English slang and abbreviations and police terminology, at
the back of this book.

LONELY HEARTS

GWYN GB

GWYN BENNETT

CHALKY DOG
PUBLISHING

Loneliness: A complex and distressing psychological state resulting from isolation and an inability to connect with others.

1

RACHEL

13TH OCTOBER 2016

The garden was illuminated only by thin leached light from the windows of the house; the curtains opened for that purpose. The dark, moon-less sky meant a thousand shadows had been born, but only one had made her heart pound, turning her skin cold and sending the blood pumping in her veins.

She knew they were watching again and cursed herself. How stupid not to have realised they wouldn't have just given up. Now she'd left herself vulnerable.

Her hands started to shake slightly as she locked up the shed, determined not to leave her animals unprotected. Her breathing was shallow. Muscles tensed for flight, as she listened for the slightest sound from behind: a bush parting, soft footsteps on the lawn, the breath of another on her neck.

Like last time, there was nothing.

Nothing except the endless drone of suburban London traffic and a baby crying in a house across the road, its high-pitched wailing summoning tired parents. She was surrounded by houses, by families, and couples, going about their evening routines: TV, computer games, reading, arguing, all oblivious to her rising fear and what might be about to happen.

Rachel shivered involuntarily, partly because of the cool October evening which had begun to penetrate the thin cotton jumper she'd flung on over her jeans earlier; and partly because of the tide of cold dread washing through her.

She pushed her blonde hair back from her face, pocketed the shed key, and spun on her heels to face the house. It was only ten paces, but the empty lawn gaped wide. Why were they here again? It'd been weeks since the last time and she'd convinced herself they'd gone, scared off by the presence of a man in the house. It was almost as if they knew she was alone tonight.

What if they were already inside? Slipped in unseen while she'd fed the rabbits.

Light poured from the open kitchen doorway in front of her, a threat lit up and welcoming to any passing stalker.

What should she do? Stay outside with the shadows in the open? Or trust the light and the doorway that will enclose her?

Fear won. Her legs started to move as flight and adrenaline took over. If she got into the kitchen, her mobile phone was on the table. She could almost see it from here.

Rachel walked. Each step an eternity. Nearly twisting her ankle as she missed the edge where lawn met footpath.

She was a few feet from the doorway, light bathed her pale face, making her blonde hair glow.

Her phone was just a breath away.

2
___

NEIL

13TH OCTOBER 2016

Neil leant into the bathroom mirror, plucking the last grey hair from his dark eyebrows. The demanding youth culture of digital marketing wasn't his only motivation to hold back the years.

It was as he dropped his gaze to the sink, turning on the tap to wash away his age, that the knife entered his back.

He didn't see who killed him. It wouldn't have mattered much if he had because he was dead, and thus a useless witness, long before anyone found him.

As he careered headfirst into the bathtub, he knocked his bottle of Creed aftershave in with him, smashing and spattering the white porcelain with scent as well as blood.

The pathologist later commented that his was the nicest smelling corpse he'd ever had the pleasure to be acquainted with.

By the time Neil's mobile phone rang in the sitting room, Rachel's number flashing up on the screen, his heart had stopped pumping.

Neil would stay forever young.

CLAIRE

13TH OCTOBER 2016

DI Claire Falle had an epiphany lying naked next to the man who'd shared her bed for the past three years. He would never make her happy, a fact backed up by the dull ache between her legs instead of a pleasurable post-orgasmic throb.

In truth, he'd bored her for months, but it had been convenient. The same reasons so many coppers get together, an understanding of the crap you have to deal with and the shit hours. Unfortunately, Claire no longer wanted convenience. She wanted passion and her own space, neither of which she'd been getting since Jack moved in.

He'd also been getting a bit too heavy lately, broody even. Jack had started talking forward, not just weeks or months, but years.

'This would be a good investment,' he'd said the other night. They were sitting on the sofa, dinner finished, watching *Game of Thrones*. It was one of those rare occasions they were on their own in the flat, without one of Jack's buddies over for a beer. All of a sudden, he'd just come out with it and handed Claire his iPad. Claire expected him to show her a savings account or the latest Kickstarter hit, but instead he'd offered up an estate agency site with an ad that said, "Great neighbourhood. The perfect family starter-home." Claire hadn't known what to say.

Thankfully, Khaleesi and her dragons took that moment to catch Jack's attention, and she was spared any further awkwardness.

4

CLAIRE

14TH OCTOBER 2016

The morning's rude awakening at the hands of her mobile phone saved Claire from any further embarrassing conversations about settling down. She resented the call, though; it was supposed to be her day off. She and Jack were planning to go to Great Yarmouth for a couple of nights. Even if she didn't want to play happy families with him, she missed the sea and could have done with getting out of London. The brown North Sea wouldn't have been a patch on the clear blues and greens of her Jersey childhood waters, but the fresh salty air would have been welcome. She needed to clear her head.

'We've got a murder. Get here as quickly as you can. Leave is cancelled. Sorry.' Detective Chief Inspector Robert Walsh's East End accent came at her down the phone, matter of fact. He gave her an address.

Jack stirred and opened one eye at her. 'Who's that?'

'Bob. I've got to go in. Sorry about today. Why don't you see if Matt's free?'

'Yeah, whatever.' Jack rolled back over.

She was relieved he wasn't going to create a scene. He

knew the score with the job, but her lack of upset at not being able to spend time with him seemed to have gone unnoticed. She'd deal with what's going on in her head another time.

Claire disappeared to the bathroom and took a moment to gaze in the mirror while the shower heated up. She needed a haircut. Her auburn hair was looking scraggy around the edges. It had been a sharp mid-length bob. Maybe she'd try something different next time. More layers might last longer, although when next time was going to come was anyone's guess. She couldn't see herself getting time off for a haircut for a while, not with a murder inquiry on.

The shower dragged her into a state of full consciousness, and when she returned to the bedroom, Jack had fallen back asleep. His mouth was half open, black hair tousled, and he was making little snuffly snores like an upturned hedgehog. She took a moment to look at him, trying to rekindle the way she'd first felt about him three years ago, when just seeing him had made her want to unbutton his trousers. What had killed that passion? Familiarity? Too much of a good thing? Did she simply not find him intellectually stimulating? Had they crossed that line when you know there's nothing left to discover and what's there is simply not enough?

When they'd gone to bed last night Jack had farted, wafting the bed sheets at her, 'Smell the amber nectar.' He'd laughed. She'd got stroppy. Maybe she's prudish or doesn't have a sense of humour, but the laddish behaviour turned her off. She got enough of that at the station. At home, things should be different. Shouldn't they?

She thought about her mother and her parents' thirty-eight-year marriage. She couldn't imagine her dad doing that. Did her mother ever think like Claire? Ever feel the need for an affair just to know she's still capable of passion and lust? Claire couldn't see that either.

Claire had no urge to kiss Jack goodbye, instead, she slipped out of their bedroom and left him sleeping. Her mind buzzing with the prospect of a new case.

THE MAIN ROADS of Shepherd's Bush were already choked with traffic, and as she walked to where she'd parked her car, Claire could hear the rumble of the overground Tube trains. In the distance were the muffled shouts and mechanical noises of the massive building site that was once BBC Television Centre. It was being slowly transformed into apartments, restaurants, and a hotel. She'd hate to think how much even a one-bed flat would cost with their 24-hour concierge and underfloor heating. She'd heard a two-bedroom unit was nearly one million. If that's true, then there wasn't much chance of one of those unless you were already a TV celebrity. Besides, she could think of plenty of places she'd rather be than Shepherd's Bush. There's only so much landscaped gardens can do to detract from the overwhelming grey urban sprawl.

Claire reached her car, but only just managed to escape the parking space because the white van in front and VW Golf behind had boxed her in so tightly there was barely enough room to turn the wheel. The CD player switched on with the engine, and Adele kept her company for the journey.

It was easy to tell when she'd got close to the location of the murder. The London street changed colour, multicoloured residents' cars replaced, or blocked in, by the fluorescent yellow of emergency vehicles. Those at home were twitching their curtains. Those at work would return to a very different street to the one they'd left, but one which would temporarily be united in neighbourly gossip. People who'd not said as much as 'good morning' to each other in years would stop and chat about the terrible goings on.

Despite it being a Friday, a small crowd had gathered outside the flats where the murder took place. Among them Claire could see a couple of local journalists, already tweeting something, desperate to be the first with the next update. They won't have much to go on yet, and she certainly wasn't going to give them anything. Nevertheless, as she walked past and into the building, she saw their phones go up and heard the electronic clicks of their cameras.

'DI Falle, can you tell us who it is?' They knew she wasn't going to, but guessed they were hoping she'd turn round for a better shot. She wouldn't give them that pleasure. Her colleagues were bad enough as it was about the media attention she gets. Some sleazy tabloid had named her 'Baton Babe' last year. Armed only with her truncheon, she'd risked her life to overpower and arrest some knife wielding nutter as he'd threatened a playground full of terrified kids. They wouldn't have given a male copper that tag, would they? Yet in the same sentence as commending her bravery, they'd commented on her 'arresting good looks' and great figure. It wasn't fair. She'd worked hard to be seen as an equal, and they smashed that down with one badly written article.

A young PC directed her up to the third floor where Scenes of Crime Officers had taken over half the corridor. She donned the protective clothing and went in search of Bob.

The flat was nice, expensive TV and sound system, quite minimalist in other ways, especially the galley kitchen. She guessed it was probably a bachelor pad for a young but well-paid professional.

A pack of cleaning materials and cloths lay scattered on the floor just outside the bathroom. Claire quickly surmised that the distraught Eastern European woman being calmed down in the corridor was probably Neil's cleaner who'd discovered his body.

Bob spotted Claire and beckoned her towards the bathroom. Inside, two Scenes of Crime Officers were working: marking, measuring, photographing, and taking samples. The corpse was still upside down in the tub. He was only wearing boxers, so it was easy to see just how much blood had drained down the plughole, with more of it sprayed around the walls. There was one large puncture wound in his back, the bloodless skin giving the impression of cut pastry.

'Looks like the attacker stabbed him in the back while he was standing, and he then fell into the bath.' Bob didn't waste time with pleasantries. She could see him logging and assessing the scene like a well-programmed scanner.

'Why didn't he see them in the mirror?' Claire was standing in the doorway and it was clear the large mirror above the sink gave a good view of the whole bathroom.

'Tap was still running when the cleaner got here, so perhaps he had his head down over the sink. Maybe he knew the attacker. There's no sign of forced entry.'

Claire nodded in thought. 'Mirror could have been steamed. What's that smell?'

'Creed. Expensive stuff.' Bob motioned to the smashed bottle that could just be seen under the corpse.

'Nice.' She took another look at the scene, recording the details: the tweezers on the floor by the sink, the row of expensive hair and body treatments. This was a man who took pride in his appearance.

She looked at the upside-down corpse again. She couldn't see his face, but from the toned body she could tell he was a young man. For a moment Claire allowed herself to see him as a person, not a case. Then her eyes moved on.

The drips of blood running down the white tiles reminded her of a poem she used to love as a child. Something about two raindrops having a race down the windowpane. She could even remember the book, *When We Were Six* by A A Milne. But this wasn't a scene for a child's eyes. The drops of blood had dried and congealed in place. Race over.

When it was clear in her head, she backed out and took a look around the rest of the flat. A mobile phone had been dusted for fingerprints and was being bagged ready to be given to the investigating team.

'Three missed calls,' Margaret Taylor, the senior SOCO, said to Claire. 'All from the same woman.'

'Thanks.'

In the kitchen, she saw one plate on the side next to a single wine glass.

'Looks like he ate alone,' she said to Bob, who had come up alongside her.

'Unless the killer took away their plate and glass knowing we'd find their DNA!'

Claire frowned and nodded. These days the level of information on the Internet and in TV crime dramas meant even the less cerebrally endowed criminals could make their job harder.

'The flat belongs to a Neil Parsons,' said Bob, leafing through some letters and paperwork. 'Looks like our bathtub man likes the camera,' he added, nodding at a gallery of photographs showing a handsome young man with various gorgeous women and groups of drunken men. In every photograph, Neil was the centre of attention.

Claire saw the face of their bathroom corpse for the first time. Twinkling blue eyes, all-year round suntan, and meticulously coiffed hair. Good looking, but in a self-absorbed kind of way.

'Maybe his ego was his downfall,' she replied.

'Crime of passion. I'll bet fifty quid on it,' said Bob.

Claire raised her eyebrows at his certainty. Then something drew her attention to the small desk by the window. Neil's laptop sat waiting to be collected for evidence, but it was the papers that caught her eye.

'SoulMates Dating Agency. You wouldn't have thought someone like him has a problem meeting women, would you?' She flicked through the printed pages of profiles. Smiling women all hoping to meet their Mr Right. They'd be disappointed if they were pinning their hopes on Neil. Some pages had ticks or crosses on them.

'Any sign of drugs?' Claire asked to the room.

'Nothing so far,' one of the SOCOs, the thin pasty one with eyes like a weasel, replied.

'Let's get back and get set up,' Bob said to her, already heading out the flat.

Claire took one last look around. The place was crawling with SOCOs, hard to see it as a home and not a crime scene right now. She'd come back again later.

'Did he drive a car?' she asked the uniformed officer at the door.

'We're looking for it,' he replied. 'Got an Audi key but parking's a mare round here so it could be a couple of streets away.'

'OK, thanks.'

She left, knowing in a few hours she'd be reacquainting herself with Neil on the autopsy table.

RACHEL

14TH OCTOBER 2016

She wasn't used to being a victim, feeling vulnerable, the cold grip of fear. Rachel woke after a disturbed sleep to see the chair she'd jammed against her bedroom door lit by the pale autumn morning sun.

A wave of nausea washed through her, the result of too little sleep and the memory of her slow progress through the house last night. Clutching a large kitchen knife, she'd locked every door and window before going into each room, opening every cupboard in the house and checking she really was alone. Once she felt able to show her back to a dark room, she'd peered carefully through the curtains into the back garden, searching for signs of someone out there.

At the end of the garden, where the fence became hedgerow, she'd seen a shadow and the flash of electronic light, a mobile screen. She'd tried Neil again. His presence would scare them away, but he hadn't picked up.

Eventually, Rachel barricaded herself into the bedroom, staying fully clothed, ready for action.

In the daylight, and with a tired mind, she began to

question the events of last night. Had there really been somebody there? Was she just being paranoid? Was it the tiredness making her jumpy, sending her heart racing when a loose strand of hair fell across one of her eyes?

Rachel headed into the shower, locking the bathroom door and relishing being able to relax under the hot water which pounded her skin, turning it flush pink. This had to stop, she told herself. She won't be bullied like this. Neil couldn't be relied on. She couldn't rely on anyone, for that matter. She'd get dressed, go out, and investigate. Maybe get some security cameras fitted, find out if there really was someone watching her, and if so, who. She had the day off because she was working tomorrow, Saturday; it meant she could get ready again for the night-time. The daylight would give her courage.

Once dressed, the first thing Rachel did was check on the rabbits. It was comforting to pick them up and feel their warm bodies against hers. She sat for a few moments watching them tuck into the lettuce leaves, chomping through them from side to side like manic old typewriters working through a sheet of paper. Their simple needs and complete ignorance of her fear gave some respite. She hadn't felt this vulnerable since she was eleven years old.

RACHEL

FEBRUARY 1994

Rachel knew there was something wrong even before she'd opened the tired wooden door into their farmhouse kitchen. Her right shoulder ached from carrying the schoolbag, which bulged and threatened to burst its zip, spewing out the books inside.

She'd no idea why she was nervous. What had changed? What had made her uneasy—but for a moment she hesitated—preferring the pain from her shoulder to the possibility of what was beyond the door. She re-traced the circle of the smiley face she'd made sometime last week, in the dusty grime of the opaque glass window. Then, smile renewed, she pressed down on the metal handle and entered.

The kitchen was empty, devoid not only of her mother but any scent of cooking. The air hung undisturbed, holding its breath for fear of scattering the dust particles gliding on the shafts of light.

'Mum!' Rachel shouted into the house. Her dad would still be in the fields or working with the herd in the milking barn. There was no reply, so she scanned the kitchen worktops for a note. They were empty. The gadget-less surfaces wiped clean, breakfast things long since washed and put away. Nothing to be seen, except the kettle and the stains and gouges of family life.

She took her coat off, putting it over the back of a chair. She was thirsty after the walk home, so headed to the fridge to get some of the unpasteurised milk her father always brought in each day. The fridge was another surprise; it was full. The shelves packed with food: ready-made meals, pasta, sausages, and yogurts. Her mum had obviously been shopping, blown the month's budget in one go by the look of it. That wasn't like her. Maybe she'd won some money, come into an inheritance? Perhaps they had visitors? Had Rachel forgotten a birthday or other celebration? Even at eleven, Rachel knew money was a bad word in their house, its mention always a precursor to arguments and tears. She poured herself a glass of milk. One thing they always had in abundance.

Just as she'd finished tipping the cold creamy liquid down her throat, she heard him. The noise made her freeze, ears straining, goosebumps rising on her neck and arms. What was it?

She heard it again, a wounded animal moaning. Was it a cow injured? No, the sound was coming from inside the house. Should she run into the yard? Seek out her father or George and Reg, the two men who'd helped him with the cows for as long as she could remember?

Rachel's heart pounded in its small frame and she stood shock still, taking tiny, panicked breaths that barely made her chest move. She reached out for the wall to steady herself, placing her palm against its cool surface.

There it was again, a deep guttural moan. Something was dying in pain. Slowly she stepped forward, edging towards the hallway and closer to the noise, one eye on the back door in case she needed to escape. Her instincts told her running was going to be much better and that whatever she found beyond the kitchen couldn't be good. She stayed. An invisible force pulling at her inquisitive mind.

Into the hall now, there was the moaning again. It was coming from their sitting room. She stopped a moment, listening so hard her ears almost hurt.

'Sally,' she heard. It was her dad calling to her mum, although his voice sounded strange. Relief flooded through Rachel, freeing up her fear shackled legs. Did he need help? She rushed into the sitting room.

The sight of her father on the floor alone, bent double, his face glistening with grief, eyes red raw in pain, kicked her right in the stomach.

'Dad?' she asked. 'Are you OK?' He looked up, the vacant gaze of the shocked. Rachel's eyes dropped to his feet. He had his boots on. He never wore his boots in the house.

'Rachel!' He tried to stand, but the effort was too much.

Rachel remembered to breathe.

'Dad, what's wrong? Are you hurt?'

He snorted back more tears and shook his head.

'Where's Mum?' He was really scaring her now. Dads don't behave in this way; adults shouldn't be like this. It wasn't right. 'Dad,' she said it more quietly, instinct kicking in, and knelt on the floor beside him. His dirty boots had left smears of mud and cow excrement on the carpet, the brown merging in with the copper swirls of the pattern. Her mum would be so cross.

'Dad,' she said again, touching his hand this time.

'Your mum,' he said at last, looking up at her. 'Your mum has…'

Rachel's body tingled with the alarm of fear. She nearly clasped her hands over her ears, not wanting to hear the next words. She knew, from the state of her dad, that they'd be words to change her life forever. Bad words.

'Your mum has gone,' her dad said finally, gripping onto her arm. He seemed to battle to form the words in his mouth, face contorting in the struggle. 'She's dead,' he finally said, with more effort.

'No. No,' Rachel heard a voice like hers come from somewhere, and she pulled her arm free, as though breaking the connection would stop him. Stop this nonsense.

'Car. She had a car crash,' he continued, glazed eyes not focusing on her or the result of his words.

Rachel collapsed; all strength gone. Her mum dead? No, she couldn't be. She was here this morning. She kissed her before she left for school. Warm and very much alive.

A surge of adrenaline kicked in. She scrambled to her feet and ran out to the yard where her mother parked her car. En route, the threadbare hall carpet nearly tripped her up, catching her toe in its skeletal fibres, and slamming her shoulder into the wall. She didn't feel it.

She burst out of the kitchen into the fresh air. Even that had turned sour. The space where the car should be was empty, just a dirty brown stain where the oil leaked.

Back into the house, up the stairs. She wasn't in their bedroom. She wasn't in the bathroom. Nothing but her things and the lingering scent of her.

Rachel pounded back down the stairs to the sitting room. Her dad was still on the floor, exactly where she'd left him.

'Why Mum?' She shouted at him, 'Why?'

There was no answer, just sobs. Her dad not even half the man he'd been that morning.

They sat like this until the room grew dark, and Rachel shivered with the cold. Or perhaps it was shock. When she finally got up off the floor, her legs were shaky. She walked, like an elderly woman, over to the old electric heater in the corner and flicked it on. She watched the element inside until it was glowing red, her eyes blurring over, gaze fixed. For a second she forgot and then it hit her again, a two-ton truck of emotional bricks ramming into her consciousness, splitting open her heart. Why would God do this? He's cruel. Or maybe he doesn't exist at all. How can he be a good God, why would he take her mother from them? How can her mother be here this morning and gone by the afternoon?

She turned to look at her father. He was rocking back and forth, clutching his knees and staring ahead. Should she get some help? But who? They didn't have any relatives living near, in fact they had very little family at all.

Outside she could hear the herd being led from the milking barn, their hooves clattering on the cobbles and the odd shout from Reg or George as they shoo-d them along. How can life carry on as normal when the heart of her very being had been ripped out?

7

CLAIRE

14TH OCTOBER 2016

The team had already kicked into action back at the station. The Major Incident Room almost assembled. Everyone was nose-to-screen or setting up equipment. As Claire walked in, a man overtook her with a trolley laden down with a large shredder and two more computer screens. Another man followed, wheeling two large whiteboards. Claire recognised the woman who greeted them. It was Lena Kowalski, who was Office Manager on her last case. She hoped this one would be more successful.

Claire scanned the room for other familiar faces. There were a fair few, and it looked like a good team. Everyone wore the look of people completely focused on the task.

'One hour,' shouted Bob above the bustle. 'I want as much info as possible on our victim.' He disappeared behind a computer screen and before being swamped by various officers seeking or giving him information.

Claire sank into her chair and logged into the system. This was her first murder enquiry at a full Detective Inspector rank. She'd been assigned to Bob, the Senior

Investigating Officer, with the idea that she worked towards Assistant SIO. Claire needed to impress. She knew there were a few eyebrows raised at her promotion, and a few noses put out of joint after the last enquiry. It was never easy when you knew your colleagues failed in their duty of care. Jackie Stiller would still be alive today if they'd taken more notice of her situation. If they'd taken more notice of what Claire had said. She deserved the promotion, but there was a little part of her that couldn't help feeling she'd profited from someone else's misery and misfortune.

The intel was already coming in. Their corpse in the bath was definitely Neil Parsons, 31, and no previous. Claire looked into the eyes of the dead and wondered what they'd seen or done, which had led to them being closed forever. He was just one year younger than she was; a good-looking guy, completely unrecognisable from the purple-faced corpse in the crime scene reports.

She still saw each case as a life, a human being. That was important. She'd met a DCI last year who'd crossed that line. He'd become numbed by the daily acquaintance of death and violence, and it had turned his heart black. There's no coming back from that.

'Hey, Baton, want a coffee?' Claire bristled. Detective Sergeant Lewis was a mate of Jack's and consequently his naturally irreverent personality was decidedly over familiar. To say Claire hated that nickname was an understatement. Trouble was, everyone at the station knew it, so she was an easy target.

Claire swallowed hard and breathed in deeply. Sod it, she would have one. If he was going to irritate her then he could bloody well fork out for a coffee.

'Yes, thanks, Lew. Latte.'

'No sugar, right?' He beamed back at her.

She wondered why he didn't get that broken tooth in

the front fixed. Maybe it took the focus from his balding head. She berated herself for being such a bitch.

'Right,' she replied, forcing herself to smile back. Last time she'd looked in his face it was after he'd been racing Jack with Jager Bombs, just before he'd run into the bathroom and puked the whole lot back up again. Jack had simply crawled into bed and attempted to initiate sex by pawing her roughly and breathing alcoholic fumes that would have been enough to keep an Olympic torch burning for the entire Games. Finally, he'd fallen asleep on the job before rolling off and snoring for the rest of the night.

Claire had lain awake working through an imaginary crime scene, visualising the autopsy report which would show death by alcohol poisoning—after she'd carefully smothered him with his own pillow. She didn't of course. Instead, she'd lain awake for most of the night, occasionally slapping him or rolling him over in an effort to stop the noise, but unable to escape to the sofa because Lew had crashed out on it. She'd earned a bloody coffee.

One hour later and they were all assembled, an expectant buzz of chatter as DCI Bob Walsh stood up.

'OK, I want your full attention.' The room fell silent as his voice reined in the dozen or so men and women who had been discussing everything from the state of Neil Parson's bank account to why the sergeant's wife was asking for a boob job for her birthday.

'Right. This one's spotless, no previous, a seemingly respectable young professional. No signs this is a burglary. It's going to attract attention. We need a quick result. Sarah, you took a statement from the cleaner who was first on the scene?'

'Yes, sir.' DS Sarah Potter jumped to attention. 'She said everything was exactly as she'd expect, and it was only the sound of a tap running that took her to the bathroom where she discovered the deceased. "Lovely man", is how she described him. Had a few women through the flat, and the neighbour corroborated that—on the bedroom side— if you know what I mean. But no sign of any criminal activity.'

'Any chance he could have been an escort?' Bob queried, his mind and half the room's working overtime on the bedroom noise issue.

'Nothing so far, just a good-looking bloke,' Sarah replied.

'Who's assigned research?' Bob's fact hungry mind had already moved on.

'Me, sir.'

'OK, Tom, what you got?' he barked at the nervous DS. Tom Knight was one of those young men who'd yet to fill their frame; an Alsatian puppy growing into his paws. His blond hair was thin and wispy, which added to the youthful effect.

'So,' he started, consulting his screen, 'Neil Parsons, 31, works for Crowther and Taylor as a Digital Marketing Exec. We've requested bank statements and phone records. He's paid well. Enough for a good lifestyle for a singleton. We've got officers at his place of work now taking statements.'

'Neighbours?'

'Nothing so far of any consequence, just say he's a nice bloke, and it's a real shock. All have clean records.' Tom looked up at Bob apologetically.

'CCTV?' Bob moved on, throwing his query towards the back of the room where Sam, a civilian analyst, was half listening and half engrossed in a screen.

'Nothing at the flats, unfortunately. System broke a week or so ago and the caretaker hadn't got round to fixing it. We've got two at a small supermarket and a bookies along the road running south. Two more which are ours at lights going north and west, but the area is by no means watertight. We're plotting the potential escape routes and checking CCTV now.'

'I want maps on the board,' Bob said. Sam nodded.

'SOCO?' Bob called out to Margaret Taylor, Scenes of Crime lead.

Margaret snapped to attention. 'Obviously preliminary, but it looks like they've been careful. No signs of a forced entry, so potentially someone he knew. Looks like a large blade, meant to kill. No evidence of a struggle. The autopsy should confirm a single wound to the back, which did the job it intended, so the killer likely knew what they were doing. They would have got sprayed. From the blood patterns I'd say we're looking for someone tall and well built. We'll get a more detailed estimate once we've modelled it.'

Bob nodded, taking it all in. He sucked in some air to fertilise his thoughts.

'OK, so chances are we're looking at a male killer and potentially premeditated?'

Margaret nodded. 'One thing I would add is that there's a knife block in the kitchen, only sharp knives in the flat, and none of them are missing.'

Bob turned to address the room again. 'I want a list of possible motives and suspects on this board by lunchtime. The number of women could be important. Is he scamming them, or even blackmail? Is it a disgruntled ex-lover or cheated husband? I want every inch of his financial affairs checked. Sam, we need CCTV commandeered and looked through within a half-mile radius. The killer could have parked up and walked to the flats rather than risk a vehicle being seen. Anyone gives you any crap about handing over footage, pass them on to me. If this guy was sprayed, how did he get away without someone noticing? Lewis, track down the victim's friends. We've got a family liaison officer with the parents in Cornwall. If they come up with any names, I'll let you know. Take Tom with you. I want to know where Neil Parsons went, what he liked to do, and who he did it with. The rest of you see the Action Manager for your tasks.' Bob turned to Claire now. 'Falle, you and I are gonna go see the woman who called our victim three times last night, find out what she knows and if she realises her impeccable timing.'

8

CLAIRE
14TH OCTOBER 2016

When they left the station, a pale October sun was taking the chill out of the air, but it was still hazy. Claire wondered if Jack had gone to Norfolk after all. Would have been a nice weekend for it. Forecast said it would hit 18 degrees over the next two days.

'Hate cases like this,' Bob was moaning. 'Nothing to go on, no bloody clue why someone would want to skewer Neil Parsons. I still reckon it's a crime of passion.'

'Could be,' Claire agreed. 'Certainly sounds like he's got the potential to have picked the wrong woman. But what I don't get is why there's no forced entry. He was in his boxers so he's not going to have invited someone in—other than a lover or really good friend. So if it's an angry husband, how did they get in?'

Bob frowned. 'If you're asking me, I think it's looking more likely the killer is a pro.'

'What you mean a hit man or something?'

'Not unheard of, is it? Passions run deep. The jealous will do anything. A single wound intended to kill isn't your usual frenzied attack by an angry spouse.'

Claire thought about her and Jack. She couldn't imagine being that upset that she'd kill someone if he was having an affair; but then it was probably more about pride than love. She'd give him a call a bit later, see if he'd gone. If he had, then that would mean she'd got the flat and bed to herself—bliss! Typical that she'll probably not be getting that much time to enjoy it. They'd be at the station until late and then up again early, unless this girlfriend of Neil's provides a revelation.

She looked out the window as they sped through Hammersmith. White plastic sheeting, ripped and shroud like, flapped in the branches of a skeletal tree. Ghostly rubbish.

'Do we know anything about the woman we're going to see?' she asked Bob, turning to look at him.

His hair was white around the temples and pewter grey elsewhere. He was concentrating on the road so his eyes had creased at the corners, brow furrowed. On his left cheek a neat, straight white scar prevented any stubble from erupting. It was the result of being a little less attentive than he should have been when arresting a schizophrenic who'd just murdered his parents and was convinced Bob was taking away their bodies to harvest their souls for some devilish army.

'Not a lot apart from the fact she doesn't appear to be married, although that doesn't, of course, rule out a jealous boyfriend.'

'She not work?' asked Claire.

'Day off apparently, which is lucky for us. She knows we're coming, but I haven't told her why.'

Claire nodded in acknowledgement and resumed looking out the window. Bob started tapping a tune in his head on the steering wheel. It was impossible to tell what song it was, and for Claire it was irritating. She was relieved when he stopped to change gears; his wedding band clunking against the steering wheel as his hand returned. He never talked much about his wife and kids. They have two boys, both grown up, but never any talk about what they're doing, if they've come home for a visit. As far as Claire could work out, and according to Jack, Bob's wife, Debbie, lived her own life. She'd long ago given up the dream of marital bliss and instead lived from new kitchen to new appliance, bridge to bowls. Claire wondered who Bob was at home where his rank meant nothing.

He'd been a father figure to her in the last year. It was to Bob she'd turned for advice when she hadn't known what to do in the Jackie Stiller case. They'd worked together briefly on an enquiry a couple of months before, and she trusted him. Some people are like that, they get your trust and your respect just by being them. Bob wasn't one of the ambitious ones, but he was a damned good copper. Claire could forgive him for his annoying steering wheel tapping.

They drove across Hammersmith Bridge Road, trundling over the suspension bridge. Claire looked up at the Georgian structure, wondering how it had survived the pounding of modern vehicles, and not cracked and crumbled down into the murky brown waters of the Thames.

Gradually bedsit land gave way to middle-class family suburbs. Windows covered with blankets, and doorways paired with panels of buzzers for the multitude of flats and bedsits, become neatly curtained and well-maintained homes. If you paid the price you needed to for a house in the London suburbs, then you were going to look after it.

Big white pillared house fronts with arch shaped windows and immaculate gravel drives lined the road, before slightly more modest and modern properties lead them into Barnes. The landscape became leafier, green sports fields and parks. Along Rocks Lane, trees not houses framed the roadside.

They reached the tip of Wimbledon Common before heading down Parkside and off up a side street. Claire was jealous already. Her tiny excuse of a flat in Shepherd's Bush had no open space of its own, and its only views were into other people's windows or the back of the Indian takeaway next door. On hot nights they were constantly bombarded with the smell of spices, the choice of suffocating in the heat being less preferable to death by Tandoori.

Bob peered through the windscreen. 'Number 32,' he said.

Claire scanned the houses on both sides and pointed to an opening in hedges. There was no gate, just a short gravel drive which they pulled into, behind a black Corsa.

'This must cost a whack,' said Bob, voicing what they were both thinking. 'I'd struggle to afford this on police wages.'

Claire scanned the facade of a neat 1950s house. The garden was minimalist, designed for easy care. Windows clean, not like the dust spattered windows of her flat. Other than that, there was no character, no ornaments or themed door knocker, nothing stuck to the windows or visible in the darkness of the house inside. No indication of who lived there.

She got out and knocked.

There was no reply. Bob, who had caught up with her after pocketing the car keys, also knocked. Nothing. They stepped back from the front door and surveyed the house. Its blank eyes stared back, unblinking.

'She definitely said she'd be in,' Bob said, pulling his

mouth into a downward grimace. He stepped forward and knocked again.

To the left a green side gate, presumably to the back garden, was just visible. It was from there they heard the sound of a woman's voice. They exchanged glances, confirming they'd both heard something, and walked to the gate. Bob tried the latch. It opened.

The pair of them entered a reasonably sized back garden, a mix of lawn and patio, bordered by fencing and thick hedges and framed by the blocks of flats and other houses. At the back of the garden was a large shed, and in front of that a trim, denim-covered bottom was bending over, tending to two rabbits in a large run.

'There you go, Reg,' the blonde head said.

Claire could tell that Bob was appreciating the tidy arse in front of him because he didn't say a word to disturb her.

'Miss Hill?' Claire called out as they crossed the garden towards her.

The blonde woman in front of them jumped, startled, spinning round fast.

'Sorry, I didn't mean to startle you,' Claire began, and saw the fright dissipate on her pretty face. The woman in front of her was verging on petite, slim with blonde hair just beyond shoulder length. She wore make-up, but not much, just enough to enhance her blue eyes.

Bob spoke next, spell broken.

'Ms Hill? I'm DCI Robert Walsh and this is DI Claire Falle. I called you earlier.'

'Yes, of course.' Rachel's face relaxed a little more, and she gave them a tentative smile, but it soon clouded over again. 'You didn't say what you wanted…'

Her question hung between them. Bob batted it away.

'Is there somewhere we can talk?' he asked. Rachel

seemed to shake herself out of whatever thoughts were rushing round her mind.

'Let me just make sure these guys are secure and we can go inside.' She bent again, closing the top of the run, gently rubbing the nose of one of the inquisitive rabbits.

Claire looked at the shed where a small toolbox sat by the door with a new alarm lock ready to be fitted.

'Have there been shed thefts round here lately?' She nodded at the box and both Bob and Rachel looked at it too.

Rachel hesitated, looked at Claire, and then away again.

'No, not that I'm aware. I keep the rabbits in there at night, so just making sure they're secure.'

Claire got the distinct impression that she was holding something back.

'There.' Rachel made one last check on the rabbit run. 'This way,' and started walking towards the house.

'No, Mr Hill?' Bob asked, with the nonchalant air of a police officer digging for info, but trying not to sound like he was questioning.

'No,' she simply replied, before leading them through into the sitting room at the front of the house. 'What's this about?' Her face again registered the worry behind the question. Thick lashes quivered over her blue eyes as she scanned the faces of the two police officers in front of her.

Bob and Claire sat down, a cue to their host to do the same. She hovered before realising they wouldn't start until she too was seated, and so slowly settled into the opposite chair. Expectant.

'Miss Hill, could you tell us your relationship to Neil Parsons?' Bob launched straight in. Claire would have engaged in a bit more chit chat first, put her at ease, but Bob was keen to get on.

A ripple of surprise flowed over her face. She was clearly taken aback.

'Well, he's a client at the agency where I work and we're friends of sorts, I guess… Is he in trouble?' She looked from one to the other.

'Miss Hill, I'm sorry to tell you that Mr Parsons was found dead this morning.'

'Dead! Why? How?'

Both police officers were watching her every move closely. The shock seemed genuine. Bob avoided her questions.

'There are several phone calls on Mr Parson's mobile from yourself. Were you expecting to see him last night?'

She shook her head.

'Not expecting. I was calling to see if he could come over and help me with something, that's all.'

'Three calls?' Bob pressed.

'Yes, I thought maybe he'd missed them because he was driving or on a Tube or something. You know how noisy London is, it's easy to miss a phone call.'

'Were you in all evening?' Bob continued.

'Yes, I was. Why? Oh my God, I heard on the news that a man had been murdered in his flat. That's not Neil is it?'

The colour very visibly drained from her face now. Claire looked to Bob.

'I'm sure you appreciate we're currently conducting our investigations and so we can't share any information with you.'

She nodded.

'Could you tell us how long you've known Neil?'

Rachel shook her head and Claire wasn't sure if it was sadness, disbelief, or she didn't want to answer.

'If you'd like a moment?' Bob's voice softened.

Rachel seemed to pull herself together and continued. 'I've known him about three months. He joined the dating agency, SoulMates, where I work. We didn't date or anything, that's not allowed. He was just easy company and used to come over for dinner and a chat occasionally. He's one of those guys who like female company, seems to prefer being around women to hanging out with a bunch of lads.'

Claire noticed she was still talking about Neil in the present tense.

'He has three sisters, so I guess that might be why.' Rachel trailed off.

'Do you know who Neil might have been seeing?' Bob asked.

'What, girlfriend?' Rachel clarified.

Bob nodded.

'We'll have records of who we paired him with, but to be honest, I think there were several over the months. He seemed to be looking for someone who was going to blow him away, stop him from needing to keep on looking, if you know what I mean. That's why he joined SoulMates.'

Bob thought a moment.

Claire took the opportunity to ask a question.

'Did he ever mention if he was seeing someone perhaps he shouldn't? Someone who was married or attached, maybe?'

Rachel turned her gaze to Claire. Her eyes looked into hers, and Claire could see her wondering why she'd asked that question.

'Not that I'm aware of. He never mentioned anyone outside of the agency. I'm sorry I can't remember who he'd been paired with. The last time we spoke it was a quick chat at one of our events.'

'So you keep records of who each client is dating?' Bob

asked again. Claire could see he was grasping onto a thread of hope this case might get solved quickly.

'Yes, of course, but I can assure you we're not Ashley Madison. We want to help people find long-lasting relationships and so screen our clients to make sure they're not married. I am…'

A knock on the front door interrupted Rachel mid-flow. She frowned.

'Excuse me,' she said, rising to go to the door.

Claire was by the window and as Rachel went to open the front door, she looked at who was outside. A young guy stood holding a bouquet of white lilies wrapped in black.

Claire tapped Bob's shoulder to tell him to look. He raised his eyebrows, and they listened to the exchange in the hallway.

'For me?' They could hear a surprised Rachel say. Then the door closed, and it sounded like she took the flowers through into the kitchen. One minute passed. Two minutes. Five. When eventually she returned to the sitting room, there was a new look on her face—a look of fear.

'Everything OK?' Claire asked her.

'I…' Rachel seemed to wrestle with what to say.

'Have you recently had a family bereavement?' Claire pressed.

'No.' Rachel almost whispered back.

'Miss Hill,' said Bob. 'Is something wrong?'

Her face twitched, and she fumbled with her sleeve. The vulnerability made her look younger.

'They were for me.' She looked at them both, from one to the other.

Claire wasn't quite sure what she meant. Obviously they were for her, they were delivered to her house.

'They were lilies,' Rachel continued. 'For me, "Rachel RIP". I think I'm being stalked by someone.'

UNKNOWN

14TH OCTOBER 2016

Outside in the shadows, someone was watching. They had seen the two police officers arrive, watched as the flowers were delivered. The expression on Rachel's face was definitely worth the effort. It was annoying that the cops were now involved, but it didn't matter.

What do they make of Rachel Hill? Did the man find her attractive? Was the woman officer sympathising with her?

Rachel thinks the police will bring her protection, but she is so wrong. She has everything to fear and no one to help her.

Rachel will be alone again tonight, but she won't be on her own.

CLAIRE

14TH OCTOBER, 2016

Claire was on to the florists straight away.

'Not very original, is it?' she said to Bob.

'No, but it's effective, an easy threat. My bet is they paid the florist cash and there's no CCTV.'

Bob was proved right.

Before they left Rachel's house, Bob called for some uniformed back-up to make sure the house and garden were secure. Local patrols would also be asked to include the street on their routes, to act as a deterrent.

Claire went round the back of the garden to where Rachel said she'd seen someone last night. The ground was well trodden with some definite footprints in the earth. As it was the outskirts of London, pretty much everywhere had been walked over by someone, but she called it in to Margaret and her SOC team. They could get a quick imprint of the shoes before it got dark, just in case they found any at Neil's flat and could compare.

'Did you find anything?' Rachel asked her when she got back to the house.

'Footprints, nothing else.'

She looked upset.

'Why didn't you call us last night?' Claire questioned.

'I didn't think it would be taken seriously. Not being rude, but you read these stories in the papers where women go to the police and either nothing happens, or they're made to feel guilty themselves. Look at what happened to Lily Allen, and she's a celebrity. I wasn't even 100% sure it was about me, not until the flowers came,' she replied.

Claire understood. She knew that when it came to stalkers, the record book wasn't exactly great. With only 1% of recorded cases making it to prosecution, it was one inequality in law she'd like to change, especially after what happened to Jackie Stiller. She'd sworn she'd make sure she always listened to victims so she could stop another tragedy like Jackie's.

'We will take it seriously, I promise,' she reassured her. 'I've asked our Scenes of Crime team to come and take some casts of the footprints. We'll collect whatever evidence we can.'

Claire went to find Bob, who was just finishing a phone call.

'Control logged a call from a neighbour. Saw someone loitering last night. Uniform attended, but they'd gone. I'll get someone to take a statement from the neighbour, see if they got any kind of look at our stalker,' he told her.

'What about timings? Does it fit in with Neil's murder?' Claire asked.

'Potentially. We've no idea if they're connected, but seeing as we've come here today after seeing the phone calls Miss Hill made, and they knew each other, I'd say we need to take this seriously. I don't want another corpse on my hands.'

. . .

Back at the incident room, the place was buzzing with activity and the smell of various police canteen lunches, eaten at desks, hung in the air. On the board, someone had put up social media messages posted by Neil. Bob went straight up to look. *Home alone with an M&S curry #nightin*. The Twitter post was accompanied by a photo of the plate they'd seen at the flat earlier, complete with food. It was posted last night at 7.46 p.m. There were two other tweets which both referred to great nights out and had an *@madmikey888* tagged in. Michael Stratton was listed on the right-hand side under 'Known Acquaintances'.

'Someone in touch with this Michael Stratton?' Bob asked Tasha, the team's Action Manager.

She checked her screen. 'DS Lewis is on his trail, sir,' she replied.

Bob nodded.

'Funny thing is, sir,' she added. 'Michael was prolific on social media, about twenty tweets a day, every day, only he's posted nothing in the last couple of weeks.'

Bob raised his eyebrows and looked back at the board. 'Get someone to find me all they can on both men's social media accounts, would you?'

Tasha nodded and got to it.

Claire checked her watch. It was nearly 2 p.m. and the duty pathologist was doing them a favour, rushing through the post-mortem to help the investigation. She needed to get to the morgue in half an hour to see what he'd found, but she'd enough time to do a little bit of digging first.

She wanted to know more about the dating agency and Rachel Hill. Could someone from the agency have killed Neil and be after Rachel, too? SoulMates had a Facebook page with over 1600 likes, and it was full of the usual stuff you'd expect. Blog posts and articles on how to find your ideal partner, how to choose the perfect outfit, what star sign are you most compatible with etc. Not surprisingly, there was nothing that would suggest that it was a hotbed for vicious murderers. Seemed like they ran loads of local events, though. An ideal hunting ground for a stalker.

She googled Rachel and to her surprise, apart from her bio on the SoulMates agency website, there was nothing about her at all. No social media accounts, no other record of her having worked anywhere else. She jotted that down, too. Could she have had another name or even identity? Or was she really one of those rare people nowadays who avoided having an online presence?

Neither Rachel nor Neil had anything in the police records. They were a squeaky clean couple. But one of them was dead and the other being threatened. What was the connection?

THE DUTY PATHOLOGIST had already done the worst work by the time Claire got there. Although she was OK with dead bodies and had seen some horrific murders, she still didn't like seeing somebody get opened up. Put her off eating meat for several days. Mark Rodgers was doing the medical examination, and he knew that about Claire. He'd been chatting to her one day as he started the opening up process and had witnessed her getting paler and paler. It wasn't for everyone. She was glad it was him on the job today, for lots of reasons.

The first thing that hit Claire as she walked into the examination room was the overpowering aroma of Creed aftershave. She sniffed and wrinkled her nose, not entirely sure if it was a good thing or not. If she ever smelled the aftershave again, she'd be forever reminded of Neil's body laid out on the metal table, but she had to admit it beat gastric odours and cleaning fluids.

'Best smelling cadaver you've ever sent me.' Mark smiled at her. 'You can tell it's good stuff, still pungent even now.'

Claire grimaced back at him and smiled.

'I'll get you a bottle for Christmas.'

Mark was a good-looking bloke, a bit older than she'd usually go for, in his mid-forties, but she liked his quiet intelligence and gentle manner. He had jet black hair, slightly wavy, and twinkling green eyes which had smiled too often and created deep creases around them. The kind of guy you knew you could rely on. Mark loved his job and treated all his charges with respect. He was also damned good at spotting even the smallest detail. She knew he felt it was his duty to make sure he helped bring people to justice and find answers for the bereaved. She'd often wondered what he dreamt about at night. Was his sleep haunted by the bodies he spent his days with, or could he shut the door here in the evening and lock them inside?

'Straightforward,' he said, nodding at Neil, and headed to his computer screen where a camera was still plugged in. Claire skirted around the examination table and joined him at the screen. He was scrolling through a gallery of photos. Every single inch of Neil's body, inside and out, was visually recorded. Mark stopped towards the beginning of the storyline, where the camera focused on the wound in Neil's back.

'Simple, one entry wound, but whoever did this knew what they were doing. You see the way the wound isn't a neat cut?' Mark zoomed in on the photo, pointing to the edges of the stab wound which were jagged. 'The killer knew how to do the job quickly. Stick the knife in here and slash at the heart, that's why there was so much blood. Your victim would barely have known what was going on, it would have been quick, almost instantaneous.'

'Right,' said Claire. 'Any ideas on murder weapon? Or clues about what kind of person we're looking for?'

'From the scans and X-rays of the wound, I'd say the angle indicates a right-handed man and a little taller than the victim. Perhaps just tipping over six feet. The blade was eight inches. You can see where the guard slammed into the victim's skin as he rammed it in. I'll need to do some more tests, but I'd wager it's something like a hunting knife.'

'You said "he"?' Claire questioned.

'Yes, this took a fair amount of force to drive the knife in so far and fast. Combined with the fact it's a knife crime and they're six foot plus, I'd focus on finding a male. I'm not saying a woman couldn't do it, but it's a lot less likely.'

'Anything else?' she asked hopefully.

'Your victim looked to be a fit, clean-living guy who looked after himself, apart from some damage to his skin from sunbathing. Obviously, no toxicology back yet, but there's nothing to indicate any substance abuse. He had, however, had sex recently and lots of it.'

'OK thanks, Mark, appreciate it.'

'No worries, stop by sometime when we haven't got a dead body between us and I'll get you a coffee.' Mark creased his face at her again, and Claire felt herself doing the same back.

'Thanks, I will.'

As she left, Claire looked back at him, bent over the remains of Neil Parsons, concentrating on his work. You couldn't get two more different people, Mark and Jack. She'd barely given the latter a thought today. Perhaps she should call him.

· · ·

'AT LEAST HE DIED HAPPY,' was Bob's response when Claire told him about the autopsy findings.

Claire tried to hide her irritation. Trust a bloke to focus on the one piece of information that contained the word *sex*.

'Ties in with Margaret's initial analysis of the blood spatters,' she actually said. 'Anything back on the stalker yet?'

'Nothing. Neighbour couldn't see clearly, just saw a hooded figure lurking at the edges of the garden. I've pulled up Google Earth. There are several routes someone could take to get to that point. There's a lane just the other side of the neighbour's house and an open communal garden behind. It wouldn't be difficult.'

'She doesn't have any kind of social media presence. There's nothing on Rachel Hill at all.'

'We'd better arrest her now then.' Bob didn't mask his sarcasm, but it had a humorous tone. 'Since when has not having social media accounts been a crime?' he asked.

'It's not, but it is a bit odd.'

'Well, bloody good for her. Maybe she hates all that crap. We're not allowed social media accounts either, it's not that unusual.'

'I know, I wasn't suggesting ... I was just wondering if maybe there was something in her past she's hiding from. Something that's come back to haunt her now ...' She could see Bob was glazing over. 'Just thought it was odd, that's all.'

Bob started to walk away. 'Don't wonder, find hard evidence and facts. Tell everyone I want them assembled with everything they've got in ten minutes.'

He headed out of the incident room.

Claire felt like a cadet again after that conversation. She didn't know why she'd brought it up; it had just been niggling her. Who doesn't have a Facebook or Twitter account nowadays?

She knew where Bob was going. He'd lock himself into one of the toilet cubicles and stay in there for the full ten minutes, if not longer. It's what he always did when he needed to clear his head.

When she reached her desk, there was a latte and jam doughnut waiting for her. Lew gave her one of his broken tooth grins from across the desk and she smiled back at him, with a little more warmth this time.

11

RACHEL

14TH OCTOBER, 2016

As the dusk settled on the garden, Rachel said goodnight to her rabbits. She picked up the female and burrowed her face into her soft fur. The smell of fresh sawdust mixed with the tang of ammonia reached her nose. The rabbit snuggled into her, enjoying the attention and the soft massage from Rachel's fingers.

'You're going to be safe, Amber, I promise,' Rachel whispered to her before kissing her warm ears and placing her back into the large cage with her mate. The male was inquisitive as usual, interested to see what treats she might have brought them this time, and as he leant his head out Rachel bent down and kissed his forehead. 'You're a greedy guzzler, Reg.'

A bag of lettuce sat on the side, and she could see he'd smelled the succulent leaves in the air.

'Here you go.' She tipped the bag out onto the cage floor, a pile of green tasty joy for the rabbits, who immediately tucked in.

With them distracted, she closed their cage and took a small lock out of her pocket. If the stalker managed to get past the shed alarm, at least they wouldn't be able to open the cage door easily. She put images of fire and other violence out of her mind. Rachel didn't even know if the rabbits were in any danger, but the thought of them out here on their own, while she was safely locked in the house, made her feel uneasy. She'd toyed with the idea of bringing them inside. If she emptied out the cage she could just about manage to carry it to the house while Reg and Amber were in the run, but a part of her was hoping this would just go away. Maybe the police attention would scare the stalker off, and her life could return to normal.

She set the shed alarm and returned to the safety of her house. This time she'd locked the door behind her when she went out in the garden. The possibility of someone invading her privacy, entering her home unknown, made her stomach churn. She wouldn't make it easy for them.

One of the police officers had gone around every single window with her, checking the house was secure, and now she double bolted the doors behind her. He was a nice guy, the policeman, about the same age as her but already engaged. She could see it in his eyes, the glow of contentment that comes from a full heart. It made a nice change from the empty loneliness of so many of the dating agency clients. She could still feel his trail of warmth in the house.

Now the house was silent again, and she could breathe in relief. A return to her natural state. She was hungry, but for a few moments she sat in the armchair in the sitting room, staring absentmindedly at the pair of pottery dancing hares on the hearth. She might even put the fire on later. Fill the small wood burner with fuel and listen to it crackle and pop as the flames consumed their sacrifice. What she needed now was for the soft silence to envelop her, its familiarity a comfort blanket, an antidote to the uncertainty of the day.

Each room had its own acoustics and sound floor. This one, the sitting room, faced onto the road, but she could barely hear the world passing by through the double glazing. Sometimes in the day a bird would sit on top of the chimney and its song would find its way down and into her living room—muffled and amplified by distance and the chimney flue. At times she thought she could open up the wood burner and the bird would fly out. It seemed that clear and near.

Her mind switched, once again, to Neil. All day she'd thought about him, about what might have happened. She couldn't believe he'd been murdered—he was so full of life —so desperate to stay young and energised. She knew the police would wonder if there was a link between his death and her stalker. Could there be? If only she knew who it was that watched her.

The flowers were a shock. Whoever it is knows her name. It wasn't just a random weirdo who had seen her, latched on to her, and become obsessed with her. The stalker wanted to scare her. It was personal. This latest fact had definitely upped her stress levels, even though she realised that must be exactly what they'd intended, and she wasn't about to give them what they wanted.

The two CID officers who came round earlier seemed nice enough. The older man was a classic career copper, but the woman; she had an edge to her. Maybe it was her age and ambition, or the fact she's a woman, but Rachel could feel she was more intuitive and relied on gut feeling, not just straight facts. That gave her more confidence that they'd find Neil's killer, whether it was anything to do with her stalker or not.

He didn't deserve to have his life taken like that. Neil

loved living. He was a fireball bouncing off the walls in her house when he visited. Occasionally they'd sat and got serious, talked about the future, his hopes and dreams or the childhood he'd idealised. Often his chat would revolve around his latest date, or the weekend's plans. Neil wasn't lonely because he had himself, that's what really mattered to him. She found him easy company because he wasn't interested in her, in quizzing her about her childhood and past life.

His parents must be devastated. He was their only son, a boy they'd doted on. She could imagine their house filled with photos of every stage of his existence. What a horrible way for it all to end. She could almost hear their hearts being ripped apart. Grief like that can't ever be mended.

12

RACHEL

FEBRUARY, 1994

The first night without her mother, neither of them went to bed. Rachel's dad refused to eat or drink. He stayed curled up in a ball on the living room floor. She stayed with him, afraid that if she let him out of her sight, he too might disappear.

Rachel tried so hard to keep her eyes open, but they betrayed her. It became too difficult to raise her lashes, and they dropped like weighted safety curtains at the end of a performance. Every time she closed her eyes she saw her mum, heard the crash of the car, and watched her die. Sometimes she was engulfed in a raging inferno of fire, other times crushed to death like a beetle beneath a shoe. Every time she was terrified, in pain, alone with no one to help her.

What sleep Rachel got wasn't restful. In the dark recesses of her mind, her loss took on a thousand different demonic guises. Exhausted with wrestling her emotions and imagination, she eventually slipped into a deep sleep, but waking was cruel.

She opened her eyes to morning light. Dry, scratchy,

swollen lids. For a few seconds she thought it had all been a dream—until her eyes focused and she saw where she was, lying on the sofa with her father curled up foetal-like in front of her—still in his outside boots. Cold reality stripped her of any vestige of hope.

She'd opened her eyes to a world without her mother.

Instantly her head began to pound, her mood a cloak of lead around her shoulders. Dehydration, lack of sleep, and shock took it in turns to hammer at her brain.

She looked at her dad. His complexion was so pale it was almost transparent. A screen drawn back on the window of his human frailty overnight. What would her mother do? How could she help?

First, she had to satisfy the itch of disbelief which wormed around her mind. She got up quietly, so as not to disturb her father, and slipped out to the yard. The damp cold February night had left a film of dew upon everything, creating a sheen on the old tractor which lay lopsided, one wheel off—and long since lost—just outside their garden gate. It was a sorry excuse of a vehicle, but the only one in sight. The oil patch was there, still exposed.

Back inside and upstairs, just her footsteps and her breath. Her mum's dressing gown hung behind her parents' bedroom door and she burrowed her face into the soft velour breathing in the scent of her mother. If Rachel closed her eyes and stayed wrapped in its comfort, she could pretend like it hadn't happened. Or step inside her mum's wardrobe and become enveloped by her clothes—transport herself to her own Narnia where her mother waited, smiling, arms open.

The thought of her mother embracing her squeezed a hot tear from each eye. She shuddered, and her mind returned to her dad downstairs. Brushing the tears from her face with her sleeve, she headed back down.

It's difficult when you're eleven, when your world had been ripped apart. It's difficult suddenly finding yourself the main carer.

'Dad, you need to drink a cup of tea. Sit on the chair, I'll take your boots off.'

Rachel placed the mug of steaming tea on the small table next to his chair. She'd put a spoonful of sugar in to help with the shock, like she'd seen on one of the TV soaps her mother used to watch.

The room was warm. The little electric heater had finally taken charge of the temperature, but her dad felt cold. His pale, grief mottled face looked at her as though he didn't even recognise who she was. He allowed himself to be guided up from the floor and into his armchair, where he sat awkwardly. A guest in a home he didn't recognise.

Rachel knelt on the floor, unlaced his boots, and eased them from his feet. The mud had long since dried and crumbled off them, leaving a sprinkling of brown and black in front of his chair. He placed his socked feet down into the mess, oblivious, and she cursed herself for not having thought to get his slippers ready first.

'Dad, you need to drink your tea.'

She lifted the mug and placed it in his hand, supporting the weight in case he didn't respond. Like an automaton, he took the tea to his lips and sipped.

Buoyed by this success, she returned to the kitchen and made him some toast. The smell of the cooking bread and sweet jam awakened her own hunger, and she made herself a piece. Its taste shocked her mouth with the flavours and her stomach lurched into activity, churning at the prospect of sustenance. She ate half a slice before the guilt made her take it all into the sitting room.

'Eat some toast, Dad,' she said gently, tentatively. This

was a role she wasn't used to. At first, he didn't respond. 'Dad, here...' She placed a piece of toast in his hand and at last he looked at it, although his face remained impassive. Rachel encouraged his hand towards his mouth, and he took a bite, chewing it slowly. There was no hungry eagerness to his eating, and if she left him, the toast would just sit there. It was a slow process, but she managed to get a whole slice into him before he took the plate and put it down, shaking his head when she asked him to eat the other. Progress. He was communicating.

Around forty-five minutes later some colour returned to his cheeks, and Rachel watched her father slowly return to her. She'd no idea of the time, but the sound of knocking on the kitchen door brought her back into the real world.

It was Reg and George wondering where her father was.

'Y'all right, missy?' Reg looked uncertain, peering into the kitchen behind her. 'We wondered where your dad was, like? You not gone to school?'

Rachel's throat tightened. This was the first time she's had to say it aloud, give it a physical existence.

'My mother, she was killed yesterday in a car crash.' The words came out, an announcement before a performance—not true, not real, just acting.

Both men gasped. 'No!' said Reg, and they exchanged glances.

'Good God,' exclaimed George, then more gently, 'Where's your dad, love? Is he OK?'

'He's ... He's inside.' Perhaps they'd help. 'Do you want to come in?' Rachel opened the door wider and let the two men enter. The prospect of grown-ups in this strange new world, a relief.

The two men, both in their fifties, were dressed for the

cowshed. They pulled off their boots and left them outside. The normality of it all bringing home just how different life had suddenly become.

As she closed the door, Rachel saw the smiley face on the window. Her mind flickered back to yesterday afternoon and using her finger she smeared the smile into a big downward grimace.

13

CLAIRE

14TH OCTOBER, 2016

I t wasn't the greatest board in the history of police investigations, and that fact showed on Bob's face. Claire knew he'd be getting it in the neck from above, keen to get this wrapped up. She'd also spotted Julian from the press office, lurking in the background with his notebook. The media loved a clean-living murder victim, Neil connected to their readers far better than a scummy drug dealer's death. The headlines would, no doubt, make people feel uneasy in their beds tonight, so the media liaison was keen to get out a release that showed some progress in the investigation.

Their lack of suspects was stressing Bob, who now also had Rachel's well-being forefront of his mind. Throughout the briefing he paced back and forth in front of the room, an agitated bear twisting his wedding ring on his finger.

Lew had been unable to track down Neil's friend, Mike, but he did at least know which club it was they frequented, so Claire could guess where she'd be spending the evening. She was tired. It had been a long day and a slight headache had settled at the back of her eyes—

probably too much screen work. Jack flashed into her mind again. If he was still at home, he'd wonder if she was coming back. She really should call him.

'Right, it's 6.30 p.m. We've no definite suspects and no real motive apart from the possibility this could relate to his womanising. We have a potential link with Rachel Hill's stalker. They knew each other so could whoever's obsessed with her, be the one who killed Neil Parsons? Is this a jealous delusionist who thought Neil was seeing Rachel? She called him on his mobile the night of the murder. Could the killer have seen her number and name flash up on Neil's phone? Did Neil know or do something he shouldn't and now the killer thinks Rachel could also be involved?'

Bob paused to survey the faces of his team. They stayed silent.

'What we do know is it looks like whoever did this is either a professional, or someone who has researched this meticulously. This wasn't a heat of the moment attack. They carefully planned it. The killer left no traces. So how was he not seen? How did he get into the flat? I want every person in that block of flats investigated. They're all suspects for now. It would be by far the easiest explanation of how they were able to do this without trace. Get their names and divvy up the work.' He directed this to Tasha, and Claire saw her nod.

She took the few moments of silence to speak.

'The one link we do have between Rachel and Neil is the dating agency,' she offered to Bob. The SoulMates name sat on the board in black and white but to Claire, it throbbed red. 'Could well be some anti-social nutter on their books.'

'Yup,' agreed Bob. 'And that's why you and I are going over there first thing tomorrow morning.'

Before tomorrow morning there was still this evening and the nightclub reccy. It would be useful to see where Neil hung out and who it was he liked to spend his time with, plus the elusive Mike could show. His name currently sat on the potential suspects list and while there was no obvious reason why he would have chosen to murder his best friend, they needed to rule him out and see if he had any information.

Before she could brave a nightclub, Claire decided to get something to eat. The sugar rush from the doughnut Lew had bought her had long since subsided and she was craving something savoury. Heading back to her desk for her purse, she couldn't avoid Lew sitting hunched over his keyboard, concentrating on his screen, face illuminated by the blue light. He'd bought her two coffees and the doughnut. She felt obliged to ask him. Trouble was, if you ask one person, you have to ask the others too. She could end up with a massive tea and coffee order that she just didn't have the energy to deal with right now.

Instead, she sat down at her desk and sent Lew a message. '*Off to the canteen, want anything?*'

He looked up and smiled at her. A new message from him appeared in her inbox. '*Flat white cheers.*'

'Jack on tonight?' Lew asked out loud.

Claire shook her head. 'No, we were supposed to be off for a long weekend.'

'Ah, hazard of the job for you Brangelinas.'

'Brangelinas!' Claire exclaimed. 'Yeah right. Anyway, we're still together.'

'Still together? Yeah, I know,' replied Lew, puzzled.

'You do know that Brad and Angelina have separated? Right?' she asked him, bemused.

'No! No way. Really? Brangelina is no more?'

'Yeah, they split in September. It was all over the news. I can't believe you don't know.'

Lew looked genuinely shocked and turned to the young PC next to him who had been patiently sorting through records.

'Yo, Duster, you know that Brad Pitt and Angelina Jolie have split?'

'Yeah, sure, course,' he replied, a little bemused.

Lew shook his head.

'I don't believe it. What hope is there for the rest of us mere mortals?'

Claire smiled and headed off to the canteen, suspecting he was now googling the Hollywood couple rather than getting on with investigating Neil Parson's death.

Claire was just heading down the corridor, thinking how awful it must be to have your private life splashed across the world news, when her phone started to vibrate in her pocket. 'Mum and Dad Home' came up on the screen. She answered it.

'Hi.'

'Hello, love,' it was her mum, 'you at home?'

'No, Mum. I'm still working.'

'Oh sorry, do you want me to ring off?'

'No, it's fine, just on the way to the canteen.'

She wondered how many times her mother was going to apologise during this conversation.

'Everything all right? How are you and Dad?'

'We're fine. Mary Gruchy had a car accident last week, you remember Mary?'

'Yes, of course I do, Mum.'

'She broke her pelvis and arm. Drove into a granite wall. Pressed the accelerator instead of the brake in her new automatic. I don't know how she's going to manage in that house on her own. Your dad is taking me out tomorrow to the cinema. We're off to see *Deepwater Horizon*, not sure what it's about. I'd rather see *Girl on a Train*, but your dad isn't interested in that. We won't be getting any sweets at the cinema, far too expensive. I might buy a bag of Maltesers from the Co-op to take with me. How are you?'

Claire was used to her mum's verbal diarrhoea, a symptom of a day spent on her own.

'Fine thanks, Mum, just got a new case today so busy.'

'Oh, I'm sorry to disturb you. Your dad used to like the first days of a case. Said he loved the buzz of it all. They're building a new police station here now, you know?'

Claire thought back to her childhood and the rare times her dad was actually home.

'Yup, you told me, it must be ready soon.'

'Yes, I think so…' Her mother trailed off. 'Did I tell you that Mary Gruchy has had a car accident?'

'Yes, Mum. You OK?'

'Me? Yes, I'm fine, it's Mary who isn't. I wasn't in the car, you know.'

Claire had arrived at the canteen now, and the inane chatter from her mother was rejuvenating her headache.

'No, look, sorry, Mum. I've got to go now.'

'OK, of course, sorry to take up your time when you're busy. Give us a call soon. We miss you, you know.'

'I know, I will, bye, Mum.'

Claire pocketed her mobile and studied the canteen menu, but she wasn't really concentrating. She doubted her dad was missing her, and that conversation with her mum was a bit weird. Her mother could ramble and talk about the most mundane things for hours, but that took rambling to a new level. She guessed her dad was out again with his old police buddies at the golf course. Her mother gets lonely in the house on her own, and she could be quite adept at making Claire feel guilty for not being around.

It was nearly twelve years since she left Jersey for university in the UK and she'd never been back—apart from holidays. It wasn't that she doesn't like the island, she does, it's just it can be career limiting. Thankfully for people in Jersey, murders and serious crimes are few and far between. Her dad used to get excited about cases they wouldn't even investigate over on the mainland. The low crime rate was a great bonus for those living there, but not a great way to get career experience if you're an ambitious police officer.

She considered getting something hot to eat, but then decided against it. A full belly on a late night after a long day was more likely to slow her down and make her sleepy. She chose a salad with lots of bacon pieces and cheese and got another latte for herself and a flat white for Lew.

As Claire was paying, a big hoot of laughter came from a group of uniformed men who had just finished up and were on their way out of the canteen. It was Jack's posse, the bunch of guys he hung out with and who invariably ended up round their house drinking beers. They were all right, most of them, a bit immature for her liking, and she winced when one of them caught her eye and they drifted towards her, enveloping her in their group.

'Claire. You good?' James Baxter beamed at her. They called him the Ginger Whinger, but he was probably the smartest of the bunch.

'Yeah, fine, James, just starting a new case.'

'Craig had a good collar today, didn't you, mate? Although it's made him feel funny.'

The other men smirked, and Craig raised his eyes to the ceiling.

'Arrested one of those killer clown pranksters,' Craig

explained to her. 'The prat was terrifying a group of pensioners on Putney Heath. This lot won't let it drop.'

Claire wished she could come up with a clown one-liner to join in, but her mind was blank, like it always seemed to be in these situations.

'Boys!' was her lame response and all she could think of saying as the group moved on, joking and laughing and slapping the brunt of their fun on his back. Her response went almost unnoticed. Thankfully.

Claire followed them out and Jack flashed through her mind again, but her hands were full so she couldn't call. She'd ring him later.

Zero:Ten was what she'd call a middle-class nightclub. They'd gone to town on the decor and the drink prices and cocktails would preclude anyone on an average wage from being able to afford a boozy night out.

Bob had assigned her and Lew to the task of checking out Neil's stomping ground while he reviewed all the day's work. She knew attention to detail was his thing. He'd be wanting to make sure he'd not missed anything in what they'd found so far and what they still needed to find. She also knew he was more of a fan of Frank Sinatra than the latest dance club mix.

On the way to the club, Lew was his usual unsubtle self.

'So, how d'you feel about this Rachel being stalked after what happened in the Stiller case?'

He took Claire by surprise. She knew people realised it had upset her, but everyone has to deal with things. You either get on with it or you spend a few sessions talking it through with the duty psychologist. Did she come across as being that weak? Or had Jack been talking?

'It's different. This time we're being forced to take it seriously and not writing her off as some neurotic air head.'

Lew stole a quick glance at her.

Claire tried to change the subject.

'You're not planning any more Jager Bomb nights at ours again, are you?'

Lew laughed and the ensuing reminiscing lasted until they'd pulled up outside Zero:Ten.

It was early, but the club bouncers were already on the door. Claire and Lew weren't in the usual clothes they'd go clubbing in, but they had both changed into slightly more relaxed outfits. Nevertheless, the bouncer could still spot they were police at first glance. He was in his fifties, built like a brick outhouse, no neck, and his arms were thicker than Claire's legs. As they approached, she saw him say something on his radio microphone—no doubt warning management that they were arriving. She wondered if that was an old habit born of years working in rougher clubs than this one, or if there really was something illegal going on inside.

He introduced himself as Tony and was actually quite friendly, especially when they said they were investigating Neil's murder.

'Terrible,' he said, shaking his head. 'Nice bloke, charmed the ladies no end. Mikey will be gutted.'

'We haven't been able to contact Mikey to tell him,' Claire replied. 'Do you know where we'll find him?'

'No, haven't seen him in for a couple of weeks,' the bouncer replied. 'Neil's been coming in on his tod, not quite so frequent like, but yeah, come to think of it, not with Mikey.'

Tracking down Michael Stratton had just become their priority number one.

14

RACHEL

14TH OCTOBER, 2016

I t was on evenings like this that Rachel would like a glass of wine or something stronger, but she wasn't going to revisit that period of her life again and so steered well clear. Besides, she needed her wits about her. The last thing she wanted was to dull her senses. Somewhere out there was a person who wanted to hurt her. She'd no idea who or why, but she certainly wasn't going to make it easier for them.

It was too early for bed, and so instead she tried to focus on doing a bit of work. She'd taken on a couple of new clients this week and needed to suggest some suitable dates for them. She loved this part of her job, the buzz of possibility, the swell of hope ahead of each date. Deborah was in her forties, divorced three years, and with two teenage children. She was quite self-deprecating, probably a result of her bad marriage and the fact her ex went off with a woman ten years younger. She was actually attractive both inside and out, and so Rachel paired her with two men she knew Deborah would never normally pick because she'd think them out of her league. They were also both nice guys, she'd be in good hands. Rachel smiled at the thought of Deborah's dates. She'd find someone, she was sure of it.

Rachel couldn't help it. Her mind kept going back to Neil. Dead. Murdered. His life taken violently, and for what?

This house had been her sanctuary for twenty years, but now she felt like dark shadows had crept in under the door. The spectre of Neil's murder swirled in front of her, but in the corner of every room stood another black shadow—the threat of the stalker. She wanted to close the curtains to prevent anyone from looking in and watching her, but that felt like she was blinding herself. She'd have no idea if they were out there or what they were doing.

She imagined pulling the curtains open and seeing a face right up close to the window, eyes staring at her. Skin bleached white by the lights. She could be surrounded, oblivious.

Even work couldn't help her settle and she kept getting up and going into the kitchen, lights off, to peer into the darkness of the garden. The glow that was the London outpost of Wimbledon Village helped with the illumination. So far she'd seen nothing. Perhaps the police presence had scared them.

The card the female detective gave her was propped up against her mug rack, DI Claire Falle. She said to call her if she was worried or saw someone, although she' also said to dial 999 if she thought she was in any danger. How would she know if she's in danger until it's too late? Until they're upon her? Rachel hadn't felt this upset in years.

15

RACHEL

FEBRUARY, 1994

Thinking about her mother and the fact she would never see her again, took up the whole of Rachel's head and heart. It was day two, a full 24 hours from hearing the news, before she felt even remotely able to look upon the world outside her inner pain. What she saw was her dad, a man who she'd always looked up to, loved and felt secure with, gone. In his place was a crumpled bag of human bones, riven with a grief that saw no boundaries.

Reg and George had stumbled and muddled their way through an awkward conversation with her father. She'd hoped the arrival of adults would solve things, not bring her mother back—she wasn't that childish—but bring some semblance of normality into their grief-stricken world. She soon came to realise that most adults are befuddled and afraid of the extreme emotion grief creates.

Reg and George looked embarrassed and wary of the toll this beast called grief had taken on her father. They muttered platitudes and quickly returned to safer ground, promising to look after the cows for him. Her father nodded in reply, but looked as though he couldn't care what they were saying or what they'd do.

Rachel thought of the cows in the barn, oblivious, and was grateful they'd be fed and watered. For a moment she wished she was one of them, chewing and poo-ing, just worrying about the next mouthful.

The conversation between the men was brief. Practical. Rachel followed them back out to the kitchen, just in case a magic solution to their situation appeared.

'You all right, missy?' Reg asked.

Even at eleven, she could see from his face that he was hoping she'd say yes, that he didn't really know what to do next if it was a no. She hesitated.

'We'll be fine,' Rachel replied.

Overnight she had aged far more than just one day. Yesterday she believed adults, especially her parents, could fix everything, knew everything. Now she realised they can be as vulnerable and clueless as the cows in the barn.

Reg and George put their boots back on and scuttled back to the safety of their own world. Rachel closed the door and prepared to return to her new reality.

Before she could gather herself, the sound of guitars broke into the silence of the house. And then Elvis's voice.

'*Hold me close, hold me tight…*'

It was her mother's favourite album, the record she played every time she was in a good mood, at home cooking or just relaxing. She'd grab Rachel's hand and dance with her, making exaggerated movements to the music and the words as she sang the song.

Rachel didn't move, transfixed by the weight of the memories as the hypnotic swirl of music transported her mind.

When Elvis finished and the silence returned, Rachel became aware of her own breathing and the occasional drip from the tap, before more gentle guitars wafted through the house and 'Love Me Tender' filled the void.

Why was her dad doing this? It was torture listening to the songs her mother loved so much. Elvis's voice, sad and lost, filtered through their home and their heads. Rachel imagined her father sitting bereft. '*For my darling, I love you and I always will.*'

She couldn't move. All she could see was her mother, the flash of her smile. Spinning as she danced, hair flying. Calling to Rachel to join her as she flitted around the house. She couldn't be gone. How can someone so alive be no more?

Rachel gripped on to the empty work surfaces in the kitchen, a grinding pain in her gut.

She didn't want to go back into the sitting room, to see the stranger that had replaced her father. Instead, she went upstairs to her parents' bedroom and sat on their bed looking at the room. Her mother had sat in the same spot on this bed, putting on her make-up every morning— except this one. She didn't have many things, but what she did own sat abandoned on top of the chest of drawers, which once belonged to one of Rachel's grandparents.

Rachel reached out and touched the bottles, running her fingers over the same smooth, cool surfaces her mother would have done. The coldness emphasised their abandonment.

The perfumes were mostly small tester sizes, no big expensive bottles of Chanel. Her mother's favourite, a miniature of Thierry Mugler's Angel, took centre stage. Rachel picked it up. It was almost finished, but the smell instantly brought her mother back to her. She slipped it into her pocket. It would be her own genie in a bottle to conjure up her mother whenever things got too hard to bear.

Rachel felt tired, weak even, her legs and arms heavy. Tiredness stroked her eyes with its promise of an escape from reality. She focused on her memories, playing short clips of her mother in her mind. Then the tiredness wrapped its arms around her, and she leant into it, curling up on the bed and willing release.

IT WAS the cold that woke her. She shivered on top of the bed. This time she didn't need to struggle to think where she was or what had happened.

Elvis had stopped singing and the silence in the house set alarm bells ringing. She jumped off the bed and quickly headed downstairs to find her father.

She needn't have worried. If it wasn't for the fact she knew he'd had to get up to turn the record player on, she wouldn't have believed he'd moved at all.

'Dad, do you want a cup of tea?'

Rachel's voice seemed to startle him. 'Rachel!' he said, as though seeing her for the first time since it happened. 'I'm sorry, love.'

Relief flooded through her. He was coming back to her. She went to him and hugged him, wrapping her arms around him, seeking a familiar, safe harbour. His arms stayed on his lap. Nothing. Not even a brief pat on her back. His rejection was a new pain to add to the chronic ache of her grief.

Rachel returned to her sofa and to watching her father. If only she knew what to do to help him. Who could she ask?

Outside it started to rain, hard. It was coming down in straight streaks of water. She tried to focus, to see the drops, but it was impossible. Occasionally they'd fly slant ways across the window, driven by a gust of wind which smashed them into the glass pane. The windows rattled in sympathy, disturbing the curtains with their suffering.

She could hear the raindrops tinkling into the drains, pattering onto leaves and foliage and banging on the rooftops. Why did it rain? Without rain and water there couldn't be life, so what magic occurred to create this natural wonder? How do we know it will continue, that the pitter patter she heard now, like the rustle of a million leaves, wouldn't just suddenly stop forever? We couldn't take anything for granted. If her mother could be snatched from her, then so too can anything. The rain, the sun, her father. Anger rose in her. Why do we even exist when all we do is die? What point is there to anything?

16

CLAIRE

14TH OCTOBER, 2016

When she arrived home, it was immediately obvious to Claire that Jack wasn't there. The flat was dark and silent. When he's in, it was filled with him—music, TV, PS4—there was always something on and usually more than one thing. She'd come back and find him living out his firearms fantasy with *Call of Duty* or knocking back the beers with a couple of guys from the station. He seemed to hate being home alone; he needed his pack around him. The flat was a constant backdrop to his busy life and Claire ended up an extra, waiting on the sidelines for the principal actors to clear the stage. Tonight, though, she had the stage all to herself. Her only regret was that it was late, she was tired, and she wasn't going to get to enjoy a full evening home alone.

She turned on the lights and went round pulling curtains, pausing to look out the window. Two of the Indian takeaway staff, food-spattered aprons on, were having a quick cigarette out the back near the bins. She noticed some mould on the inside window frame, cultivated by condensation, and inspected the paintwork.

When she looked outside again, the men were staring up at her and so she nonchalantly pulled the curtains closed. She couldn't quite shut out the neon glow of the takeaway sign, which stayed like a yellow stain on the fabric.

It looked like Jack had left some time ago. There was a light flashing on the phone, and she listened to the message. It was Matt, Jack's best friend.

'*Yo, dude. You wanna catch the footy tomorrow? We're meeting at The Crown if you're around.*'

That meant Jack hadn't gone to Norfolk with Matt. Claire looked at the time. It was 9.45 p.m., not too late for her to ring him. He was probably in a London pub somewhere, tanked up, ready to roll home after closing and shatter the silence like a thunderclap.

She called his mobile, but it rang out. She tried again and then sent a text. *Hi where r u? I've just got in. C*

The text went, but her phone didn't buzz back at her with a reply. Wherever he was, it was probably noisy. He'd get back to her later.

One good thing about living with Jack was that there was always alcohol chilling in the fridge. She nearly finished an already opened bottle of white wine and plonked herself down on the sofa to watch the ten o'clock news. The death of *Coronation Street's* Hilda Ogden, actress Jean Alexander, was in the headlines; as too was the acquittal of former footballer, Ched Evans for rape. The case had been going on since 2012 and been a controversial one. He'd always insisted he was innocent, but there was criticism from some. The appeal court allowing the cross-examination of the victim's sexual history was one reason why; as too was the offering of a £50,000 bounty to anyone with information that could bring about his acquittal. It made Claire think back to what Rachel said earlier about being nervous to report her stalker. It's not always clear who gets put on trial.

Her mind was still buzzing with the case and the day's caffeine intake, and so she finished the wine, hoping to dull her brain. She was more successful than she expected because she fell asleep on the sofa before the national news had finished.

Claire woke up feeling cold and confused, just in time to witness the end of *The Graham Norton Show*. The heating had gone off and some sitcom about a bunch of flatmates was coming on the TV. She couldn't bear all these cosy *Friends* style set ups and so she hit the *off* button on the remote. Her neck was stiff from where she'd let her head loll back into the cushion, and the empty glass of wine still sat on the table in front of her. She was more tired than she'd realised. Claire reached for her phone, shocked to see it had gone midnight. There was no message from Jack, and he was obviously not home.

Where was he?

17

CLAIRE

15TH OCTOBER, 2016

W hen you're on a new murder case, there was no such thing as a weekend. Every day was a working investigation day. Claire had sent Jack another text at 3 a.m. telling him to get in touch and let her know where he was, but she guessed he'd probably crashed out on Matt's, or someone's, sofa.

Her alarm woke her up at 6 a.m. again and she felt dazed and heavy-headed from the broken sleep. There was still no news from Jack, but she wasn't worried. He knew she was working a case and so wouldn't be home much—he'd always find somewhere to go rather than be home alone.

She sent him another text to say she'd be at work all day and probably this evening again, then headed for the shower.

Bob was already in by the time Claire rocked up. It was still not even 8 a.m., but she guessed he'd been there a while, a spent coffee cup and what looked like the remains of a bacon sandwich, were on his desk.

'All right?' he asked her in the way of good morning.

'Fine,' Claire replied. 'You been here long?'

'Since just before 7, wanted to get a head start. We're going to the dating agency for 9 a.m.' He looked up at her for confirmation, and she nodded back.

'Lew is on his way to Mike Stratton's flat. Can you go through the Current Situation Reports, catch-up with progress and see if we've any matches to our MO on the HOLMES computer? This could well not be their first attack.'

Claire was annoyed. She should have been in earlier if she wanted to impress and show she could lead an investigation. It was her own stupid fault for drinking the wine last night. She should have read the CS reports and checked through the police computer systems to see if anyone had spotted any links or fresh evidence.

'Sure thing,' she replied. 'Need a coffee?'

'No, I'm good.'

And so, their day began.

When Lew returned and reported that Mike Stratton was not only not at his flat, but actually gave the lease up two weeks ago, the buzz in the room rose noticeably. The hounds thought they could be onto the scent of a fox.

'Don't all sit around waiting,' Bob shouted at the room. 'This might turn out to be a red herring, or another dead body. Keep looking at that CCTV and going through the gathered statements. I want Michael Stratton tracked down now.'

'You heard from Rachel Hill?' Claire asked Bob.

'I called her first thing. She didn't see anyone last night, but she can't be sure. Maybe they saw us and it's spooked them. Either way, I've told her to remain vigilant. We'll have to put off our agency visit. We need to focus on this Stratton guy.'

Lew plonked down onto his seat opposite Claire and yawned.

'I hate the earlies,' he said to anyone listening.

Claire wondered if she could ask him if he'd heard from Jack, without it sounding totally weird that his girlfriend hadn't. She decided against it and instead texted Jack again. He'd never done this before, just disappeared without a word. Jack knew she couldn't go to Norfolk because of the case. He couldn't be blaming her for that, surely?

Jack's whereabouts were distracting her from work, and that annoyed her. She needed to be 100% focused on this case. They need to get their killer, and she needed to prove she was up to the job. Typical of Jack to be trying to get her attention, even when he wasn't around.

'Found the parents,' DS Sarah Potter shouted out triumphantly, bringing a hush to the office. 'They moved last year into one of those retirement estates in Essex.' Bob looked positively delighted.

An hour later, the team watched as he rubbed his head. Michael Stratton's parents said he'd gone travelling, backpacking through Asia, but they hadn't heard from him for a while, and they had no idea of his current position. His work confirmed that he'd been on a zero-hour contract and one day had just told them he wasn't coming in again. The parents did say it was a little out of the blue. Someone in the team got confirmation from immigration that he'd left the country—on-board a flight to Vietnam two weeks ago. Michael Stratton was highly unlikely to be their murderer, unless he'd somehow snuck back into the country.

'I want him found,' Bob barked to the room. 'Why has he left in a hurry? What's he running from and is this connected to Neil's murder? The timing is too coincidental and for someone who has always been active on social media to suddenly clam up, suggests he's lying low. Did the pair of them have any business dealings together? What else links them besides their friendship? I want him tracked down in Vietnam and I want him questioned.'

18

RACHEL

15TH OCTOBER, 2016

She was trying really hard not to be paranoid. Coincidences happened, right? How could it possibly be anything to do with the stalker when the rabbits had been safely locked up in the shed all night?

Amber was poorly. Off her food and sitting in the corner of the hutch with her ears forward. Reg was keeping away from her. But he wasn't his usual cheeky self either, sensing his mate was ill. She'd been a little quieter than usual yesterday, but Rachel hadn't thought much of it, suspecting that the banging and noises associated with fixing the alarm system to the shed were the likely cause. Now she wasn't so sure. She'd keep them inside today; it was getting a bit too chilly to keep putting them out, anyway. Perhaps she'd got cold yesterday in the run.

Rachel stroked her gently, willing her hands to be healing hands, her touch to send the right vibes through her fingers to make Amber well and draw the illness from her. She stayed with her as long as she could, one eye on her watch. She was working today and needed to walk to the Tube station. They were back-to-back with clients, so she couldn't be late.

She locked the shed and headed inside, heavy-hearted. She knew some people would ridicule her for how much she adored her rabbits, but she didn't care. They were easy company. It was nice to have something to take care of, no strings attached. Rabbits were so uncomplicated compared to humans.

As she got into the kitchen, Rachel heard the letter box open and something drop onto the hall floor. Probably just another bill or some letter trying to persuade her to open a savings account with the amazing interest rate of 1.25%. As she walked towards it, she could see it was neither.

Rachel picked up the letter from the floor and turned it over so she could see the address written on the front. She wasn't sure what it was—it couldn't be the innocuous printed label—but alarm bells jingled through her body. Here she was being paranoid again, reading danger into everything she saw and touched. What was wrong with her? She needed to pull herself together. She toyed with the idea of leaving it on the kitchen table while she went to work, but chances were it was nothing at all and she would have spent the entire day worrying about it.

Rachel carefully opened the envelope, gingerly tearing the paper as though it contained a booby trap that would jump out and startle her.

Inside was a single piece of paper, A4 folded over. Probably just a marketing letter. She took it out and unfolded it.

I'M WATCHING YOU

was printed in big letters across the length of the paper. Her head swirled, and she reached out to steady herself. When was this sent? Before the police came round? She looked for a date stamp on the envelope, but there wasn't one. If this went through the mail, then it must have been posted before the flowers were delivered. Should she ring the police? Maybe there's some kind of forensic evidence they could get off the letter and envelope.

Why were they watching her? Who are they? The hairs on her neck were up again, and her stomach churned, pushing bile up into her throat. She imagined prying eyes everywhere she looked, everywhere she went. Her first instinct was to call in sick and stay at home, hide away from everyone and everything—but that wouldn't help. This person had already infiltrated her home with their poison. Perhaps she was safer outside where there were people. Among those she knew at the office. She hated this feeling, hated it. Rachel willed herself to get angry about it instead of feeling paranoid. She needed to fight this intruder in her life.

19

RACHEL

MARCH, 1994

Today Rachel's grief was an angry snarling cat, disdainful of the world and hiding her fear behind claws. Tomorrow it might find her at the bottom of a pit; dark, slippery mud sucking her down. A place where only despair could survive.

The unlucky recipient of her cat's claws was the Assistant Head from school, Miss Mayhew, who had come searching for her when her persistent non-appearance had been reported and it became clear their home phone wasn't working. In truth, Miss Mayhew had also come because of the school netball team she coached. They had an important match next weekend, and Rachel was a key player.

It was far from perfect timing. Rachel had been trying to make an omelette, but nothing had gone right. She dropped eggshell in, burnt her wrist on the pan, and it ended up more scrambled egg than anything resembling a neat flat omelette. It made her angry. Nothing was going right. Then when the burn on her wrist stung and pained, she cried—hot, angry tears. To add insult to injury, her father just stared at the lunch she had struggled to make and while she ate hers, she watched his go cold, congealing on the plate in front of him.

Ten minutes later Miss Mayhew rapped on the front door.

At first, Rachel just froze. She knew it wasn't George and Reg—they never came to the front door. She waited for her father to respond.

The caller knocked again.

'Dad?' she questioned.

He looked at her, something flickered in his eyes, but not quite a spark enough to light a response.

Rachel opened the front door to Miss Mayhew, which was both a relief and a panic. Her familiarity, a face from her old life, was comforting; but Rachel also realised she was there to find out why she wasn't at school.

'Rachel!' Miss Mayhew exclaimed, as though seeing her was the last thing she expected. She gave her a wavering smile. 'Are you OK? Have you been ill?'

Rachel shook her head. She wasn't sure what to do, but she guessed she should let her in. She stepped aside and opened the door wider.

Miss Mayhew took her cue, stepping over the threshold nervously, a shy cat venturing into a neighbour's house.

'How are you?' Miss Mayhew tried again.

Rachel swallowed hard.

'We missed you at school and netball practice. Your telephone seems to be out of order. We were worried, so I thought…' She had followed Rachel into the sitting room and the sight of her father crumpled in his chair, a half-eaten plate of egg yellow mush on the table beside him, made her stop. 'Mr Hill. How are you? I've come to see Rachel. She's missed quite a few days at school.'

Her dad looked at Miss Mayhew. 'I'm sorry,' he said.

Rachel felt his discomfort, saw Miss Mayhew staring, and wanted her to stop looking at her dad like that. 'It's my mum,' she said to her. 'My mother died. She was killed in a car crash two weeks ago.'

Her dad looked at Rachel, eyes tearing up, and Miss Mayhew's hand flitted to her mouth.

'Oh, my God. I'm so sorry.' Now it was her turn to feel uncomfortable, imposing on their grief. 'I, we had no idea.'

Rachel dropped her head. She didn't want to see the new look on Miss Mayhew's familiar face.

'Is there anything we can do?'

Rachel shook her head. Her dad was staring at the floor.

'Please, if I can help at all…' her teacher continued. 'I'll make sure everyone at school knows. We'll arrange that you can catch-up on what you've missed.'

Rachel gave a half smile, more wry than thankful. Miss Mayhew eyed the door.

'Thank you,' her dad's voice made both of them start, and they turned to look at him. 'Thank you for coming,' he repeated.

It was Miss Mayhew's turn for a half smile. Only hers was more sympathy than anything else. She took her cue. 'I'd better get going.' She looked at Rachel, eyebrows angular furrows of concern. 'You take care, and I'll visit again soon. Just let us know when you're ready to come back to school.'

Rachel was irritated by her sympathy. She wasn't sure why, but she was. 'I don't care about school,' she blurted out, because it was true. She didn't. She didn't care about anything, her life had been torn apart. There were no boundaries, no roads to follow. She was adrift on a sea of emotional upheaval with no rock to cling to.

'I know it's hard,' Miss Mayhew's eyebrows furrowed

deeper, 'but you might find coming back to school, being with your friends, takes your mind off things.'

That's when Rachel's cat claws sprung, finding a bravery she didn't know she possessed. 'Do you think school will make me forget my mum is dead?'

Miss Mayhew took a startled breath. 'No... I...'

'I don't want to go to school. We are fine. We don't need your help.'

The Assistant Head teacher looked at the slight eleven-year-old girl in front of her, body rigid, jaw clenched, and hands in tight fists. 'I'm sorry for your loss,' she said to them both again. She was no match for a child's grief. She took a deep breath and turned, letting herself out of the house.

Behind her, Rachel watched through the window, eyes glaring, until she saw her drive out of their yard.

THE PRESENCE of a stranger in his house seemed to spur her father into action—only it wasn't positive. An hour after Miss Mayhew had driven her white Mini away, he got up and went to their drinks cabinet, lifting out a bottle of whisky and a dusty tumbler. He sat down and poured himself a glass, then another. He didn't stop until he could no longer see to pour, and his legs were unable to lift him from the chair. Then finally, he slept.

Rachel couldn't bear to watch him, so she went upstairs to her room where she cleared some space on top of her chest of drawers. She rummaged in the boxes in her wardrobe, a jumble of childhood memories and imagination: plastic toys, broken pens, and thrown away make-up containers, ribbons and rotting elastic bands, and an envelope with photographs. Aunt Alice, her dad's sister, had visited with a friend. It had been a fun week of picnics and trips. Afterwards, the friend, Trudi, had posted Rachel copies of some photos she'd taken.

The envelope was busting with laughter and smiles, and there was one of Rachel and her mother. She was standing, her mum's arm holding her close. Nothing but happiness on their faces, which were framed by a sunny Norfolk coastline.

She propped the photograph up on the drawers, next to the bottle of Angel and a small ceramic cow her mother had bought her one summer. They sat there, gathering the dust which silently settled on the whole of their house.

THE FOOD IN THE FRIDGE, freezer, and cupboards ran out, and Rachel was forced to walk a mile to the village shop for supplies. Once the whisky had dried up, her father also made the effort to go, bringing back a mismatch of basic foodstuffs and the occasional bar of chocolate for Rachel. When she ate it, the sweet, creamy texture made her feel guilty. How could she be enjoying something when her mum lay alone, cold, unable to taste life's pleasures?

Eventually, Rachel plucked up the courage to ask her father about the funeral.

'Funeral?' he questioned, the very thought seeming an abhorrence. 'I can't go to a funeral.'

Rachel's heart beat faster with distress. She didn't want to upset him, but she couldn't let this alone.

'Daddy, I want to say goodbye to Mummy. Surely…'

'I can't say goodbye to her. She's gone, that's all you need to know.' His face crumpled and spasmed.

'Has she… is she already?…' Rachel asked quietly, afraid of his response but desperate to know where her mother was.

Her father didn't answer at first.

'Please, Daddy… Can we visit her sometime?'

Finally, he answered.

'I can't… I'm just not up to arranging a funeral,' he added, looking up at her, pleading. 'You understand, don't you? We'll go visit her soon. Just the two of us, OK?'

It was Rachel's turn to nod. It would have to do. Just the two of them. That would be the signature of her life from here.

Apart from the odd trip to the shop, when she avoided people as much as she could, Rachel didn't interact with the outside world for the next week or so. Reg and George knocked on the door every couple of days and she left them to talk cows with her father.

In bed at night in the darkness, Rachel thought about her mother lying alone and cold in her silent grave. No one to say goodbye to her, no one to whisper prayers and last messages of love. She took to talking to the photograph on the chest of drawers and sometimes she thought she could even hear her mother reply.

The only constant voice in her life was Elvis. Her father played the songs over and over. His voice permeating the fabric of the house.

She could hear the years in Elvis's recordings. They came from another time and place, a great distance from the here and now. Another world, where try as he might, her father did not belong – and neither did Rachel.

She wondered if her mother had met Elvis in heaven. Would he still be singing up there? Would her mother break from listening to him to look down on them? Does she see the pain her death has caused?

From downstairs, Rachel heard the dining-room door swing open hard, banging the brass doorknob into the stone wall. She didn't need to hear what was next to know what her father was doing. She could see him cross the room to the side cabinet where the bottles of spirits were hiding, barely touched for years, only coming out at Christmas and the odd birthday. Now their time had come. One by one they were being hoisted into the light, their bodies wrung dry of liquid before being left abandoned in the sitting room.

Rachel found them the next morning, spent soldiers in a battle of depression which reached new depths each day. Sometimes her father sat slumped in his armchair with them, other times he managed to stumble up the stairs to seek the comfort of his marital bed. He wouldn't wash the sheets. He wanted everything the way her mother left it. Their house was cloaked in aspic, the jelly-like state of grief seeping into their existence and slowing down time itself.

Night-time was the worst when everyone else was in their homes. In the day she could hear the gurgle of a tractor engine in the fields, the hum of cars in the lane, or the chirrup of birds busy with their daily routines. The cows were constant reminders of life, their mooing, their hooves clattering as they walked from field to milking barn and back again. Reg and George carried on as they always had done. Outside in the daytime, it was as though everything was the same.

At night there was nothing. Nothing but her and her own existence. It was as though the night threw a dark shroud over their house, preventing her from seeing or hearing life going on around them. She found no purpose in her life but to look after her father and hope he returned to her.

One morning Rachel woke to the acrid ammonia of urine and damp bedclothes. Her shame was another layer upon her grief. She washed the sheets and duvet cover and scrubbed at the mattress, but the yellow stain remained.

Her body's betrayal of what her mind kept hidden. She took to sleeping on an old towel, relieved that at least there was no one but her mother's smiling photograph to witness her shame.

The morning post was a succession of white. Her father ripped them open and tossed their contents into an unruly pile by his chair. For some, he didn't even do that. The only colour in their morning postbox flutter was a single red envelope—a condolence card from Miss Mayhew and the school. 'So sorry to hear about your loss,' it said, as though somehow they'd mislaid her mother. 'Our thoughts and prayers are with you.' Rachel wondered where God was when he decided it was OK for her mum's car to career off the road.

She waited for her dad to tell her to go back to school.

He didn't.

20

CLAIRE

15TH OCTOBER, 2016

Claire and Bob left the rest of the team to carry on sifting through Neil Parsons' life as they headed off to the SoulMates dating agency.

'We need to know every woman he saw at this agency.' Bob managed to keep mentoring her even when he was driving. Claire also knew it was his way of keeping the momentum going. He's known for not letting a case slump. 'Maybe Neil mentioned something to one of his dates, or they witnessed something. Or maybe one of them is jealous or has a jealous ex-lover. But we won't mention the link with Rachel, not yet, let's treat her just like the others. First, we need to clear it with her that she doesn't mind her colleagues knowing, and second, I don't want word getting out to the press about her stalker. It might be totally unconnected.'

'What about the men at the agency? If we work on the premise that someone stalking Rachel killed Neil, then that could mean a jealous man. Maybe there's a client who is fixated on her and thought Neil was seeing her.'

'Yup, could be, you're right, everyone's a suspect, and

that includes the staff. Wish I knew why Stratton has done a bunk. It's like he just doesn't want to be found—that has to be connected.'

The agency was located in a busy Fulham street and so finding a parking space reduced Bob to swearing, even with their police car status. They finally got there, after he'd nearly arrested a van driver for obstructing a police officer.

The agency entrance was discreet but stylish. At least, it was once. Now its style was fading somewhat. A French café, and a hair salon that encouraged you to create a fresh new you bordered it. Claire wondered if the SoulMates clients had tried its potential for a new beginning.

The agency doorway led to a flight of stairs with what was once expensive carpet throughout.

'Places like this must surely struggle nowadays, what with all the online dating,' mused Claire.

'Big business though, all this stuff,' said Bob, waving his hand at the gallery of happy smiling wedding photographs that lined the staircase they were climbing. 'Everyone wants somebody, don't they?'

Claire left that question hanging. Jack sprung back into her mind, and it reminded her she still hadn't heard from him. She also wondered what Bob's 'someone' consisted of. Was he happy with his wife? How could he be when he never talked about her? Although, if she thought about it, Claire hadn't exactly been that verbose about Jack either. How many people ended up staying in relationships just to prevent loneliness from stalking their lives?

The office reception had plush leather couches and a top of the range coffee machine, which Bob immediately helped himself to. Behind the desk was a petite woman with black hair pulled back from her face and tied in one of those figure-of-eight styles at the back of her head.

Claire admired the hairdo. She could never figure out how to do it herself and how it could stay there all day. It certainly wasn't a practical look in her line of work.

'Can I help you?' the figure-of-eight head asked.

'Yes, DI Claire Falle and DCI Robert Walsh. We're here to see Edward Scott.'

'Of course, no problem, please take a seat and I'll let him know you're here.'

If Claire wasn't mistaken, there was a slight flicker in the woman's face when she had told her who they were. Either that or her lack of sleep was making her oversensitive. She turned and headed back to Bob, who was lounging on one of the sofas. In front of him was a glass coffee table on which sat a jug of water with lemon pieces floating on the surface. Claire poured herself a glass —trying to avoid a lump of lemon sploshing into her water and splashing her—maybe the caffeine in her bloodstream was making her jittery.

'You could get bloody paranoid coming in here with all these smiling couples, it's like something from one of those mass weddings that Moonie cult holds.' Bob was flicking through a large album containing more photographs similar to the ones they'd seen on the stairs.

'Yeah, but I wonder how many of them are still together,' Claire cynically whispered with a smirk, just as the agency owner appeared out of a door in front of them.

Edward Scott was a large man in many ways. Tall at six foot three, he was well built and clearly had an appetite that was more than healthy. His ebullient character burst into the room with him, dominating the space.

By the time Claire and Bob had walked from reception to his office, they knew Edward Scott preferred to be called Eddie, that he set up the agency in the early nineties with his wife—who no longer worked there because they discovered all day and all night with each other could be a little too much. She now ran a wedding planning business from home instead. They were also informed that the dating industry was worth around two billion pounds globally, and he loved his job.

It wasn't until they'd all sat down that he seemed to stop to draw breath. Claire suspected he was just one of those people who are naturally chatty but wondered if nerves were also coming into play.

Bob spotted the breath and immediately jumped in.

'Mr Scott, as I explained on the phone, we're here investigating the death of one of your clients, Mr Neil Parsons,' he began.

'Terrible, terrible.' Eddie shook his head.

Bob continued. 'Did you know Neil well?'

Eddie looked a little shocked.

'Me? No. I never actually met him. Don't have much to do with the clients nowadays, to be honest, I leave that to my team. I'm the back-room guy.'

'Would it be possible to have a list of all the women Neil saw through the agency, please?'

'That's confidential client information, that is,' Eddie jumped in fast.

'I understand client confidentiality, but we are investigating a murder, Mr Scott. The murderer could be connected to this agency, but we're not going to be able to say if they are or, just as importantly for you, if they're not, until we've looked into it. One date might also have witnessed something that has a direct bearing on our case. I assure you we will be completely discreet when conducting our enquiries.'

Eddie's face was stony.

'I could arrange for a warrant, if you'd prefer,' Bob added. Claire knew he was bluffing on this one. At the moment they'd have a tough job persuading the powers to be that a search warrant at a dating agency was connected enough to their case to be needed. It was a well-used tactic that still worked.

'Oh no no no, that won't be necessary.' Eddie Scott's face wobbled with the exertion of his head shaking. 'I'll get the list of names for you. I can assure you that our clients are well vetted, we don't accept every applicant. This is a high-end agency, you know.'

Claire had been looking around his office as they'd been talking. There was a welcome absence of smiling, happy couples, and the room looked more like a bedsit than an office. There was a sofa to one side with a TV and a small fridge. He had an iMac on his desk, but if she wasn't mistaken, it was one of the older models. The whole place could do with a bit of a revamp. It looked dated. On the face of it, it was unlikely he was going to want to turn away fee paying clients. She wondered if he and his business partner wife had a family. There was no evidence of them in his office, not even a photo of her, which Claire found a little unusual for someone who was supposedly passionate about hooking other people up.

There were two pictures on the wall, one of the sun setting over the Thames and the other a group shot. Claire recognised Rachel in the group along with Eddie and the figure-of-eight haired woman, who had a short bob in the picture. Rachel looked exactly the same, although she was clearly more relaxed than when they'd seen her yesterday. There were two others in the shot, a man and another woman—heavily made up and looking like she was posing for *Vogue* rather than a staff photo.

'Is that your team?' Claire asked.

Eddie didn't need to look where she was pointing, but Bob did.

'Yes. I'm lucky I have a good team. All been with me for several years. They enjoy working here. A good-looking bunch, don't you think?'

Claire didn't answer but changed tack.

'Is there any client that you've ever had cause to eject from the agency, especially in the last year? Someone who might bear a grudge?' she asked.

Eddie thought for a moment.

'Male or female?'

'Either,' she replied.

'Well, there's one woman, she's been an absolute pain, I cancelled her membership about ten days ago.'

'Did she go on a date with Neil?' Bob interjected.

Eddie humphed. 'She's been on a date with virtually every man on our books. She's a cold fish, I can tell you. Not unattractive but just… well, difficult.'

'OK, if you could let us have her details please,' Bob continued. 'And which member of staff would have looked after Neil, you know, arranged his matches and interviewed him?'

'That would be Gary.'

Bob looked at the photo. 'Is he in today?'

'He is, but unfortunately, he's back-to-back with clients. Saturday's our busiest day of the week. As you'll appreciate, most people are at work Monday to Friday and can't get away to come in here.' Eddie had noticeably quietened a little. 'Look, this isn't going to get out is it? That Neil came here. You're not seriously suggesting that SoulMates could have had anything to do with his murder?'

'We are just investigating every avenue, Mr Scott. We have several lines of enquiry but as I explained, one of your clients could have witnessed something while out with

Neil, or perhaps he's said something to Gary which might give us a clue.'

'OK, well, please, you know, this is my business, if word gets out…'

'We will be discreet, Mr Scott. There is no need for the agency to be linked to this publicly—not at the moment.' Bob, ever the professional, added a caveat.

'OK, I'll get Sandra to print you out that list.'

Eddie rose. An air of serious thought had settled on him, the earlier enthusiasm dampened. 'She can also sort you an appointment with Gary—for your investigations,' he quickly qualified.

Bob gave a half smile.

'Thank you, Mr Scott. We'll be back in touch.'

Sandra was the figure-of-eight haired receptionist who turned out to be very efficient. She had the list of Neil's dates and their contact details ready within minutes. She also provided details for Rosa McKenna, their *former* client.

'So sorry to hear about Neil,' she said as she handed over the information to Claire. 'He was such a charmer. They're dropping like flies around here—we won't have any clients left soon.'

Claire's ears pricked up. 'What do you mean, have there been other deaths?'

Sandra suddenly looked panicked as she realised the implications of what she'd just said.

'Well, some, Todd Fuller died last week—not murdered like Neil though… I didn't mean… you know…'

Eddie had been talking to Bob, but seeing the papers get handed over, he wound up their conversation.

'Did you get everything you needed?' he said to Claire, interrupting. 'Sandra will sort out a time to talk to Gary.'

'Thank you, yes,' Claire replied.

Sandra was now avoiding her gaze and pretending to be busy on her computer.

'Thank you, Mr Scott.' Bob was keen to get back and on with their work.

Claire gave one last look at Sandra and as soon as she was outside, scribbled down the name 'Todd Fuller' in her book.

21

CLAIRE

15TH OCTOBER, 2016

Claire managed to set off for home before 7 p.m., which was a result. She was tired. They were hoping to hone in on Mike in Vietnam tomorrow, but they needed Asia to wake up first and respond. One of the young detective sergeants, who was pushing for promotion, had volunteered to stay on and man the phones and email. He benefited from still living at home with his parents and therefore having no responsibilities to deal with—and no one to complain if he got back late. His rival for promotion had a baby on the way and an uncomfortably large and cantankerous wife. He'd already headed out the door.

With no new leads and no obvious suspects or motives, the team was still scurrying around in all directions trying to get a scent. Claire knew Bob thought it was some cheated husband who was responsible, but she wasn't convinced. Something told her the key lay within the dating agency. Neil was a client and Rachel worked there. Now he was dead, and she'd got some stalker hanging around and sending her veiled threats with flowers. Could

Neil have received any threats in the days leading up to his murder?

As she pulled up outside her flat, her mind buzzed with all the potential directions the case could take them. By some amazing miracle, she managed to get a car parking space almost directly outside instead of having to walk half a mile. She could see why Jack fancied the idea of that house. Maybe he was right. Maybe if they had a house, there would be more space for them, she'd feel like they were less on top of each other. She looked up at the flat windows and from their dark returning gaze she could tell he still wasn't home. She surprised herself when she felt a little disappointed.

Claire nearly slipped on a discarded burger bar wrapping in the gutter, just a couple of feet away from a lamppost bin. Further along, she could see the cardboard container for chips. She couldn't bear slobs who dumped their life's detritus wherever they liked. Perhaps that's something she inherited from her father. She remembered him jumping out of their car at traffic lights in St Helier years ago. The driver of the car in front had just dropped rubbish out of his window. Her dad had flashed his police badge and ordered the embarrassed driver to get out and pick it up again. She couldn't quite remember her mum's reaction, but she'd been proud of her father that day. It was events like that which had spurred her on to follow in his footsteps and join the police. A crusade against injustice and bad behaviour that she wanted to carry on.

The reality was that even if she'd seen the slob who'd chucked his takeaway dinner wrappers onto the London street, she knew the paperwork and hours required to charge him with littering wouldn't be worth it. Not when there were murders and rapes to solve. Still, it niggled the hell out of her, she'd love to have given them an official mouthful.

They shared their flat door with downstairs—the owner. Her name was Emma, and she was a divorced single mum with two teenagers, a boy and a girl. She worked hard. Claire saw her going in and out at all hours and wearing different shop uniforms. The kids were polite; it was only rarely she heard loud music. Jack's PlayStation was probably the noisiest thing in the house, he insisted on having the sound up loud to get the full effect.

She entered through the front door, and into the small, shared hallway. The door to what would have been the downstairs sitting room was blocked off, and another internal front door led into her landlady's flat. Claire's front door was at the top of the stairs, which were the same internal stairs that came with the house originally and somehow looked slightly out of place in the new arrangement.

Claire couldn't be bothered to cook from scratch tonight, so she took a lasagne out of the freezer. That would do her with a few peas. It was going to take almost an hour to cook, so she got changed and settled down to call her parents. The earlier phone call with her mum had been niggling away at the back of her mind.

The flat was quiet, not even any sounds from downstairs. It was a welcome relief from the buzz of the day.

Her dad picked up.

'Hi, Dad, it's Claire, how are you?'

'Ah, hello. Susan, it's Claire.'

He always did this, told her mum she was on the phone the second she was through, as though he wanted to hand the phone over as fast as possible.

'I'm fine. Had a few rounds of golf this morning with

Richard and Don. Very pleasant day. Do you want your mother?'

'I've just started a new case, murder enquiry.' Claire scrambled to keep his attention.

'Oh yes.'

'Yes, not going to be an easy one.'

'Well, the criminals aren't there to make our job easy, are they?'

'No…'

'Shall I get your mother?'

'Is Mum OK? Only she seemed a bit confused earlier when she called.'

'Of course, she's fine, I'll pass you on to her.'

Claire sighed and closed her eyes, resigned.

'Hello, love, are you at home?'

Her mum's voice sounded jauntier, more relaxed than earlier, but distracted.

'Yes, sorry about this morning.'

'No problem. Do you mind if I call you back, love, only *Strictly* is on?'

'No, of course. You do know you can pause it?'

'Yes, but your dad likes to watch it live. I'll give you a call back.'

'OK, speak later.'

Claire ended the call and sat in silence, imagining her parents in their living room. Her dad would be in his armchair, feet up on the footstool, her mum on the sofa. Their house had barely changed in decades. Her dad's police medal and the photo of him at Buckingham Palace, still centre stage in the sitting room.

She sighed again and picked up her mobile. There was a missed call from Jack, the phone was on silent. How irritating. She turned the sound on and instantly called him back, but it went to voicemail. He must be in Norfolk—it was the only explanation. He'd know she was going to be flat out on the new case, so he'd be avoiding disturbing her. She could imagine him in the arcades now, trying to win some silly stuffed toy. He'd spend an absolute fortune before he realised the machine was rigged and then go and drown his sorrows in the nearest pub.

She'd got one more evening alone tonight, and she was going to enjoy it. She might even have a soak in the bath, open a bottle of red, watch something that she'd recorded, and Jack didn't want to see. A bit of 'me time'.

Claire couldn't help it, but her mind wandered back to the case. She never got a chance to check out the name Sandra, the receptionist at the dating agency mentioned. She must do that in the morning.

The lasagne and peas were welcome sustenance. She hadn't realised how hungry she was, and she took a sip of her wine – it was good. Not one she'd bought, probably a bottle brought along by a guest at some point. She was halfway through her meal and a recorded episode of *Who Do You Think You Are?* when her mobile rang. Neither she nor her phone recognised the number, and she nearly ignored it, but she couldn't.

'Is that DI Falle?'

'Yes it is, who's speaking?'

'It's Rachel, Rachel Hill. I think someone's outside again. I'm sorry to call in the evening, but I wasn't sure what to do. I've had a threatening letter and now they're out there.'

Claire put her wine glass and fork down.

22

RACHEL

15TH OCTOBER, 2016

Rachel turned the blue stone ring round and round her finger as she stared out the back bedroom window into the dark garden. She'd definitely seen something: a shadow, the flash of a mobile screen. They were out there watching her house right now. She was sure of it.

She'd been careful with her own mobile, keeping it down and the screen off so they couldn't see its light. Should she call 999? That seemed a bit drastic. She wasn't actually in danger right now. Was she? The business card for the police detective was in the kitchen. But if she went downstairs, she'd lose sight of them, then she wouldn't know where they were, what they were doing. She should have put the police officer's number into her phone that would have solved the dilemma.

If she'd taken Gary up on his offer of dinner tonight, maybe the stalker would have been scared off again. She'd declined. What if Neil had died because of his friendship with her? She didn't want to think about that kind of responsibility, but she had to, for their sakes. Maybe she needed to be on her own until this got sorted.

If she stayed here at the window she could watch them, see where they went, until hopefully they left. But what if they didn't? What if they were waiting for the people in the houses all around to go to sleep and then they were going to make their way into her home? How could she even be sure that there was only one of them? That there wasn't someone else creeping up the stairs right now while she looked outside?

She bit the inside of her mouth, the pain a good distraction to her fear. The earthy, iron taste of the blood sent her brain into an even higher state of anxiety.

If she stayed up here, she was trapped. She had to go down.

She had thought about making a quick dash out the front door. If they were out back they might miss her, but that relied on there only being one person, and what if they heard her? She could run, but maybe they could run faster. Then there was the prospect of coming back home to an empty house, not to mention the question of where she would run to.

Rachel took one last look out the window and toyed with the idea of taking a photograph, but realised it wasn't going to do her any good. It was too dark, and the figure was hidden by the large bushes at the back.

She picked up a can of deodorant, holding it ready to squirt in the eyes of anyone she might encounter, and she made her way downstairs to the kitchen.

DI CLAIRE FALLE was obviously eating when she picked up and there was a voice in the background which must be the TV, because it immediately quietened. If Rachel was worried about being fobbed off, then she needn't have been concerned as the police officer was instantly sympathetic. She told her to sit tight and keep her phone with her. For once in her life, Rachel did as she was told.

It was more difficult to see from the ground floor. The bedroom enabled her to look over some of the low bushes, but down here, at eye level, they merged into one. She couldn't see if they were still out there, but DI Falle was true to her word and within a couple of minutes she heard sirens getting closer. Her adrenaline rose. If they caught him, if she could find out who it was…

An hour later, DI Falle was standing in her kitchen nursing a mug of hot tea. The two police cars, which had screeched to a halt outside her house, had gone—the officers leaving empty-handed. Whoever it was had skipped away over the back somewhere. They'd searched everywhere, but there was no one to be seen.

Rachel worried that DI Falle was going to think she'd made it all up, and she was studying her closely.

'I've requested regular drive-bys. We should hopefully have scared him off tonight anyway, but just to be sure,' she was saying to her.

Rachel pulled out her trump card.

'I had a letter this morning, too. I put it in a bag, just in case you could get something off it.'

She picked up the envelope and A4 sheet of paper, which she had carefully placed inside one of her large freezer bags that morning.

DI Falle took it from her, reading the words on the paper.

'Do you have anyone who can stay with you? Or who you can go stay with?'

Rachel shook her head.

'No family, a friend?' The police officer pushed.

'No. Both my parents are dead, and I was an only child. This was my aunt's house, but she's died now too. I'm not from London so I don't have any close friends here.'

She shrugged and looked away from DI Falle's sympathetic eyes. It was a welcome relief when her mobile phone rang.

'DI Falle… Yes, sir, I'm here now…'

She walked her conversation into the hall, leaving Rachel to put the milk back in the fridge and stir her own tea. Her hands were shaking slightly. The after-effects of the adrenaline and the chink of the metal spoon on the china mug jarred her nerves. She went to the back door and checked again that it was locked. She'd already double checked it at least twice.

DI Falle's voice carried from the hall. 'Yes, I will. I'll stay for a bit, make sure she's fine… OK, Bob, night.'

Rachel turned as the police officer re-entered the kitchen, and she gave her a tentative smile.

'I'm sorry to have called you out on a Saturday night.'

DI Falle smiled back. 'You're fine. I was only sitting home alone with a TV dinner. You were right to call. Let's go take a seat and I'll get some details from you.'

'Would you like a biscuit or anything? I've got some chocolate cake,' Rachel offered.

'Actually, yes, thank you. I wouldn't mind a slice. Could do with a sugar hit.'

The two women settled into the armchairs in the sitting room, cups of tea and cake by their sides.

'I really appreciate you taking this seriously,' Rachel said. She was well aware that lots of other women hadn't got this kind of treatment.

'It's my job.' DI Falle said. 'We need to make sure you're safe and I'd like to catch whoever's sending you threats.'

'Maybe I should have taken Gary up on his offer of dinner. He was going to come round, but I said no.' Rachel surprised herself that she found it so easy to confide in this woman. Maybe it was her professional concern rather than judgemental sympathy. 'Gary works with me at the agency,' she qualified.

'Yes. Does he often come round?' DI Falle asked.

'Not often, just sometimes. He's a nice guy, and he likes to get out of his bedsit. He loves to cook, but he can't really do it properly there. I let him take over my kitchen, he's good.'

'Does he know about the stalker?'

'No, I haven't told anyone at work.'

'He was Neil's consultant, wasn't he?'

Rachel nodded.

'Did he know Neil came round occasionally, too?'

'Yeah, I think so. But you know Gary's gay, right? He isn't interested in me like that.'

It was DI Falle's turn to nod in understanding.

'Did you have to come far to get here?' Rachel asked her. She couldn't help it, but whoever she talked to she always felt herself slipping into interview mode. It was force of habit from trying to glean information from the agency clients, to get to know them and find them a good match.

'Shepherd's Bush, it's fine.'

'I'm sorry. Does your boyfriend mind you working such long hours?' She was doing it again. Being nosey.

'No, he's a police officer, too. So, at what time did you notice that there was someone outside?'

DI Falle was actually quite easy to talk to. Rachel

warmed to her, even though she knew that what she was doing was her job, trying to calm her down and make her feel better. It was nice to be on the receiving end for a change. It was always her being the sympathetic ear to the clients at the agency. She'd got used to giving and not expecting back. The trouble was, she would only be there for a short time. Soon DI Falle would leave and Rachel would be alone again in the house. Her home was fast becoming a prison. She was under siege from an enemy she didn't know.

23

RACHEL

MARCH, 1994

When Social Services came to call, her father was out in the yard. He'd taken to wandering aimlessly around the farm whenever he wasn't too drunk to stand. She'd see him from the window, staring at the empty pens when the cows were out in the fields, as though he was watching a ghostly herd. Today it meant there was nowhere to hide from their questions and paperwork.

Rachel saw them walk into the kitchen and she was an angry terrier, hackles up, barking in defence of her father whose awkward gait and fiery breath told tales on him.

They requested an audience alone with her father, but Rachel stood firm.

'We're fine. I'm fine. We don't need your help,' she told them, before her father had the chance to open his mouth.

There were two of them. An older woman, thickened waist and shapeless clothes, with an officious air and face that had seen it all before—and much worse. The younger one was fresh and eager, scanning their home, taking in the dust and unwashed floor, the bare necessities and lack of luxury. She followed on the heels of her mentor like an attentive gun dog.

Rachel's terrier instinct was quick to spot she was the weaker of the pair.

'Why you staring?' she attacked, aiming her bites squarely at the younger woman. 'Mind your own business,' she said again.

The older woman calmly defended her colleague. 'Hello, Rachel. We are here to ensure you and your father are managing. You haven't been to school for several weeks and your dad can get into trouble.'

Her firm tone made Rachel's snipes sound immature and spiteful—even to herself. Her dad could get into trouble? What will they do, take him away, lock him up? Take her away?

'Dad?' Rachel pleaded.

'Mr Hill, I really think it's in yours and Rachel's best interests if we sit down and talk things through. Just us.'

He looked at them and then at Rachel's pleading face, before reluctantly nodding.

'Rachel, you go up to your bedroom for a bit. It'll be fine,' he said, attempting a weak smile.

Betrayed, Rachel gave a last withering look at the two women and turned, tail between her legs, back to her den of safety.

She took refuge in her parents' bedroom, where she could be as close to her mother as possible. Reverently, she slid open her mother's drawers, seeking familiar things to bring her back. Her hairbrush, a brooch. The scarf she wore on the rare evenings they went out. She slipped on one of her mother's rings. It had been her favourite, given by her dad one Christmas Day, when life had been full—the future framed by their family happiness. It was only costume jewellery, a ring of blue glass stones, cut six sided and placed like a flower on a metal mount that seemed to be brass, but perhaps wasn't. Rachel didn't care what it was made from. They could be real diamonds set in platinum, but it wouldn't be worth any more to her.

The light caught the stones, throwing round rainbow reflections onto the wall. A myriad of full stops. Her mother would never return to wear their glitzy decoration again. Her life had reached its own full stop.

The social workers stayed for around an hour before Rachel heard the click clack of their heels outside and a car engine roar into life. She rushed to the window and for a moment she couldn't see if there was somebody in the back. It looked like a head. Had they taken her dad away? Then the car turned out of the yard and she realised it was just the seat headrest silhouetted.

She ran downstairs to find him sitting in his chair, a little pile of leaflets, pamphlets, and paperwork on his lap.

He looked up when she came in. 'Sorry, love,' he said. 'You're going to have to go back to school.'

Tears flooded her eyes, and she ran straight back upstairs to her bedroom again. The prospect of leaving her safe cocoon was terrifying.

She flung herself on to her bed in frustration, catching her hair in her mother's ring. She held her hand up, trying to find the sparkles again, moving her hand this way and that—but all she could see was a dull glow reflected back. Her mother's light disappearing. Dissipating into the environment. Her brightness fading.

'WHAT'S WITH YOU?'

The question came at Rachel, a torpedo into her consciousness. As her eyes looked up, taking in the row of expectant faces in front of her, she became aware of the salty taste on her lips and the dampness of her cheeks.

Stella Wainwright stood in front of her, an almost amused look on her bratty face. 'Well? What's up with you?'

George Roger's eyebrows flickered, and Nancy Cooper's mouth narrowed.

'My mother's died,' Rachel half whispered.

'Liar!' Stella came back at her. She had her hands on her hips now. 'You're a liar. I saw her in Norwich last week. She was fine.'

'She was killed in a car crash a few weeks ago.'

Rachel's voice didn't sound like her normal voice. She wasn't really sure where the sound came from, like a TV playing in another room.

'Liar.'

Stella shoved her spiteful face closer into hers and the audience fizzed with anticipation.

Rachel wasn't sure how the fist flew so straight and fast through the air, but she felt the crunch against her knuckles as Stella Wainwright's nose buckled under the blow.

MISS MAYHEW DROVE HER HOME, a journey of adult false cheerfulness and inane chatter. Rachel didn't want her to come in, to have her invading their privacy again, but she insisted. She was relieved when they discovered her dad was sitting at the kitchen table with George and Reg, not slumped in his chair with a bottle. They had the farm books spread open. Records of the herd and the accounts, numbers and words Rachel didn't understand.

Her dad jumped up shocked when Rachel and Miss Mayhew walked through the door.

'Rachel! Are you OK?'

'I'm fine,' she replied and despite herself, despite all her attempts at braveness, she couldn't help but run to him and fling her arms around his waist. Refuge.

'There was a small incident at school,' Miss Mayhew explained, with loaded words. 'I thought it best that Rachel came home today. Can I have a quick chat?'

Rachel's head tingled, and a shiver ran down her spine as her father's hand briefly rubbed her head before he pulled away. 'You wait here a mo,' he said to her. She wanted to cry, but she wouldn't, not in front of everyone.

'Y'all right, missy?' Reg asked tentatively, trying to appear cheerful. He wasn't as good at it as Miss Mayhew. The two men looked at each other. An awkward silence fell on them as heated whispers carried from the hallway.

The front door opened and closed, and her dad returned to the kitchen.

'Bloody outrageous. They said you'd got to go back to school and then they don't look out for you. Good for you girl, I'm glad you bopped that little madam.'

Relief washed over Rachel, and she wanted to run to hug him again, but she didn't. This was the most animated she'd seen her dad since it happened. He was pleased with her. If she had her fighting spirit, maybe he will get back some of his.

The next day Rachel was disappointed to discover they expected her to return to school.

'But, Dad, isn't it better that I stay with you?' she pleaded.

Her dad shook his head. She was finding it harder to read his expressions now that his stubble has turned into a beard, but nothing could hide his eyes and the sadness in them.

'You have to go, love. It's for the best. Just stand up for yourself and any trouble with the kids go straight and tell the teachers. I'll meet you off the bus, shall I? We can walk back up the lane together.'

She liked that idea. It would give her something to look forward to.

At school, the other children gathered in huddles. Stella Wainwright collected them all around her and they whispered and turned to look. Eventually, Rachel learnt to ignore them. Lucy Cocker, the previous outcast of their year group, tried to talk to her at break. The prospect of a potential friend, a fellow outcast, encouraging her on. Even Lucy got infiltrated into the Stella posse—much to her delight. She went from no friends at the start of the school day to being in a gang by the end of it. She didn't care why they were suddenly being friendly to her, just that she wasn't the one sitting alone in the corner anymore; the one that nobody chose for their teams or wanted to pair up with in class.

Rachel sat twisting the blue stone flower ring on her finger. She wasn't alone, she knew her mother was still with her. She counted down the minutes to the end of the day when she could get the bus home and meet her father.

THE BUS WAS CROWDED, children forced to stand, but the seat beside Rachel remained empty. She was glad she lived further out than most because by the time it was her stop the bus had almost emptied and she didn't have to push past stiff, reluctant bodies.

Rachel got off the bus and waited for it to pull away. The fields were dry, and it made her blink as the tyres kicked up the dust on the side of the road. As it cleared, she saw that no one was standing at the end of their farm drive. She looked up and down the road for her father, in case he'd wandered off looking at something. The road was empty. Disappointment hit her hard, as though someone had thrown a bucket of cold water on her soul.

She wandered across the road slowly. Perhaps he was a bit late and any second she would see him walking to the end of the drive. Her imagination almost conjured him up like a desert mirage.

She waited. The minutes ticked by. Cars drove past, their passengers staring at her—a lone figure on the roadside.

She waited. Kicking at the pebbles wedged into the dry earth. Sending the dust up and over her school shoes and socks, until they felt gritty and dusty inside.

She waited. Then eventually her mother said, 'I'll walk with you', and so she did.

They walked together up the half mile drive that wound between the fields of cows and the small piece of woodland that made up their farm estate.

'Told you I'd always be here for you,' her mother said to her, and she smiled down at Rachel.

When they got home, her mother hung back in the kitchen while Rachel went searching for her father. He was easy to find, slumped in his armchair, the bottle of whisky open beside him. Rachel didn't wake him. She could see he went someplace else when he slept. His face relaxed. He looked younger, almost content. She'd leave him to his dreams.

The whisky was his bridge to her mother.

24

CLAIRE

16TH OCTOBER, 2016

'We don't know for sure if Rachel's stalker is connected to the murder of Neil Parsons.' Bob had been listening to Claire's account of the evening before.

'I know, but she's frightened. It's all a little bit too coincidental isn't it? The flowers, the note.'

'It could just be someone taking advantage of what's happened, to scare her. Someone with a grudge.'

'Well, they're going to a great deal of trouble and risking getting caught.'

'Yup, I know,' agreed Bob, stretching back in his chair. 'This case is just so murky right now. I can't see anything clearly.'

'There's something else.' Claire had been dreading telling Bob this. He was in a bad enough mood already because it was taking far longer than hoped to track down Michael Stratton in Vietnam. 'When you were talking to Edward Scott yesterday, the receptionist, Sandra Jennings, she said something. She intimated that Neil's death wasn't the only one and when I tried to ask her more, she looked worried.'

'Why didn't you tell me this yesterday?' Bob sat up straight again.

'I wanted to check it out first. She gave me a name, a Todd Fuller. I pulled the report on his death this morning. It was presumed to be death by natural causes by the officers who found him, therefore it wasn't processed as a crime scene.'

'Post-mortem?'

'Nothing was found except he'd been drinking.'

'What about the family?'

'No family, well at least no one in the UK, there's a distant cousin. What if it wasn't accidental? Sandra intimated there were other clients who had died.'

'So, this Todd fellow just pegs it at home. What in bed?'

'Armchair in his lounge.'

'OK, so he slips away all peaceful while having a couple of drinks. Not a violent stabbing then, is it?'

'No, but…'

'Unexplained deaths happen. How old was he?'

'Forty-nine.'

'Well, unfortunately I know of people younger than that who have just keeled over. There's no indication of criminal intent so how can you compare this one with the violent, professional killing of Neil with a hunting knife? Neil's murder was a well-planned execution, and if you're intimating that it's a serial killer, well then, they tend to stick to the same method. Right?'

'Yes, but what if…'

'Focus, DI Falle. Focus is what solves cases, not what ifs, and our job is to find the killer of Neil Parsons.'

'Yes, sir.'

They only ever called each other by their ranks when Bob was pulling his. It always reminded Claire of when her mother would call her by her full name when she was telling her off. It was clear Bob wasn't going to listen to anything more about Todd and the agency, but there was something in the way Sandra mentioned it yesterday, combined with Rachel's stalker, that had got her antenna waving. She wasn't going to drop it, not yet, not until she'd looked into it a bit more.

DS Potter walked up to them both.

'Gary Foster's in interview three.'

It was time to interview Rachel's colleague. Perhaps Claire could slip in a few questions that might be slightly off piste without irritating Bob too much.

Gary Foster was moderately good looking in a schoolboy kind of way, slightly overweight, but well-manicured. He'd dressed casually, but she suspected he was one of those who instinctively knew what goes with what and without trying could look effortlessly smart. He looked perfectly relaxed when they greeted him in the interview room. It didn't take Claire long to ruin that.

'Neil was a nice guy looking for love,' Gary told them. 'He was one of those good-looking hunks who was fed up with one-night stands. He wanted to fall in love. There was no edge to him, you know what I mean? He could chat to anyone and get on with them.'

Claire thought how everyone always seemed to compliment the dead, as though the minute they're gone some kind of automatic respect comes into play and no one can speak ill of them. She rarely heard bad words said against the recently deceased, and yet the air would be blue sometimes if you'd heard them chatting about the victim when they were still alive. She wondered if Neil really had been as nice as everyone was saying.

'Did he find anyone special?' Bob asked him.

'No, unfortunately.'

'Is there a chance he could have been seeing someone else? Someone who wasn't through the agency?' Bob pushed.

'I guess, there's always that chance, but not that he told me. He was still arranging dates.'

'Have there been many deaths among the agency clients?' Claire asked now, completely ignoring the fact that in her peripheral vision she saw Bob's head turn and felt his eyes burning into her.

Gary's immaculate pose turned a little ragged. He shuffled in his seat and uncrossed his legs.

'Well, I'm not too sure. There have been a few, but nothing like this.'

'A few? How many, Gary?' Claire pushed now.

'I don't know the figures, but they were all natural. We've never had a client murdered before.' Gary shuffled uneasily again, avoiding her gaze.

'And is it true that the agency has been struggling financially?' She wasn't going to let go now.

'Ummh.' Gary shook his head as though he were trying to think. 'I'm sorry, I'm really not sure. It's not easy, but we're fine.'

His face was burning. Eyes ranging anywhere but at them.

'I understand that a Rosa McKenna has recently been asked to leave the agency but is there anyone else who has behaved oddly or who was told they couldn't join or couldn't stay?' asked Bob, trying to steer the interview back to Neil.

'Not off the top of my head, no. I'm sure we've refused quite a few people over the years, we are quite particular you know, but nobody stands out.' The table vibrated from the jiggling of his right leg.

'How long have you been with the agency, Mr Foster?' Bob continued.

'Four years,' Gary replied.

'And are you able to tell me where you were on the evening of October thirteenth?'

'Umm, yes, I was at home all evening.'

'OK, Mr Foster, thank you for your time and for coming in on a Sunday.' Bob wrapped up.

Gary Foster looked like he'd just been let off test piloting a one-way ride to Mars. He couldn't get out the room fast enough. When he'd gone, Claire turned to Bob and raised an eyebrow.

'Didn't you notice how nervous he got when I asked about other deaths?' she prompted.

Bob sighed. 'We are investigating the death of Neil Parsons. There are absolutely no indications at all to suggest that there have been any other murders, this is pure conjecture.'

He'd got a set look on his face. Behind it, Claire could see the numerous internal emails and pressures that were pushing him for a result.

'I agree he got shifty after you asked about the agency, particularly its finances. My guess is that SoulMates has been in financial trouble for a while. But that's not pointing us towards Neil's killer. Stick to what we know are facts. We have a body in the morgue. Find *his* killer, DI Falle.'

25

UNKNOWN
16TH OCTOBER, 2016

It had been a close call last night. Luckily, the police sirens had given enough warning to make an escape. There was still too much to do to be caught. Rachel must suffer first.

It was time to up the pressure.

She will feel too scared to sleep, too frightened to close her eyes, or be alone in her house.

Her life will be misery.

She will pay.

26

CLAIRE

16TH OCTOBER, 2016

C laire wasn't going to ignore her gut instinct. Last
time she did that Jackie Stiller was killed. She was
convinced the agency was at the centre of all this, both
Neil's murder and the other deaths; they were intertwined.
She needed to speak to two women urgently: Sandra the
receptionist and Rosa McKenna, the woman who they'd
kicked out the agency.

She started with Sandra. Sandra Jennings turned out to
be another enigma. No social media, no photographs of
her online—not even a profile at the agency. She had no
visible online presence. Rosa McKenna was a little easier
to find. She clearly had a penchant for letting the world
know her views on various things from the best coffee to
the US presidential election. It was also clear Ms
McKenna had some strong views on the SoulMates dating
agency.

Rosa McKenna opened the immaculate navy door of her
town house. She was small and dark, Claire estimated

around forty-five-ish, still fit. She obviously spent time and money on herself.

'Miss McKenna, DI Claire Falle,' she introduced herself, holding out her police badge for ID.

'Ms please,' Rosa answered, somewhat brusquely as she scanned her badge. There was no welcome in her voice. 'Come in.' Rosa looked up and down the street as though worried the neighbours might see a police officer at her door and gossip.

Claire stepped into a hall of thick cream carpet, populated only by a small gilt table containing an orchid plant, and with a large gilt mirror above it on the wall.

'Shall I take my shoes off?' Claire asked instinctively.

Rosa inspected her feet.

'No, you're fine, we're in the conservatory. Come through.'

She led her past an open door that showed a sitting room with wall-to-wall cream carpet. Claire caught a glimpse of a photo canvas on the wall, what looked like a studio shot of Rosa herself looking seductively at the camera. They carried on through the hall to a spotless modern kitchen of stainless steel and beechwood and into a small conservatory. It looked like a photograph from one of the home style magazines. No clutter and certainly no evidence of dust or cobwebs, just a few strategically placed plants and artistically pulled blinds. Claire wasn't sure if she was envious or not. It looked nice, but it also looked more like a show home than a lived in one.

'Can I get you a coffee or tea?' Rosa asked her.

'A coffee would be great, thank you.'

Claire took a seat while Rosa went into her immaculate kitchen with its silently shutting cupboard doors and put together a cafetière of coffee.

'It's shocking about Neil.' Rosa started the conversation. 'I couldn't believe it when I heard.'

'Yes. I understand you went on a date with Neil through the SoulMates agency?'

'Yes. We went to Zedel in Soho. It was a pleasant enough night, but we weren't suited.'

'When was this?'

'I knew you'd ask that, so I checked my diary. It was at the end of August, the twenty-seventh, bank holiday weekend.'

'Did Neil mention anyone causing him any trouble, or was there anything about his behaviour that seemed strange to you?'

'Absolutely not. No. We talked for hours about this and that, as you do. It was an enjoyable evening, but nothing came of it. You realise I'm taking legal action against the agency, don't you?'

'I hadn't realised that, no.' Claire let Rosa talk.

'I've been with them two years and they're useless. They don't do anything about matching people, they just take whoever and stick them together and hope for the best. I'm asking for my fees back, it's only fair.'

Claire wondered what it would be like to be a man trying to please Rosa McKenna. Her prickly exterior might hide a soft inner, but she doubted it.

'You must be angry about that,' Claire tentatively said.

'Yes, damned right I am. It's false advertising.'

'Do you know anyone else dissatisfied with the agency?'

'There are a few of them who moan, but I'm not sure anyone has the balls to do anything about it,' Rosa replied.

'Are you aware of any other client deaths?' Claire ventured into the trickier territory while she seemed to have Rosa's full attention.

'Yes, there's been a few, but not murders. There was

that chap from Kensington just a week or so ago, American sounding name…'

'Todd?'

'Yes. Don't think they quite worked out why he died. Been drinking, apparently. Last year I remember there were a few too, Mark Baxter, the Welsh guy, Jones, Robert Jones, and a women I met at the summer picnic, Louise Safferey. She died too. Can't remember why. There was another man as well. I met him and then a month or so later heard he'd gone. I can't remember his name off the top of my head, but I can let you know. Why? Oh my God, do you think Neil's isn't the first murder?'

'Please, these are just standard questions we ask everyone during a murder investigation. I'm not suggesting that any of them were murdered.' But Claire couldn't wait to get back to the station and pull up their coroner's reports. 'What about the staff at the agency, do you get on with them?'

'Gary's a lovey, real sweetheart. Eddie is charming, but useless, and it's not going to stop me suing him. Felicity is a bit of an airhead. That receptionist, Sandra, can be a cow at times. She was rude to me once, and Rachel is just so nice it's sickly.'

'Who worked with you for your matches?' Claire queried, getting the impression that Rosa wasn't one of the girls when it came to supporting her gender.

'Initially, Felicity, but apparently I upset her, so they put me with Rachel. She was nice enough, don't get me wrong, but she ended up telling me I actually didn't really need a partner, that I'm happy on my own, as though she is some kind of bloody counsellor. The cheek of it! What did she think I was paying her for? Anyway, I got Gary after that and he was just lovely but at the end of the day, if all he's got is chaff on the books then I'm hardly likely to meet my

Mr Right, am I? They guarantee success, but they've certainly failed with me.'

Claire thought that perhaps Rachel was a good judge of character. Rosa spent another twenty minutes talking about herself before Claire decided she wasn't going to get anything else useful out of her and made her excuses and left. She went with an impression of what Rosa's dates might have consisted of: her sitting across the table talking 'at' some poor bloke who was probably sick and tired of hearing about her before they'd even started the main course.

BACK AT THE STATION, she ran the names Rosa had given her through the system. It confirmed none of them were treated as suspicious. Now she needed their post-mortem reports, to see if there was any kind of common thread between them.

She found an address for Sandra Jennings, but no phone number. It was Sunday, she could be at home. Claire was prepared to take the risk and pay her a house visit. She needed to find out exactly what was worrying Sandra and what she knew.

THE ADDRESS for Sandra Jennings turned out to be a bedsit in a house run by a bubbly Caribbean lady called Clarissa. Clarissa was in her Sunday bests when she answered the door to Claire and although it was somewhat inconvenient, because she appeared to have her entire family over for lunch, she was the exact opposite to Rosa McKenna and warmly welcomed her in—even asking if she wanted to stay for lunch. Claire politely declined and explained she was there to see Sandra.

'Sandra? Oh, she's a lovely girl,' Clarissa said, clasping her hands together. 'Such a shame.'

'A shame?' Claire asked, her breath catching in her chest.

'Yes, a shame that she's gone. I enjoyed her company. We used to watch the TV together some evenings.'

'When you say *gone*?'

'I mean she left. Just upped and gone. Left me a note, didn't even say goodbye. She's paid up to the end of the month, though. Such a shame she was a nice girl. Is she in trouble then?'

27

CLAIRE

16TH OCTOBER, 2016

By the end of the day, Claire's adrenalin was pumping like there was no tomorrow. Rosa McKenna had come through with the other name, and she now had five autopsy reports in front of her. All five died within the last year, and all the deaths were unexplained. There was no way that level of deaths was normal. She hadn't got any proof to suggest they were suspicious, let alone murder, admittedly, but statistics would show that death by natural causes for all five would be incredibly unlikely—and these were just the ones she knew about.

She'd had background checks done on Sandra Jennings and it turned out she should be dead herself. Whoever Sandra was at the agency, she wasn't Sandra Jennings. The woman with the national insurance number and name she'd been using died from a brain tumour six years ago. Claire was already writing out a search warrant application while she waited to brief Bob.

The rest of the team had another day of trawling through Neil's phone records, speaking to his contacts, neighbours, colleagues, and sifting through his computer and paperwork. Claire was busting to spill her findings, but she knew she'd got to run this all by Bob first and she wasn't sure he was going to be delighted about the fact she could potentially have just increased their workload, especially as he wasn't keen on her looking into it in the first place.

Lew had been strange all day. It was almost like he was avoiding her, keeping his head down and the office joke free. Claire wondered if it was a hangover, or maybe she'd said something that had annoyed him. Either way, she was too busy with work to worry about it.

AT FIRST, the annoyance showed on Bob's face, but as Claire carried on talking, he softened, butting in now and then with pertinent questions.

'So, none of the five were treated as crime scenes,' Claire explained. 'There were the standard autopsies done, but they didn't show up anything out of the ordinary. All five had been drinking but the levels in their blood streams were not sufficient to have killed them.'

'You say one of the deaths was last week?' Bob asked.

'Yup, that hasn't gone before the coroner yet, luckily, so they've still got his body at the morgue. Obviously, I don't need to point out that this rate of unexplained deaths is hundreds, if not thousands of times above the national average. Something has to be going on.'

Claire waited, holding her breath, for her mentor to think through what she was saying.

'The fact that Sandra Jennings, or whatever her name is, has done a runner is either evidence of her guilt or evidence that she's scared for her own life.' She carried on talking, keen to ensure Bob was fully taking into account all the facts.

'OK,' he finally said. 'I agree. We can't ignore this. I'm still not convinced it's connected to Neil Parsons though because he was stabbed.'

'But the agency is the link between him, these deaths, and Rachel's stalker. Perhaps there's a reason why Neil's murder was different. Maybe it was to send a message, or it was bungled?'

Bob nodded thoughtfully.

'You could be right, but my gut feeling is that even if they do turn out to be murders, they're separate. However, as we've no other clear leads at present, get a pathologist to look over the most recent death again. But if it comes back all OK and absolutely not suspicious, then you must drop this. Is that clear?'

'Yes, sir.'

Claire beamed back at Bob. This was the buzz she loved about the job and if she was proved right, if there really was a serial killer murdering clients of SoulMates agency, then she might finally get her dad to take her career seriously.

28

RACHEL

16TH OCTOBER, 2016

The first thing Rachel did when she woke up on Sunday morning was to go and check on the rabbits. She'd had a nightmare that something horrible had happened to them, and while she couldn't quite remember the details, it had made her feel upset. The threat posed by her unknown stalker was infiltrating every part of her life and being.

The shed looked intact and untouched, but there had been a light dusting of icy sleet or snow overnight which hadn't settled everywhere, but could be seen under bushes and where there were dips and dents in the shade.

Amber was still sitting in the corner of her hutch, ears forward and not touching food. Rachel gently picked her up and looked her over. There was nothing showing outwardly, but she felt cold and her stomach looked distended. She added some more hay to their cage and sat with her, trying to tempt her with her favourite foods. Amber was unresponsive.

Rachel stayed cuddling her, keeping her warm for over an hour. It wasn't cold in the shed and she was careful not to leave the door open, but she'd set up something inside today; bring them both in to keep warm and see if that made Amber any better. Tomorrow she'd take her to the vets.

Reg was quieter than his usual self. Now and then he'd stop and sniff around for Amber, standing on his hindquarters, nose twitching, ears searching. Rachel would show him she was still there, and he'd get back to eating. The pair of them had been together for years, and he wasn't used to her not being with him.

Her concern for Amber was a distraction to worrying about her own unwelcome attention. It was constantly there, niggling at the back of her mind, but focusing on the rabbits gave her some respite. It took until after lunch to put the rabbits into their travel cage, clean out their hutch, and struggle across the garden with it into the house. She set it up in the utility room before transferring them back inside. Reg seemed unperturbed by the move, but Amber backed into her corner again and sat there moodily.

Having the rabbits in the house changed its dynamic. She could almost sense the air in the rooms shift and move to take into account the new presence in her utility room. Now there were ears in the house for her to talk to and soft warm bodies to look after. It gave her courage somehow, and as the clouds cleared to leave a bright afternoon, she decided to go for a walk on Wimbledon Common. On a Sunday afternoon, it would be busy with families and couples strolling around the footpaths with their dogs or children. She'd feel safe. It would feel normal.

She avoided Windmill Road and the constant stream of weekend visitors driving up and down. Instead, she chose to walk the paths that criss-crossed the common and skirted around the Windmill Museum; its black and white wooden top rising above the canopy of trees. The ground was thick with fallen leaves and now and then another would come spinning or floating to the ground in front of her, ready to be crushed underfoot. The smell of autumn was in the air, the freshness in the wind muted by the earthy damp decay of leaf mould. Empty chestnut and conker shells littered the ground where little fingers had prised out their prizes and slipped them into coat pockets.

She was careful not to allow herself to wander into trees where she couldn't be seen, but at the same time she stayed away from the most well-trodden paths.

The rhythm of walking and the distraction of nature began to relax her. She breathed in deeply, consciously trying to shake out the tension in her body. Her neck felt stiff and there was a pinching in the middle of her shoulders, which she'd only just become aware of. Rachel lifted her shoulders towards her ears and dropped them again, circling each one, which scrunched and crunched with the movement. It felt so good to be out doing something normal.

Crashing footsteps burst from the bushes behind her, and she spun round, instantly on alert. Body tensed for flight. The vision of an overweight black Labrador confronted her, tongue lolling, tail wagging, as he emerged through the undergrowth. It was the closest she thought she'd get to see a dog smiling. His eyes were bright and excited, his nose in raptures with the huge array of wonderful scents around him. Rachel breathed out. She smiled as he carried on his olfactory adventure, nose to the ground, ears peaked for the slightest rustle of a squirrel— although somehow unable to hear his owners who came tramping after him calling, 'Boris, Boris, here.' He disappeared off as fast as he came, making the most of nature before they returned him to the tarmac and concrete of his London home.

It was just a simple walk, but the fresh air and exercise had been exhilarating and when Rachel returned to her house it loomed at her, stark and sullied. It was no longer the refuge it once was, and although she was keen to get in and see the rabbits, she was almost apprehensive about going inside. A caged bird returning to its roost for the night.

As she opened the front door, it scraped over a white envelope on the floor. Rachel's stomach lurched, and she instantly felt nauseous. Her fears realised. She stepped into the house, making a point of kicking the envelope out of the way with her foot so that if they were watching, they'd think she didn't care.

When she closed the door, she paused before going and checking on the rabbits. They were both asleep. Reg stretched out and relaxed; Amber huddled into the corner.

The envelope screamed at her from the hallway, but the longer she ignored it, the better it made her feel, and the more she could hang on to some control of her life and feelings. She walked from room to room of her house, checking nothing was disturbed, that everything was how she had left it. Finally, she returned to the hall and stared at the white envelope.

Such a supposedly innocuous object, but the red angry capital letters on its outside, spelling out her name, told of what lay within.

Carefully she picked it up, avoiding touching the surface as much as possible, and held it by the corner in case she contaminated any evidence. DI Falle had told her to keep a journal of anything that happened and so she carried the letter into the kitchen and placed it on the table next to the notebook she had started entitled, 'Stalker Diary'. She got another freezer bag out of the drawer and put on a pair of the disposable latex gloves she used for cleaning out the rabbits. A part of her wondered if she should just bag it and leave it for the police to open, but she wanted to know what it said. It was to her, about her. She needed to know what they wanted.

Carefully, she opened the envelope and took out its contents.

It was another sheet of A4 paper, only this time the stalker had said more

I am watching you.

I see who you are seeing.

I go where you are going.

A shiver ran right through her, and she only just controlled the urge to hurl it across the room. She caught her breath and instead carefully placed both envelope and letter into the bag and sealed it. Then she took off the gloves and went to the sink to wash her hands—twice—even though she hadn't touched it.

Did that mean they were following her on Wimbledon Common? Could it have been the man with the flat cap, or the guy in the Barbour coat? She had no idea who it might be, what they looked like, or what threat they posed.

Rachel sat for a moment and in the silence, she could feel her heart pounding in her chest. It felt like it was twice its usual size, banging against her rib cage. Its effect travelled to her head where she felt the pressure mounting and an ache starting to develop in her skull.

Why?

Who was this person making her life a misery?

What had she done to deserve this? All she'd ever tried to do was to live her life helping people.

Why are they watching *her*?

It felt like someone was creeping up on her all the time. The hairs on her neck tingling with a constant flow of adrenaline. This must be how a rabbit feels, eating in the open, knowing that out there somewhere could be a hawk or a fox that might pounce at any moment if they don't stay forever vigilant. This time she was the prey, and she couldn't see what was approaching.

She couldn't think of anything else. She tried to read a book, to lose herself in someone else's story—but that didn't work. Each tick of the water pipes, bang of a car door outside, every breath that she took, found her listening. Ears straining. Heart banging.

She could put some music on, or the radio, listen to another human voice, but then she might not hear if someone tried to get in.

For the rest of the afternoon, images of faces she saw on her walk flashed through her mind. She felt almost too frightened to peer out into the garden for fear one of them would lurch at her from the gathering dusk. Was this going to be her experience every time she ventured outside the house?

How could she live like this? She had to carry on working, had to leave the house without fear. Perhaps it was time to move on, find herself a new sanctuary and escape these prison walls which were closing in on her.

She didn't feel like eating, but she forced down a piece of toast and a cup of tea. Then at just before eight o'clock was the first phone call.

Rachel didn't have a house phone, and even her mobile was a basic handset. In the past she'd not bothered about keeping it with her, but lately she'd taken to carrying it everywhere. It could be used to gather evidence in the form of photos and videos, but most importantly it was a potential lifeline in case she needed to call the police. Now, it was ringing, and she didn't recognise the number.

Perhaps it was DI Falle or another police officer

checking she was OK or warning her about something. She answered.

'Hello,' she said, but her voice was a little shaky with lack of use and tight with the fear which washed through her incessantly.

Nothing.

She could hear that there was someone on the other end. There was breathing and the sound of cars driving past in the background. Whoever it was, they were outside somewhere.

'Hello,' she said again, but even before she'd said it, she realised it was in vain.

The person on the other end of the phone just listened to her fear.

Quickly she cancelled the call and almost threw the phone down on the table as though it had just burnt her. She stared at it angrily. It had to be them. How had they got her phone number?

She toyed with turning her phone off so they couldn't call back, but that would leave her with no lifeline—maybe that's what they wanted. Maybe they wanted her to turn off her phone, and that was when they'd strike.

As she stood in the kitchen staring at her phone, it lit up again and started ringing. Same number. She ignored it. It rang and rang, screeching into her nerves until she grabbed it and turned it to silent. Then it sat on the table vibrating and lit up. A flashing warning that she shouldn't trust it.

When it at last fell silent, she closed her eyes with relief, but it was short-lived. It soon started up again, buzzing and buzzing and buzzing. She walked to the back door and peered out into the night garden. Where were they? Could they see her now?

Then, down the end, she saw a small light. A mobile

phone screen. It went dark and her phone stopped ringing. One minute passed, two, and then the light at the end appeared again and the phone behind her began its bright vibrating dance.

Anger forged through her. She ran out into the garden and shouted at the shadow, 'Who are you? What do you want?'

There was no answer, just a light flicking on in the house next door and the sound of a twig snapping, but Rachel could have sworn she heard a laugh.

29

RACHEL

EARLY MAY, 1994

Grief for Rachel was like being trapped in a jam jar. It was suffocating. She was separated from life by the slippery glass walls around her. Vulnerable. Exposed. She didn't want people prying into her cocoon of glass, peering in on her emotional nakedness. She looked out at the rest of the world, muffled and distorted. Outside of her jam jar, life carried on as though nothing had happened, and that was too painful to contemplate. Inside the jar, everything had changed. She could shout and scream, but all she heard was her own voice coming back at her.

Some days it hurt so badly that it just stopped hurting at all.

The school term continued. The bullies eventually bored of tormenting her daily, and they sloped off to find new victims. Rachel learnt a new skill, being able to meld into the shadows and not be seen. If she kept quiet and stayed out of their way, they usually just ignored her.

She sat alone at lunchtime, slowly chewing on whatever she had managed to scrape together for a packed lunch. Most of the time she pretended to be writing something, an exercise book propped up so no one could see the sad faces she doodled on the page. Other times she'd be reading a book, but she wouldn't be taking in the words. She was peering over the top of the pages at the other girls with their neatly styled hair and clean ironed clothes. She looked on enviously as they took out specially designed lunch boxes with soft full sandwiches, yogurts, snacks, and drinks. Rachel tried to hide the afterthought of a sandwich her father had made, or the hastily grabbed snack because he'd got up late again.

Their talk was foreign to her. Their lunch boxes carried images of animal characters from the *Lion King*, and they talked about *Byker Grove* and *Forrest Gump*. They whispered about boys and went shopping in Norwich or had sleepovers at the weekends. She heard names of songs and bands like Take That and East 17, but she'd never heard their music. Her dad had sold their TV just before her mum died, and now all they had was the old record player and Elvis.

Sometimes her space was invaded by a group of boys. She was invisible to them as they jostled and joked with each other, or talked dramatically about someone called Ayrton Senna, who Rachel learnt had died in a car crash. She wondered how his death could be so public, so mourned, and yet her mother's was barely acknowledged —as though she was never of any significance to anyone at all.

Instead of going out into the playground at lunchtime, Rachel chose the library where she could sit in solitary calm, at peace with her own company. She read classic novels and books on grief, hiding their covers should anyone venture in her direction. Rachel tried to make sense of what she was feeling and how her father dealt with her mum's death. She didn't ask for help because she knew

Social Services would get involved. Besides, she and her dad would manage. The books told her that there were different stages of grief and so she just needed to be patient and wait for him to learn to 'accept their loss'.

Each day Rachel rushed home to her father. To begin with, it was just a relief to see him there. Every time she put her hand on the back door handle and stepped into the kitchen, she relived that day when she'd come back and her mother was gone. As the weeks turned into months, that memory was slowly replaced by another worry—what state would she find her father in? Usually, he was already halfway through a bottle of whisky by the time she got home. On more than one occasion lately, she'd got back to find him talking heatedly with Reg and George. She'd never seen them argue before. They always put on their own unique brand of fake cheerfulness when they saw her, but even she could feel that things were slipping into decline. There were new tensions in the air, things that didn't get discussed in front of a child.

Last night she had her own row with her dad, their first since her mother's death.

'Dad, you promised to take me to mum's grave,' she'd said to him. They were eating the tinned mince, carrots, and potatoes she'd found in the cupboard. Both were pushing their food around their plates a little, but hunger kept them eating and the prospect of *cold* tinned mince, carrots, and potatoes was even less appealing.

Her dad didn't reply straight away, but seemed to be thinking.

'What's the point? It's just a grave,' he'd eventually said back to her. 'I can't afford a headstone right now. She's gone, it's not your mother there you know.'

Her dad became blurry as tears welled in Rachel's eyes.

The thought of her mother lying cold and abandoned in a dark, unmarked grave was so cruel.

'We should visit her,' she croaked out.

Her dad looked up at her, hearing the emotion in her voice, but quickly looked away again.

'OK, one day soon, yeah? I promise.'

Rachel looked at him now, there was anger rising in her, he'd made lots of promises in the last few months that he'd not kept. She was angry that he was preventing her from going to see her mum. She felt powerless, with no control over the situation. Rachel glared at her dinner, mouth pursed, trying to form sentences from the angry emotional melee in her head.

Her dad let out a big sigh. 'I can't eat this.' He pushed his plate away, food only half eaten, and went outside.

From the kitchen window, she saw him wandering the farm, back bent, a lost soul hoping that each time he returned to the house he might find home again.

THE NEXT DAY Rachel was sitting alone on the school bus, heading home and staring out the window, when the spire of St Andrew's Church caught her eye. This could be where her mother was. She didn't need her dad to come with her, she'd go and find her herself and get a later bus back. She'd even walk home if she had to. Her dad wouldn't notice if she was a bit late.

She jumped up from her seat and pressed the bell for the next stop, pushing past the other kids on the bus, oblivious to their cruel snipes.

'You sure you want to get off here, love?' the driver asked her as she got to the front. He knew this wasn't her stop.

'Yes, thank you. I'm meeting my mum,' Rachel

answered, and hopped down. The hiss and thump of the hydraulic doors soon shut behind her, leaving her alone in the town.

Surely this was where her mum would be? It was their nearest church and her mum used to love Holt. They would wander round the shops and once they even went into Byfords for cake and a drink. That was when her aunt and her friend were visiting. Their treat, they said.

Rachel hurried up Station Road towards the war monument, passing Gresham's Pre-Prep. Then she turned up Church Street and right in front of her was the church. She almost ran up the road to the wooden gate leading into the churchyard. This should be simple. All she had to do was walk around looking for the new graves, her mum's would be the one without a headstone.

At first, it was all old graves, grey stones with green and brown lichen and the names of the dead almost weathered away: Harrison, Beck... 1879, 1851... She saw some newer gravestones, black marble and clean smooth stones that remained sharply engraved, and she eagerly headed towards them. When she saw flowers lain in memory of the dead, it reminded her she had come empty-handed and she felt guilty. Her mother had had no flowers or visitors. Nothing. If only she could find her, then she could come and visit her regularly, bring flowers and look after her grave. Show her she was loved.

To the left of the entrance path were some new headstones, but no graves with wooden crosses. These all belonged to other families. Round the side of the church and down the back she hunted, seeking freshly disturbed earth. Nothing.

She started again, even more systematic this time after her excited first look. Scanning every grave. Everywhere she went the ground was grassed over and the graves decorated with headstones.

There was nothing. Rachel felt like crying, like falling onto the ground and sobbing. She'd got her hopes up. Thought maybe she would be able to find her mother at last.

She sat on a low wall near to the church entrance and took her school bag off her shoulders. If her mother wasn't here, then she must be in one of the other local churches. She could look on the map in the school library, work out where she could be, and go and visit every one of them until she found her. It couldn't be that hard. Or she could put more pressure on her dad. Either way, she had to find her mum. She couldn't bear to think of her lying alone with no visitors. It might even help her father. The books in the library said something about closure and how it could help.

Rachel sat for a while until the cold penetrated her coat and she started to shiver. She looked at the time and realised she needed to find out when the next bus was and get home to her dad. She'd never left him this long alone before. When she reached the bus stop, it wasn't good news. The next one going in her direction wasn't for an hour and a half, she'd be quicker walking. She estimated that from the bus stop to home it would be a little under an hour.

Her heart was heavy as she walked. If it wasn't for her worry about her dad, she would just sit down and not bother moving. The cars swooshed by her, gusts of automobile speed stirring her hair, which caught on her lips and irritated her eyes. She plodded on, a knot of hunger developing in her stomach, giving her a new lease of energy.

By the time she reached the bottom of their drive, her

little toes and the joint on her big toes were rubbed and sore. Despite her disappointment, her mother was there waiting for her and they walked together along the track to home. The heavy scent of the cowslips which lined the drive filled her nostrils, and the static fluttering of a kestrel about to swoop on its prey caught her eye.

As she walked, she got increasingly worried about her dad. Had he been stressing about where she was and gone looking for her? Had he had an accident because he was drunk? She knew how long the track was, but still she willed it shorter, urging on the sight of the farmhouse and its outbuildings.

When finally she reached home, the house looked dark. Although the May evening was still light enough to see outside, it was fading and anyone inside the house would need the help of electricity to see. Was her father out? Had he gone looking for her? Was he alone and upset in the darkness? She rushed inside, ready to apologise, to explain why she was late, and to hug him.

Like a homing pigeon, she headed to his chair in the sitting room. His predictability was her habit. In the fading light she saw him, head tipped back, mouth open. Asleep. His whisky bottle companion by his side. Rachel stood for a moment looking at him. The relief that he wasn't angry or out searching for her was only brief. It was soon replaced by the realisation that she hadn't even been missed.

Over dinner, once she had finally woken him, she broached the subject again.

'Dad, which church is Mum buried at?'

She watched him warily, anxious in case he got angry or upset.

Her father let out a big sigh.

'OK. This weekend we will go.' He looked at her, his face riven with grief.

'It will be OK,' she said to him. 'It's right that we both go together. I'll be there to support you.' Rachel smiled reassuringly, her heart fluttering with excitement.

Her father merely nodded, sighed again, and continued with his dinner.

To GET to the church where her mother was buried, they had to take three different buses. First, they needed to get into Holt and from there it was the Fakenham bus, Number 8. Then another change, this time onto the Norwich town centre bus, Number 24, before they got off at The Street and Hindolveston. The journey should take just over two-and-a-half hours and Rachel worked out that it was no faster than walking it—especially when the bus got stuck behind a row of cyclists. There must have been about fifty of them, their bright orange vests proclaiming they were 'Cycling for John'. Rachel wished they'd cycle a bit faster for him.

She had picked some flowers from the garden. They were plants her mother used to look after, all pinks and purples—her favourite colours. By the time they got there the flowers were wilting, their delicate petals fragile and creased like ageing skin.

It was another walk from the bus, off the main street and past houses where the gardens were far bigger than the buildings, farms with huge open fields and busy hedgerows full of life. They passed a church in the centre of the village and carried on walking to the bottom road.

In front of Rachel a huge ivy-covered tower rose from a roughly mown graveyard. Most of the headstones were ancient, many tipped and slanted, adding to the derelict nature of the setting.

'Why is Mum here?' Rachel asked him. The place looked deserted. Not a friendly community church.

'It was the only place that had room for her,' he replied, and Rachel thought about her mother lying in her coffin and being shunted from church to church because everywhere was full.

There was no one around when they get there. It had a lonely, abandoned feel to it. The graveyard was wild around the edges, roughly mown in the centre and surrounded by trees and bushes. Rachel started scanning everywhere, looking for her mother's last resting place.

'Over there.' Her father pointed.

Rachel wanted to run ahead, but she stopped herself and took her dad's hand. Together they walked towards a simple wooden cross, stuck in the ground, close to the boundary of the mown area. There was barely anything else to mark it as a grave apart from that cross. Tears sprung from her eyes that this was all there was to show her mother lay here. She knelt and placed the flowers down carefully. For a few moments, she forgot her dad, consumed by her own grief and loss. Images of her mother flashed into her mind again, and she cried. Then she turned and looked at her father. He stood motionless. A ruin of a man, the human embodiment of the church tower behind him.

WHEN THEY FINALLY RETURNED HOME, they were both quiet and her father made it obvious he didn't want to talk. Instead, he went straight to the whisky bottle and drank into the evening, interrupted only by dinner and Elvis.

Rachel couldn't get the image of her mother's grave

out of her mind. She tried to sleep, but every time she closed her eyes all she saw was her mum lying cold and alone beneath that little wooden cross. She hadn't found the closure the books promised her. There was no peaceful feeling come over her, no sense that her mother was at rest. As she stared into the darkness of the night, she felt as lonely and abandoned as her mother's grave.

Eventually, tired of tossing and turning and still thirsty from the day's outing, Rachel got up to get a glass of water. The sitting room was dark. Her father had made it to his own bed tonight, and the whisky bottle stood vigil by his chair.

She envied her dad's ability to blot out the pain with his whisky. If only she could do the same. She picked up the bottle and unscrewed the top, sniffing its contents. Her head jerked back in reaction to the strong fumes, but she poured some into the glass all the same. Maybe it tasted better than it smelled. She took a big gulp and immediately gagged. An involuntary shiver ran through her and she nearly threw up as the fiery liquid burnt her throat. It was disgusting.

This wasn't going to be her answer.

She washed away the taste with water and wandered back to bed, because she had nowhere else to go. It was another half an hour or so before eventually sleep came, but as she slipped into her dreams, she wished she didn't have to wake up the next morning at all.

30

CLAIRE

16TH OCTOBER, 2016

C laire was worn out by the end of the day. Her head pounded with the vast amount of information it had been processing, and her eyes ached at the back of their sockets. She needed a break from screens and fluorescent lighting. Besides, Jack would be back this evening, they'd only booked for two nights because they were both due on shift on Monday. She slipped off home, making sure she kept her mobile on should Bob call.

They say absence makes the heart grow fonder, and it surprised Claire to find she was quite looking forward to seeing Jack. She liked her own company but coming home to a warm and welcoming body rather than an empty soulless void was quite appealing nonetheless—even if she was likely to be wishing he'd go away again within a few hours.

She was already thinking about the fact that she was too tired for sex, but that Jack wasn't going to take no for an answer after he hadn't seen her for several days. She'd make a burst of effort that ensured a quick resolution. He'd be happy and she could get some much-needed sleep.

On the way home, she picked up a few bits from Waitrose, two of his favourite Thai curry meals, a fresh bottle of white wine, and some milk for the morning because Jack always had about half a pint on his cereal.

When she got home, Claire was pleased to see the lights were on in the flat windows. She pushed open the front door and shouted a cheerful, 'Hi.'

It wasn't obvious at first, but even without a detective's eye, it didn't take Claire long to see that something was wrong. Things were missing and there were none of the usual Jack background sounds of the TV or music. The atmosphere felt tense.

Claire hesitated, listening.

There was no immediate reply from Jack.

Her instincts went on alert and she put down the bags of shopping in the hallway, so she had her hands free as she walked into the sitting room.

She edged in and saw a figure by the window, framed by the neon of the Indian takeaway sign.

Standing watching her enter was Jack, a serious look on his face and no beer in his hand.

'Hi, you're back!' she exclaimed, smiling with relief. 'I've been trying to call you…' But the smile faded, and she stopped talking as her brain registered his face.

'Hi, Claire,' he said.

She hadn't heard him sound this serious in a long time.

As she stood there, Claire became aware that the flat felt bare. The big picture on the wall was gone, his football trophies, the silly bar sign in their galley kitchen.

'You all right?' she asked. 'What's going on?'

'I'm moving out.'

The words were like a lightning strike. She put her handbag on the floor where she was standing and sat on the arm of the sofa.

'Wow, OK, where did this come from?' she asked him, incredulous.

'You're not committed, Claire. I've tried so hard to take the next step with you, but every time you push me back. I don't want to spend the next ten years waiting for you to decide when or if the time is right to actually take some notice of me. I'm thirty-four, Claire. I want to settle, buy a place, think about a family. I can't understand why you don't either – unless I'm just not what you want. If you're not ready now, then you're never going to be.'

'OK,' she answered slowly, processing what he'd just said. It was true, she couldn't deny it. 'Did you not think about talking this through?'

'I've tried. You clam up and you know it. I just don't think you really love me. We're convenient, but we seem to want different things. It's best for both of us.'

She looked down and nodded. 'Yeah, I guess.' Then she added, 'Is there someone else?'

It was his turn to look away now. 'Yeah. Lara Phillips. Only recently though.'

'Lara in forensics?'

He nodded.

'Is that who you've been away with? Is that why you weren't answering my calls?'

He nodded again. 'I wanted to be sure I was doing the right thing. I know I am. I thought maybe a weekend away with just you and I might have patched us up, but when you couldn't go... Sorry, Claire. I'll pay my share of the rent until the end of the lease. We've only got a couple of months to go on it so you can decide if you want to keep the flat on yourself or not.'

He walked out of the sitting room. 'I've got my stuff. If there's anything else just let me know.'

She nodded

'I hope we can still be friends,' he added tentatively.

Claire gave a weak smile back, and he walked out, placing his set of door keys on the kitchen countertop.

The front door closed, and he was gone.

Claire now had the whole place to herself.

31

CLAIRE

17TH OCTOBER, 2016

It was a strange night for Claire. She felt as though Jack's leaving wasn't real. It was some kind of weird dream that she'd wake up from. For three years they'd been together, and now they're not. It won't just be tonight that she sleeps alone, or tomorrow night, or next week. Being on her own was her new reality. It felt like she was embarking on an adventure, but she was a little wary of the journey.

She'd had the urge to call her parents, but experience made her hold back. She could do without a lecture. The disapproving tuts and comments from her dad would only make her feel worse and she couldn't just talk to her mother, she always had to repeat everything back to her father, whether or not he listened.

If she was honest, it hadn't fully sunk in until she got to work and realised that she was still going to be seeing Jack around the station, along with all his friends—and more importantly Lara bloody Phillips. The bitch. She'd been looking her in the face whenever she'd seen her around, and all the time she'd been scheming to steal her boyfriend.

Then there was Lew. He must have known. Is that why he was avoiding her yesterday? He'd probably helped Jack move out, told him when she was out of the way and he could go in and get his stuff. Who else knew? Had everyone been talking about her? Laughing at her when she wasn't in earshot? Her dad always told her never to mix work with pleasure. She hated it when he was right. She made a vow to never get involved with a copper again.

She avoided as many of the communal areas as possible, stopping at Costas for a coffee rather than getting one from the canteen. In the car park, she thought she saw one of Jack's friends walking towards her and so she ducked behind a row of vans, nearly scraping her leg in the process and cursing herself for her cowardliness.

It was a sour note on what was otherwise an exhilarating morning. Bob had texted through to say they had the warrant. A team of them were off to SoulMates ready for the office opening. Claire was raring to go and determined to find out exactly who Sandra Jennings really was and where she might have gone.

'SANDRA TEXTED IN SICK,' Edward Scott was saying, jowls wobbling and eyes wide. 'She'll be at home. I've got her address somewhere.'

'Is it 26 Radeley Street?' Claire threw back at him. She watched as a single drop of sweat erupted from his hairline and ran down his forehead towards his left eye. She waited for him to brush it away and wondered if its saltiness would sting if he didn't.

'I think that's it, let me check.' He nervously tapped into his computer and then nodded enthusiastically, spraying the drop of sweat onto his keyboard. 'Yes, that's it, that's it.'

'She left yesterday with no forwarding address. We've already been round.' Claire watched her words sink in as Edward Scott sank down into his chair. 'Sandra Jennings died six years ago of a brain tumour. We, therefore, believe that the woman who called herself Sandra had stolen her identity. Did you do any background checks when you employed her?'

Eddie Scott had now taken on the appearance of sweaty white pastry.

'Oh my God. Really? Sandra?' He seemed incapable of saying anything else.

'We need to find her, Mr Scott, and we need to look through your client records. I have a lot of questions for you. Let's start by asking if you know where your former receptionist might have gone? Was she seeing anyone? A client perhaps? Did she talk of visiting anywhere or mention where she is from?'

The string of questions proved too much for Eddie Scott who rubbed his palms up and down his legs as though hoping a genie would appear and take him away. Claire noticed that the brown corduroys he was wearing were slightly worn on the top of his thighs, a habit he'd clearly had for a while.

'I just don't know. Let me get Rachel. She might be able to help us. She knows where everything is.'

'In a few minutes, Mr Scott, I've got some more questions for you first.' Claire wanted him on his own, she'd got plenty of other questions for Rachel. She was enjoying this. Bob let her run with it, holding back while she led. Eddie slumped before her.

'Mr Scott, could I ask you where you were on the evening of October thirteenth?'

He leant forward and looked at his Outlook calendar. 'I was at home. Look, do I need a lawyer?'

'That's entirely at your discretion. At present you're just helping us with our enquiries, but if you feel there is a reason why you might need a lawyer, then please go ahead.'

He shook his head. 'I've got nothing to hide.'

Claire didn't ease the pressure. 'If there is something you know which you think might help us in our enquiry into Neil Parson's death, or any other suspicious deaths, then it would help you as well as us if you tell me now.'

Eddie shook his head. He was shrinking to a schoolboy in front of her eyes.

'The woman who called herself Sandra told me that there had been several deaths among agency clients. Did you know we'd had that conversation?'

Eddie shook his head again and looked as though he might burst into tears.

'OK, Mr Scott, could you please show me where you keep your staff and client records?'

With shaking hands, Eddie Scott logged into his agency database.

THREE HOURS later Claire and Bob were standing in front of the board in the incident room, taking it in turns to sigh and make other noises that go along with deep thinking and great frustration. Claire had had a great morning. She was on a roll, but the fruits of her effort had resulted in a greatly expanded workload and a sea of leads to explore.

'Those deaths aren't connected to Neil's murder,' Bob was saying again. 'Everything tells me this is something different. I know there are links, but it's the method. It's not the same murderer—and that's IF these deaths are murder at all.'

'It might not be the same killer, but what if Neil's was a

professional hit like you said and it's the same person arranging all the deaths? If we prove that the other agency clients were killed, then whoever committed those murders without detection could be a pro. They avoided making the deaths look suspicious.' Claire was desperate to avoid the SoulMates case being given to another team because Bob, or someone higher up, decided it wasn't connected to their own investigation.

Bob didn't answer directly.

'We need to find bloody Micky Stratton in Vietnam. He's got to have information. Why else has he gone to ground?'

'And Sandra Jennings...'

'Yes. There's no reason a woman couldn't have ordered Neil's death, and the less violent nature of the others would fit more with a female profile. The other thing is, we can't be sure that this is one person acting alone...' The sighs came out again.

'We should check out Rosa McKenna a bit more, too. She has an axe to grind. Maybe she took umbrage at being rejected.'

'Maybe, but that doesn't explain the death of the woman, Louise Safferey...'

'Unless it's jealousy?' suggested Claire.

Bob had had enough.

'Too much conjecture and not enough facts, DI Falle. We are clutching at straws again. I want to find out who killed Neil Parsons, anything that looks like it could be related we can investigate, but we need to stay focused and first determine if those deaths really were suspicious before you waste any more time investigating them.'

'What about Rachel?' Claire looked at him now.

Bob was frowning.

'She could be the catalyst,' he began. 'Or she could be

the next victim. Either way, we need to keep an eye on her. Perhaps you should arrange for her to have a panic button. I'd say it's all a bit too coincidental for her stalker not to be related to this mess somehow.'

'What I don't understand is if Sandra Jennings is related to this, why would she have tipped me off about the deaths?'

'Possibly bragging, goading us. Or that's why I'm wondering if we could be looking at two working together. Perhaps she was involved somehow and didn't want to be any longer, which means she's either done a runner or we might have another victim out there.'

32

CLAIRE

17TH OCTOBER 2016

Claire knew she had to prove that the other agency deaths were the work of a serial killer. She was convinced she's right and now she had the coroner's reports she needed some expert help. A smiley eyed pathologist came to mind immediately, and she surprised herself by the way she felt at the prospect of meeting him again. This time she'd get him out of the mortuary and into a slightly more palatable environment. She didn't waste any time in emailing Mark Rodgers.

They agreed to meet at one of the quirky independent cafes in between the mortuary and the police station. The Daily Grind straddled the corner, with big windows showcasing its coffee bar seats, and a warm welcoming feel as soon as you walked through the door. They were both early, which Claire found made her heart spring.

'My treat,' she said to Mark. 'I'm going to be picking your brains.'

'Yes, but I promised to buy you a coffee,' he replied, his eyes shining and not leaving her face.

In the event, he got to the cashier before she did and

even persuaded her to partake in a caramel slice with her latte.

They sat down on some sofas, facing each other, but not so far apart she couldn't smell his musty, spicy aftershave. He was wearing black jeans instead of the usual hospital scrubs, and she noticed his broad thighs for the first time. The sight and smell of him stirred something in her, and she nearly blushed at the thoughts running through her mind. She quickly looked down at the papers she'd pulled out of a file to distract herself. It was hard when she had to look into his green eyes. She needed to pull herself together.

'Thanks for giving me the time for this,' she began, trying to keep things completely professional. 'There have been numerous unexplained deaths connected to a business we're investigating. None of them were ever treated as crime scenes because they looked straightforward. We have five that we know of all in the past year, but potentially there could be more.'

'Interesting,' Mark replied. 'That's definitely a bizarre statistical anomaly if it's not suicide or murder.'

'Exactly.'

'So we might be looking at an exhumation?'

'Ah, the good news is you have one in your mortuary right now. Todd Fuller.'

Mark shook his head.

'Not one of mine.'

'No, but could you take a look at him for us?'

'Of course.'

'These are all the coroners' reports and PMs for the others. If we can find anything about Todd Fuller that suggests he was murdered, then we will be in business.'

'OK, message understood, and I assume you want this yesterday?'

'Of course, thank you.'

Mark nodded. 'OK, leave them with me.' He took a sip of his coffee and deftly changed tack. 'So how you enjoying your new DI status?' he asked, smiling now.

'It's good, still a lot to learn, but I love the job.'

'Were there ever any repercussion over the Jackie Stiller case?'

'No, and that still gets me. If only they'd listened to me.' Claire felt her jaw harden.

'You're never going to win every one, you know,' Mark said, his voice softening. 'There will always be some that beat you or the rest of the investigating team. The key thing is to learn from it.'

'Yep, I know you're right, but it won't happen again on my watch, that's for sure.'

Claire thought back a year to the day she walked into Mark's autopsy suite and saw Jackie on his table. Staying professional then had been near impossible. He'd seen how much it had upset her. Layton Trent had gone to town on Jackie. She looked like a bus had run her over, her cheekbones and eye sockets broken. Every inch of her body showed blow after blow from an angry man who she'd barely even said a word to—let alone harmed or wronged. His deranged fixation with her had made her life a misery for nearly two years before he'd finally exploded. The authorities failed Jackie; she had nobody to protect her. Claire knew she would always see that broken, battered body and live with the knowledge that she too had failed her.

There was silence for a few moments, the jumble of thoughts and ideas swirling between them.

'Booked any holidays?' Mark asked, clearly trying to steer the conversation away from heavy work stuff.

'No, not yet. I'll probably pop back to Jersey for a week to see my parents at some point. You?'

'Toying with the idea of doing one of those eco-travel packages, you know where you get to go somewhere exciting and volunteer to help the locals or wildlife as well.'

'Wow, that sounds good, an awful lot more adventurous than me just going home for a week.'

'I'll send you the link to the website if you like,' he said.

A vision of herself with Mark saving sea turtles on some endless beach, or building a school in Africa, came into Claire's mind. It was a pleasant thought, certainly one she might explore further now Jack wasn't in her life.

33

RACHEL

17TH OCTOBER, 2016

I t had been an incredibly upsetting start to the week at the agency. Rachel, Gary, and Felicity watched as the police arrived en masse, and a pale-faced Eddie handed over the agency records and various documents. Turned out that Sandra had been lying to them all, and now they hadn't a clue who she really was. Rachel always felt there was a bit of an edge to Sandra, but now she's thinking back on everything she'd ever said or done to get clues as to why she might have lied about who she was. She'd always been tight-lipped about her private life, but Rachel hadn't found that unusual because she also kept herself to herself. Could Sandra have killed Neil? Could she be her stalker? The big question still was why?

With the office in such a state, Eddie sent them all home early. This was a double-edged sword for Rachel. She loved her job, it was really important to her, and if word got out that there was trouble it could mean the end of the agency. On the other hand, she was glad to get home early as she really needed to take Amber to the vets. She'd been worrying about her all day. This morning her eyes were half closed, and she seemed almost wobbly on her feet. Getting home early meant it wouldn't be quite such a rush to get her back out and through the traffic to make her appointment.

Every time she opened her front door, she was on tenterhooks. Would there be another letter? Thankfully, today the only thing to greet her on the hall floor was a flyer from a local church inviting her to meet God. In the daylight, the house held less fear, but every noise had her on alert, and she cautiously checked each room in the house before she felt even remotely secure.

This time it was a flying visit. She apologised to Reg with a quick cuddle, and then she and Amber got back in the car and headed towards Wimbledon Village and the vets.

She opened the Vet's door onto a wating room filled with bouncy tail-wagging Labradors, perfectly groomed Cockapoos and French Bulldogs, and hissing cats in baskets. Rachel had to queue behind an elderly man at the reception. He'd not got an animal with him, and when he turned to leave, she saw he'd been crying. She wondered what friend he'd had to leave behind today. The receptionist was trying to answer phone calls for appointments and deal with those waiting. She looked flustered.

'Sorry,' she mouthed to Rachel as she picked up the phone.

Rachel mouthed, 'No problem,' back but didn't dare put Amber on the ground for fear one of the canine patients would launch themselves at her. Instead, she placed her carry cage carefully on top of the reception desk, right next to the multicoloured knitted catnip filled hedgehogs being sold for a cat sanctuary.

Once the receptionist could talk, Rachel gave her name

and then retreated to the furthest corner, nursing Amber's basket on her lap and praying she wouldn't get worse with the stress. It seemed to take forever for the occupants of the room to be swapped for new arrivals and for their turn to come up. While they waited, she read the posters on how to prevent your pet from becoming obese or catching ticks.

The vet was a man in his late forties, and Rachel was glad it was someone with experience. He had soft hazel eyes, which smiled at her reassuringly as she hoisted the virtually limp Amber from the basket. Amber's legs splayed slightly as they slipped on the Formica top of the examination table. The rabbit made no effort to correct them or to run away.

'Let's have a look at you,' he said to Amber, and Rachel immediately warmed to him. A man who talked kindly to animals was a good one. He looked in Amber's eyes and opened her mouth, showing her orange-stained teeth. She was remarkably calm, and Rachel realised that might not be a good thing. Then he felt her body, expert fingers searching for any unusual lumps and swellings. He found one.

'OK. Put your hand here,' he said to Rachel, indicating Amber's stomach.

Rachel felt with her fingers like she'd just seen him do. Underneath her rabbit's soft fur was a large swelling. She looked up at him fearfully.

'From what you've told me and what I can see, I think she has a large intestinal tumour, and it may well have ruptured because she also has symptoms of anaemia.'

'What can you do?' Rachel asked.

His face was pure sympathy now.

'We could try to operate, but in all likelihood, she would die on the operating table because she's so weak and because of the shock. Even if she doesn't die, we might find that the tumour is attached to a vital organ and so impossible to remove. If the operation is successful, you are only going to be giving her a few months—at most.' He stopped now, letting the words sink in.

Rachel nodded.

'I think the kindest thing for her is to let her go.' He delivered the last punch.

She looked him in the face now and nodded again.

'I don't want her to suffer, if you really think her chances are that slim?'

'I do I'm afraid. She's clearly quite weak already, and to be honest she may not last the night, anyway. She's very dehydrated too.'

'OK,' said Rachel quietly, and she picked Amber up for one last time while the vet went to get what he needed.

WALKING BACK into the house with the basket was horrible. Inside was the dead weight of Amber's body. Rachel wanted to bring her home and lay her to rest in the garden she loved. She also knew Reg would be looking for her. Perhaps if he saw Amber's body, he'd understand why she won't be there anymore. Rachel knew the pain of non-closure only too well.

As she closed the front door, her mobile phone buzzed in her bag. She'd had the volume turned off ever since last night's calls, but thankfully there hadn't been any more. Eddie had said he'd let them all know if the office was going to be open tomorrow or not, so she gently placed down the basket and rummaged in her pocket for the phone.

It was a text, but it wasn't from Eddie. It was one word, *BITCH*

34

CLAIRE

17TH OCTOBER, 2016

When Claire arrived at Rachel Hill's house to deliver the panic alarm, it took her a good few knocks on the door before she answered. She spotted her peering through the sitting room curtains and reminded herself how terrifying it must be to have someone stalking your every move.

As Rachel opened the door, she held back, hiding behind it and opening it just enough to let Claire in. She'd been crying.

'Are you OK?' Claire asked her.

Rachel looked embarrassed and flushed.

'Yes, I'm fine, sorry. Everything just got to me today. I had to put my rabbit to sleep and there's all the stuff going on at the agency. Then I received a nasty text. I just wish I knew who it is that's doing this...'

'They're texting you?' Claire asked and Rachel nodded, leading her through into the kitchen where the notebook and recent letter sat.

'I had a series of phone calls last night too and they were here, outside.'

'Why didn't you call us?'

'I went out and shouted at them,' she looked embarrassed again, 'and they seemed to go away. The phone calls stopped.'

'Right, let's have a look at your phone, see where the calls are coming from. I've brought an alarm with me, something you can carry around with you at all times. It will go straight through to the control room, which means you'll get help faster. I'll show you that in a minute too.'

An hour later and Claire and Rachel were sitting at the breakfast bar in her kitchen. Rachel was making another coffee and Claire had just come off a phone call to one of the team.

Claire took a moment to look around her. Rachel's kitchen was spacious compared to her own and completely uncluttered. She didn't appear to be into modern gadgets and equipment at all. The worktops were clean and empty, not like her flat had been with Jack's stuff everywhere. His water bottle to keep his fluids up when exercising, the juicer so he could whizz up some weird green goo that was going to make him super healthy and strong. Not to mention the fake bar signs... but that was last week. This week her kitchen was also uncluttered, and Claire felt a warm glow of contentment about that fact. Not to mention the certainty that when she got home, she wouldn't have to put up with visitors and impromptu social gatherings when she was tired.

Rachel sat back down with the cafetière and pulled her out of her thoughts.

'Well, they've confirmed that the mobile phone used was a Pay-As-You-Go, and it was last used in the vicinity of your house. We'll monitor it now, see if we can track where else they go, but I suspect whoever it is won't be stupid enough to take it home with them left on.'

Rachel looked pretty miserable, and Claire felt sorry for her, she'd had a crap day. She tried some small talk, albeit with inquisitiveness as its driver.

'Not into smartphones then?'

She handed Rachel her mobile phone back, a standard Samsung flip phone.

'No, I can't be bothered with social media and all that stuff. With our clients, I notice they feel more isolated and lonely when they're hooked on Facebook and Twitter. They see everyone else seemingly having these busy, fun-filled lives and all it does is rub in the fact they're on their own.'

'Doesn't it make people feel connected to someone, even if it is online? I find I can keep in touch with what's going on back home in Jersey.'

'It can, and I'm sure it's great for many people, but if you're someone prone to loneliness and you see a person you care about doing great stuff miles away where you can't join in, it can just make you feel more isolated. People use it as a crutch, but it won't solve their problem, which is the fact they want a real relationship.'

'No, I suppose not.'

'You met your boyfriend at work, I assume?' Rachel asked. She'd cheered up a bit now her mind had been taken off the stalker.

'Err, yes, but actually we've just split up.' Claire found herself confiding.

'Oh, I'm sorry to hear that.'

'It's OK,' Claire replied. 'We'd drifted apart, wanted different things.'

Rachel looked at her for a brief moment as though she was studying her, then her face changed.

'Why were you all at the agency today?' she asked her.

'It's part of our investigation into Neil's death. I need

to ask you some questions about the agency and about Sandra. Would it be OK if I did that now?'

Rachel nodded.

'She called in sick today, didn't she? Is she OK? Nothing's happened to her, has it?'

'Do you know her well?' Claire avoided Rachel's questions.

Rachel thought a few moments.

'We see each other five days a week, but actually, I suppose I don't know her that well. We talk in the office, occasionally we all go out for team drinks and things, but if I think about it, I know very little about her.'

'No idea where she was born, where she went on weekends, what she liked to do in her spare time?'

'No. No idea at all.' Rachel looked surprised.

'And do you have any idea if she might have been seeing someone at the agency? Or if she had a partner at home?'

'No. She's very business-like, efficient. She really just avoids all the personal stuff. We spend our days talking to people about their private lives, so I don't find that unusual, just think it's an antidote to all the emotional stuff we deal with each day.'

'Does she get on with everyone at the agency?'

'Yes, as far as I'm aware.'

'Do you and her get on?' Claire pushed.

'Yes. I have no issues with her at all. We're friendly. She is OK, isn't she?'

'These are just routine questions we're asking all the staff. Do you have good relations with the rest of them, Gary, Eddie, Felicity?'

'Yeah, we're all good. As you know, I occasionally meet up with Gary out of hours, he's a nice guy, Felicity, we don't really have much in common and Eddie he's married and always seems to be busy, but it's a nice team.'

'What about clients, are there any you can think of that have caused you or the other staff any issues, or who have acted oddly?'

'No one apart from Rosa McKenna who keeps saying she's going to sue the agency. I'll be honest, I told her she shouldn't have joined. She's never going to find a meaningful relationship the way she is, she's too into herself. Rosa is one of those people who would make someone lonely if they were in a relationship with her, You know what I mean? She'd be so self-absorbed that they'd feel unloved.'

Claire nodded and couldn't stop an image of her father drift through her mind.

'I've met her,' is all Claire said.

'My job is more than just getting people to go on dates, you know.' Rachel was looking upset again. 'I know some people think working for a dating agency is silly, but we help people. Loneliness is very painful and there have been loads of studies which show it causes physical illness, depression, and other mental illness. It's not just a gimmicky Valentine's thing. Humans are social creatures, like rabbits, we all need somebody at some point and some people need somebody all the time. We help them find each other.'

Claire couldn't help but wonder if the agency could survive the investigation storm that was about to hit, but she wasn't going to make Rachel's day any worse by mentioning that now.

By the time Claire was ready to go, Rachel was looking a little better. She'd explained how to use the panic alarm and made her promise that she'd call if the stalker returned. Claire left with the letter for forensics, she'd take it in with her in the morning. She'd also get the Pay-As-You-Go phone checked, see if they could find any information on who bought it.

It was only as she headed towards home that she thought about Jack—or rather the lack of Jack.

35

UNKNOWN
17TH OCTOBER, 2016

It's useful being someone people don't look twice at. It means you can meld into the background, walk along a street and not be noticed. It means that you can survey a house and not be seen by the police officer who was pandering to the whimpering bitch.

She'd got them wrapped around her finger. If she thought she'd won this round, that the game was over, then she'd got a big surprise coming.

Rachel Hill would pay for her past.

36

CLAIRE

17TH / 18TH OCTOBER, 2016

There were little reminders of Jack around the flat. He'd forgotten his toothbrush for one thing, and Claire came across a black sock curled up under their bed, her bed, forgotten and festering. The place looked tidier and definitely felt bigger now it was less cluttered. She felt able to breathe and stretch. The TV almost looked naked without its network of wires and gadgets coming out of it. The glass shelves on which it sat had been full of handsets and controls, PS4 games, and DVDs, but now there were just their ghostly outlines in dust.

She had to admit that the walls looked bare. Were they always like that? She'd moved in here first, been in around a month or so before Jack joined her permanently. Were the walls really that barren back then, or had she had something of her own hanging there, something that reflected *her* character? When he moved in, was it relegated to a cupboard and replaced by the huge bright canvas of multicoloured skulls which he loved so much, but which left her cold?

She looked in the storage cupboard at the back of the

bedroom. Even that was now half-empty without Jack's sports stuff. She tried to remember what was in the boxes, if there were any pictures stored in the darkness. She found nothing but the vague memory of Jack coming back to the flat one day with the canvas and saying it would fill the empty wall. That was in the days when she couldn't wait to rush home to him and their life together.

Now, there was no one to watch *Game of Thrones* with, or to share a meal or glass of wine. The endless possibility of quiet nights on her own fanned out in front of her. Did it worry her being alone? How would she fill her after-work hours now the social whirlpool that was Jack had gone? Right now, Claire didn't know, but she wasn't worried about it either.

He was right of course. She wasn't ready to settle yet. She may be thirty-three, but she couldn't hear her body clock ticking, maybe she never would. It was best for both of them. She wouldn't make him happy. Maybe she never had.

Back in the living room/kitchen, she remembered the last 'gathering'. There were about twelve of Jack's friends. She was there too, that cow Lara Phillips. They'd talked until Lara had got too drunk to make any sense. Claire had swirled around them, clearing up empty beer bottles, making tea, putting pizzas on. In the middle of it all had been Jack. Jack the comedian. Jack the best game player. Jack the one everyone wanted to be with. Claire had watched it all, and she had felt a stranger in her own home, more alone than she felt now. They were Jack's friends. It was Jack's gathering and the lure of Jack, the essence of him which they all loved–and she had too once–that no longer had any draw.

She settled herself on the sofa but didn't turn the TV on. A forgotten book caught her eye on the coffee table, probably uncovered when Jack took his car and football magazines. He never liked her reading, always said it was unsociable, even though he'd sit gawping at the TV all evening if they didn't have people round.

First thing first, though, she called her parents. Her mum picked up.

'Hello, love,' Her mum cheerfully answered. 'We're fine. Managed to burn my wrist on the oven, but it's nothing serious. Are you coming back at Christmas? That ice rink at Fort Regent isn't going to be on this year, someone else is doing a little one on the Weighbridge. There's a petition online to persuade them to put it on, if you want to sign it?'

'It's OK, Mum. I'm not that bothered about ice skating, it's just something to do. I'm not even sure about Christmas yet, it's going to depend on work.'

'How is work?' her mum asked.

'Very busy. I think I might have uncovered a serial killer. It's not definite yet, but it could be a huge case.'

'Really? A serial killer?' Her mum turned away from the phone. 'Phillip, did you hear that? Claire has uncovered a serial killer.' Claire heard her dad murmur in the background. 'I'll pass you on to your father, love,' her mum said. 'Well done.'

Claire heard her mother heave herself out of her chair and pass the phone to her dad.

'Hello, Claire,' her dad answered with his police officer's voice on.

'Hi, Dad, obviously I can't talk about it, but I was just saying to Mum that the murder enquiry I'm on at the moment, it looks like I might have uncovered a serial killer.'

'You uncovered it?'

'Yeah, someone said something to me, and I

investigated it, gathered some evidence, and now we're looking at six plus deaths.'

'Good work. Make sure your ACC knows that and make sure it goes on your record and your DCI doesn't take the credit.'

'Oh no, he wouldn't do that.'

'Don't be so trusting, Claire. This could be a big boost to someone's career, immediate promotion. You could be running your own investigation and he might not like a woman promoted to the same rank as him, especially a younger one.'

'Dad, there are plenty of women DCIs now, he's very supportive.'

'What people say and what people do aren't always the same thing. What does Jack think? He not up for a promotion yet?'

Jack's rank, sergeant, and one rank below her had always been a bit of an issue with her dad. One thing she would not do was ruin her evening by telling him Jack had left. Of course, there was the strong possibility he might not think that's a bad thing, but she wasn't prepared to take that risk.

'Probably soon. So how's the golfing handicap going?' Claire deflected the conversation, and her dad was happy to talk about himself for a few minutes before abruptly deciding he needed to go as they had *The Great British Bake Off* ready to watch on pause after recording it last week, and they needed to watch it before the next episode. Claire didn't point out that as it was recorded there was no rush, and there was around 48 hours before the programme aired again.

Claire sat in the silence, letting it settle her until her stomach rumbles became too distracting. Then she cooked the ready-made meal she'd bought for Jack the night before and curled up on the sofa with the book, reading until her eyes became too dry and tired to continue. An hour later she took herself to bed, momentarily thinking about the possibility of some new exciting sex at some point in the future, before the tiredness swamped her, and she slipped into sleep.

THE NEXT MORNING, she woke to find she had spread herself diagonally across the bed. It was a good sleep, no interruptions from snoring or having someone else moving around in bed next to her. She felt positive and energised and bounced into work.

'We've got a lead on Sandra Jennings.' Lew was already at his desk when she arrived. 'I sent that agency staff photo to the real Sandra's parents, turned out they were childhood friends. Her name is Carly Watson. We're trying to trace her now.' Lew looked delighted with his find.

'Brilliant, anything on the system for her?'

'Domestic abuse three years ago. He badly knocked her around. The partner got sent down for eighteen months. We're trying to track him down now, too. He's out.'

'Good, progress at last.' Claire smiled at Lew. This was the most they'd spoken since Jack left. Yesterday was just one big awkward silence. 'Want a coffee?'

As soon as she'd said it, she wished she hadn't. Getting a coffee would mean going to the canteen and the prospect of seeing Jack or that bitch Lara. Still, she wasn't going to be scared or embarrassed to walk around. She was going to have to bump into them sometime.

The sometime, as luck would have it, appeared to be now. She spotted them the second she walked in. The two of them were by the far window, backs to her. Lara had her hand on his shoulder, and she was stroking the back of his head. He looked so happy and relaxed. Opposite them were a couple of Jack's colleagues, and one of them quickly spotted Claire. His eyes indicated that he'd noticed her. Lara's hand immediately dropped down to cradle her coffee cup, and she sat self-consciously at the table.

Claire wasn't sure whether she liked that reaction. What it did was prompt the group to break up. Lara left first, discreetly saying goodbye and slipping round the back of the food counter to avoid going anywhere near Claire. Then Jack and his colleagues got up to leave. As they drew level, he stayed back and diverted over to Claire while they walked on ahead.

'Catch you up,' he said to them. 'Hi, Claire, how are you doing?'

'I'm fine. You?'

'Yeah, good. Just wanted to see if you're OK, that's all.'

'Sure. Course I am, thanks.'

He seemed to be waiting for her to say something else, but she didn't. She concentrated on handing over some cash to the woman on the till.

'OK, see you around then.'

He smiled at her, the Jack smile. The smile that won her over when she first met him. Fit body with a Paul Newman smile. The scent of his aftershave tugged memories from the back of her mind, and she allowed herself a quick look at his retreating back.

Then she picked up the coffees and got on with work.

37

CLAIRE

18TH OCTOBER, 2016

Felicity Baxter was next on their list of agency staff to interview. They'd tried to speak to her yesterday, but apparently, she'd been too busy. It had taken some persuading, but Felicity finally made her way to their interview room where Claire and Bob found her typing on her mobile phone.

The room was already heaving with her perfume, and it was immediately clear what she spent most of her wages on.

'Give me a mo,' she said to them, barely lifting up her mascara-laden eyelashes. 'I'm just emailing a recruitment dude. Looks like I'm job hunting thanks to you lot.'

Not surprisingly, Claire felt Bob arch his back and breathe in deeply next to her.

'Miss Baxter, we are conducting a murder enquiry and while we appreciate you taking the time to come in here and talk to us, it would work in your favour as well as ours, if you were to give us your full attention.'

She looked up now.

'My favour?' she queried.

'Yes,' Bob replied curtly. 'At present, all staff and clients of the SoulMates agency are potential suspects.'

'Oh, come on, there's no way you can think I would have killed Neil! Why would I?'

Neither Bob nor Claire answered. The suggestion had served its purpose, and her mobile phone went into her handbag.

'How long have you been with the agency?' Claire broke the tension.

'About four years. I'd been a hair colour technician before that but was having problems with the chemicals, so I thought it would be a good change. You know what it's like as a hairdresser, you end up hearing all your clients' personal problems anyway, so it wasn't that much of a leap.'

'Do you get on with everyone at the agency? Staff?'

'Yeah. Eddie's a sweetheart, he's like I wish my dad was, do you know what I mean? The rest of them, they're all right. Not people I'd hang with, but they're OK.'

'How about Sandra Jennings?'

Felicity shrugged and thought.

'Fine. A bit intense, doesn't talk much, but you know…'

'Rachel?'

'She's sweet, loves her animals. Bakes nice cakes.'

'And Gary?'

'Gary's Gary. Can be a bit stressy at times, but he's fun.'

'Have you been aware of any deaths among your clients, besides Neil?' Claire changed tack now.

Felicity thought again. 'Yeah, there's been a few, but no murders.' She shrugged. 'We've got about two hundred and sixty clients and most of them are, like, in their forties and fifties, you're bound to lose some, right?'

Bob bristled again, which made Claire smile. He'd

been an absolute nightmare last year when it was his fiftieth birthday. Just couldn't get his head around the fact he'd reached half a century.

'Did you know Neil?' Bob asked now.

'Not really. He was Gary's client. I've obviously seen him on the system. We matched him with some of mine. Nice looking bloke.'

'So you've no idea who he was seeing, if he had any issues with anybody at the agency—staff or clients?'

'No. There'll be records of who he booked dates with, but nobody really mentioned him or anything. Oh, the only one who I do know is a pain is Rosa McKenna. She's a right cow.'

'WE KEEP GETTING Rosa McKenna's name mentioned.'

Bob and Claire were standing in the corridor after Felicity Baxter had left, getting a bit of fresh air after leaving the interview room door open to de-fragrance the place.

'I went round to see her. She was home alone when Neil was killed so no one to corroborate her alibi, but I didn't pursue it because we'd been looking for a man. She was also helpful in giving me the names of clients who have died.'

'Have you checked to see if she's got any links to our friend in Vietnam, Michael Stratton?'

'No.'

'Well, get on to it, get cross-referencing everyone we have on that board, double check all their alibis, and see if we can find any connections.'

Bob disappeared off for some peace in the Gents bathroom, and Claire slunk back to her desk. There must be a pattern, something to join the dots.

38

CLAIRE

18TH OCTOBER, 2016

'We've got her.' Lew rushed over, a huge grin on his face. 'They're bringing in Carly Watson aka Sandra Jennings, now.'

'Excellent,' Bob said. 'Progress at last.'

It was the first smile Claire had seen on his face all week. Earlier she thought he was going to have a heart attack. He was on the phone to somebody at the Embassy in Vietnam and clearly getting more and more frustrated by the fact they didn't seem to be making much effort to find Michael Stratton. He'd gone into the countryside on some trek, well away from Wi-Fi and the hand of the law —apparently!

Claire marvelled at how, despite the incident room being packed out, the entire team had managed to avoid going anywhere near Bob's desk for the last hour—perhaps the survival techniques they taught at the training academy really did work.

Two hours later, once Carly had finished with the duty solicitor, Bob and Claire walked into the interview room.

Claire was buzzing. Could this be the moment the investigation really took off?

Carly Watson looked a whole heap different to the calm and organised Sandra Jennings. A scruffy ponytail had replaced the neat figure-of-eight hair style. She'd cried away most of her make-up and was pale, red-eyed, and distinctly petrified. Question was, who or what was she scared of?

'Before you ask my client any questions, she would like to make a statement,' the solicitor next to her began as soon as the recording was on.

She was a small grey mouse of a woman, but with the eyes and stare of a hawk. Carly sat next to her, hanging her head.

'Carly Susan Watson would like to apologise for the inconvenience and any distress she has caused. She fully admits that she has been living under a false name, but this was not for any criminal purpose and no financial gain has been made. Carly was subjected to years of brutal domestic violence at the hands of her former husband, Mark Farley. He was sentenced to eighteen months in jail but has since been released. Carly fears for her life and that of her daughter and it is for that reason, and that reason only, that she decided to hide from Mark Farley with a false name.'

Carly's solicitor looked up from reading out the statement, ready for the interview to begin.

'If you hadn't committed a crime, why did you run as soon as we visited the agency?' Claire jumped right in. It couldn't be that simple. Carly must have something else she was hiding.

Carly looked up at her.

'I panicked. After I spoke to you, I realised that you might investigate the agency and discover I'd been lying about my name. I was also worried the newspapers might get involved and he'd see me somehow.' She sniffed, rubbing her nose on the back of her hand. 'You've no idea what it's like to live in fear every day of your life, to worry every time you drop your daughter off at school in case he finds out where we are, snatches her, hurts her. You see these cases on the TV, where some jealous or spiteful ex-husband murders the children to get at the wife. That's my worst fear and I know he's capable of it.'

'You could have asked us for help.'

'What could the police do until he's threatened or attacked us?'

'When you spoke to me, you could have explained the circumstances rather than running.'

'I didn't want to get Eddie into any trouble. He's such a lovely guy, he's been an absolute rock for me.'

'Mr Scott knew that you were living under a false name?'

'I wasn't doing anything wrong. He wanted to help me, to protect us.'

'Were you and Mr Scott having a relationship, Carly?' Bob asked now.

'No, it's not like that. He's just a genuinely nice person. He's not interested in me in that way.'

'So you don't have any issues, let's say, with people who are in relationships or men generally?'

Carly looked shocked now. 'No. No, of course I don't. I know not every guy is like Mark. He is a complete bastard. I thought working there might restore my faith in men, actually.'

'And has it?' Claire was curious.

'Eddie has. There's been loads of people he's helped through the agency.'

'Do you have any idea who might have wanted to kill Neil Parsons?' Bob asked now.

Carly shook her head.

'No.'

'Can you tell us where you were on the evening of October thirteenth?'

'Yeah, I knew you'd ask, and we were having dinner with Clarissa and her family.' She hung her head again. 'I feel terrible just moving out like that. I was with her from about six to midnight.'

'You told me that Neil wasn't the only agency client to have died, that there were others. Was this something you were concerned about?'

'I was beginning to wonder... I don't know, but something just told me it was a little odd.'

'Odd?'

'Yes, it's just there seemed to be so many. I manage the client accounts you see and they all had one thing in common.'

Claire and Bob both looked at Carly expectantly now.

'They were the clients we'd had on our books the longest.'

'All of them?'

'Yes, apart from Neil. If you look at how long they'd been with us, how many dates they'd been on, the ones who died were those who had been on the most dates and had been members the longest. I used to think that maybe there was a reason for that. You know they were just not the kind of people who others fell in love with because they were depressed or something, but it niggled me.'

'Did you mention this to Eddie?'

'Yes, but he doesn't see people the way I do, he's very trusting and couldn't believe that something bad was going on.'

'Why didn't you contact the police before about this?' Bob asked. 'If you really thought that there was an issue?'

'Well, I think you know that. It's why I've ended up here. Nobody else seemed to think their deaths were suspicious, and I wanted to keep a low profile.'

'Did you suspect that someone at the agency might have been involved?'

Carly looked thoughtful, then shrugged.

'I don't know. I read a lot of crime thrillers, so I was thinking about the motive. The only one who seems to have it in for Eddie is Rosa McKenna. She found out that some of the photos in the books and on the walls aren't really clients, and she knew the agency was struggling financially. I'm not saying it's her or anything, but she's the only one I know who had threatened Eddie. She'd dated just about every one of our male clients, and not a single one of them was either good enough for her or wanted to see her again. Doesn't that tell you something about a person?'

CLAIRE

18TH OCTOBER, 2016

Rosa McKenna wasn't too pleased about having to come into the station to be interviewed, but Bob was insistent.

'She wants a bloody home visit, does she? Well, I want her in here, out of her comfort zone. Tell her it can be voluntary or it can not. Up to her. I'm too busy trying to track down a murderer to drive round for a coffee and chat.'

Claire did as she was told and quietly admitted to herself that she enjoyed laying down the law to the hard-faced Rosa McKenna.

They released Carly Watson with a caution and on the proviso she was available for further questions. Claire also put her back in touch with the domestic violence team and asked them to see if her ex was still a credible threat.

The fact Carly's name change and disappearance appeared to be nothing to do with the case meant they were back to square one. Eddie would have to answer a few questions though, but as Rosa was next in the interview room, she was certainly not going to be in for an easy time of it.

Once Carly was dealt with, Claire tried to catch-up with as much of the information gathered by the team as she could. There was still no further news on the elusive Michael Stratton. They'd been through all the CCTV around Neil's flat, and nothing had been flagged up. Everyone had been cross-checked to see if there were any connections besides the agency, and that had drawn a blank. Neil's killer had now earned the nickname the Invisible Man, and Bob was getting more irate by the hour. Cue Rosa McKenna. Claire had a sneaking suspicion Bob wasn't going to warm to her.

'I'm really not very happy about having to come in here like this. I do work you know,' Rosa berated Claire and Bob before they'd even said hello.

Bob smiled thinly. 'I'm sure Neil Parsons wasn't very happy about being murdered, which is why we are undertaking an investigation to find out who killed him.'

Rosa bristled at his snipe, but it shut her up. Claire suspected she wasn't used to people standing up to her. She was dressed in a pinstripe suit today, which made her look even less human than she had when Rachel saw her at home. She reminded her of one of those robotic alien characters off *Doctor Who*.

'Thank you for coming in to answer a few questions,' Bob began. His voice carried a slight undertone of sarcasm that only those who knew him would detect. 'I'd like to ask you first how you knew Mr Parsons and where you met?'

'I've already said this.' Rosa McKenna looked at Claire as though she had the IQ of a chimpanzee. 'Neil and I met for a date on August twenty-seventh at Zedel in Soho.'

'Thank you, Ms McKenna, and that was the only time you ever met Neil?' Bob pushed.

Her face changed a little now. A small wave of uncertainty flowed across it. She didn't change her demeanour; the change was subtle, but for Claire and Bob it was a marker.

'Yes.'

'Only, I've been reading Neil's application for the SoulMates agency, and it was noted that his friend suggested he join after a recommendation from yourself.'

The wave of uncertainty changed from a gentle lap to surfing proportions.

'Well, yes, but that was just a brief encounter.'

'What was, Ms McKenna?'

'I bumped into a guy at a club. He had worked at Stalton and Jones for a couple of months, where I work, and he introduced me briefly to Neil.'

'Briefly?'

'Yes, we chatted for a bit. He mentioned that Neil was single and just wasn't meeting the right girls. I suggested to Mike that he tell him to join SoulMates.'

'Mike?'

'Yes, Mike Stratton, the guy who used to work with me, they were really good friends—so he told me.'

'When was this?' Claire asked now.

'Actually, I think it was August, the beginning. I think Neil joined up mid-month.'

'You think?' Bob chipped in. 'He signed up on the twenty-fifth, according to his application, and the first matches were sent to him by the twenty-eighth. Your profile wasn't in the matches sent.' Bob scanned the agency records for Neil Parsons and showed them to Rosa McKenna.

A tidal wave ripped across Rosa's face now, disturbing her rigid features, making her face flush red and her mouth twist.

'How were you able to go on a date on the twenty-seventh with someone you hadn't been matched with?' Bob pressed.

'Look, I have done nothing wrong. I met Neil that first time and liked him OK? I thought he was hot, and wanted to go on a date with him. I just used my brains and engineered it so that we could meet properly. What's wrong with that? As a premium member, you can choose to contact people. I looked out for his profile and as soon as it was available, got Gary to contact him for me. It's all above board, just ask Eddie.'

'How well do you know Michael Stratton?' Bob changed direction now.

'Not very well. He was a temp, worked in our department for a couple of months last year that's all. Really outgoing, was a complete charmer, the kind of guy who'd get on with both men and women. He was fun.'

'Are you still in contact with him?'

'No. I saw him once more after August, at the same club, the Zero:Ten and that's it.'

'With Neil?'

'Yes, with Neil and some woman.'

'Some woman?'

'I don't know who she was, long dark hair, petite, loads of make-up. I think she was a girlfriend.'

'Whose?'

Rosa shrugged and shook her head.

'Couldn't tell you. I didn't hang around after I knew they were both there.'

'Why leave?' Claire asked.

Rosa looked at her, fixing her gaze.

'Has someone you fancied ever snubbed you? I'd really liked Neil. I'd hoped he was going to like me, but he didn't give it a chance.'

'You were angry at Neil?' Bob jumped in now, purposefully goading.

Rosa frowned and scowled at him. 'Look, I don't have to be here, you know. If you're going to in any way start implying things, then I'm going to call my lawyer. In fact, I'm going to do that right now. I think I've answered all your questions.'

She rose from her chair, picking up her handbag.

Bob held his hands up. 'Actually, I do have some more questions, Ms McKenna, if you wouldn't mind staying seated?'

'Actually, I do mind. I need to get back to work and you need to stop harassing me and get on with finding out who murdered Neil.'

With that, she grabbed her jacket, hoisting it off the back of the chair and swooshing it onto her shoulder, nearly hitting Claire in the face as she went.

She left Bob and Claire sitting there in her wake.

'That went down well then,' Bob said. 'She's a buttoned-up tight-arsed madam, isn't she?'

Claire smiled.

'You could say that, but is she capable of murder?'

'She's a control freak, that's what she is. Certainly wouldn't commit a murder herself, but could she have someone doing it for her? Possibly. But she's going to really have to be a bitch if she's killed him just because he won't go out on a second date with her.'

'Maybe it's just the ones she really likes. She can't bear them rejecting her and going out with someone else.'

'Possible.' He nodded. 'Right now, possibles are all we have. The key to Neil's death will be found once we've tracked down Michael Stratton, I'm sure of it. Nobody disappears into deepest, darkest Vietnam unless they're hiding from something, or perhaps worried about someone. He did after all introduce them. In the meantime, let's do some more digging on the delightful Ms McKenna. We need to be sure she's not lying about her alibi, or her relationship with Stratton.'

40

RACHEL

18TH OCTOBER, 2016

Eddie sent a text first thing to say the office was closed for the day. It was the first text she'd been grateful to receive lately, as it meant she could spend some time with Reg, who'd been looking listless and not eating much. He was still in the utility room and she was going to keep him in there, close to her, where he was safe and warm.

Rachel was also glad for the time to think. It was looking increasingly like the agency might go down the tubes with the latest setback and that was a big blow. She loved her job. It was important, even though she knew people just didn't understand that. She was going to need to start looking for another way to continue doing her work.

In all honesty, the whole situation with the stalker had also tainted her enjoyment of the house. It was compromised, invaded. The housing market in London was phenomenal right now, so maybe it was time to move on, get away from whoever it was that had been disrupting her life. She wasn't running; she was just being pragmatic.

Having the day off would give her the chance to contact agents and get them round.

The house wasn't exactly untidy, but Rachel walked from room to room, looking at what she might need to sort out, trying to view her home from a buyer's point of view.

Her phone buzzed with another message. She expected Eddie's name to pop up on her screen again, but it was just a phone number and the words,

Not working today Bitch?

Rachel swayed a little with the shock of it, her eyes ranging around her. She ducked out of sight of the windows. That meant they had to be out there now to know she hadn't gone to work. She immediately forwarded the text to DI Falle. Within a few minutes, a police car had arrived, and she saw two officers in her back garden checking the area.

A few minutes later, there was a knock at the door. Assuming it was one of the police officers, Rachel went straight to answer it. Her guard was down.

When she opened the door, there was no one there.

As the two policemen reappeared from the side entrance to her garden, empty-handed, something at her feet caught Rachel's eye. She saw the note first. *This should have been you*, and initially she couldn't make out what the brown, mud covered thing was on her doorstep, so she bent down a little to peer more closely. Through the mud she saw white teeth. White rabbit's teeth stained with orange. Rachel recoiled in horror. The two police officers rushed over and looked at what she was staring at. Rachel stood there, hand over her mouth, stifling the urge to scream.

'It's my rabbit, Amber, he's dug her up from the garden where I buried her.' She finally said, looking up at them wide-eyed and shocked. 'Why? Why are they doing this to me?'

41

UNKNOWN

18TH OCTOBER 2016

That was so exhilarating. And the expression on her face…

It's time to play the final hand.

I'm coming for you, Rachel Hill. I know your secret and I am going to make you pay.

42

RACHEL

MID MAY 1994

To begin with, Rachel thought she was dying. Blood was never good, was it? She must be ill. Her first instinct was to call out to her dad, but she knew he'd still be sleeping off last night's whisky, and besides, she didn't want to because of where it was. She was embarrassed.

She started to think maybe this was God's way of helping her be with her mother again, in heaven, but Rachel wasn't ready to die yet. She was scared. Her lower stomach felt like something was squeezing and pulling at her insides. Stretching them out until the flesh almost ripped. The pain, sharp and dull at the same time, was what had woken her and then she felt the stickiness of the blood between her thighs. When she pulled back the duvet, shock hit her as she saw the red which had seeped through her pyjama bottoms and onto the bedsheet.

She rushed to the bathroom and, using a hand mirror, tried to see where the blood was coming from. She could walk. The blood wasn't pouring. As the panic subsided, she remembered the lessons at school. Could this be what they called a period? There wasn't any talk of pain like this, but the rest of it fitted.

She went back to bed and lay, foetal like, clutching at her tummy, rocking to and fro when the pain got too bad. Maybe she could go to the doctors or look at the computer in the school library, get some information—if she could manage to walk down the lane to the bus.

It was hard to wash the blood from the sheet and her pyjamas. Rings of rusty red, like some deadly tide lines, remained, and she had to scrub at them with soap to make them fade. Even with the scrubbing the stains could still be seen. She left them to dry over the back of a chair in her bedroom. Her father never ventured in there.

She found an old vest, long since grown out of, cut it in strips and then wrapped them around her panties. It felt like a big lump between her legs, but at least there were several layers to go through before the blood could seep into her clothes.

Walking to the school bus was a struggle. Now and then the pain would increase, and she'd be forced to stop, clutching at her stomach. Even without the sharp pain, her back ached as though in sympathy with her womb.

The ride to school was a blur. She was so self-conscious. Everyone must know. She must look different. Sitting down eased the pain, but it didn't go away and the bulge of vest strips between her legs was uncomfortable.

She could barely concentrate in lessons. The urge to rock back and forth through the pain was huge. The last thing she wanted to do was sit rigidly upright on the plastic classroom chairs, but she did for fear of drawing attention to herself. She tried to think of her mother, what she would have said and done, as wave after wave ripped at her insides.

What if the blood had come through? When the bell went for end of lesson, she hung back as the other kids got up for break. She hoped they'd clear the classroom so if the blood had leaked through her trousers they wouldn't see.

A group was gathered round a magazine near to the front and weren't going anywhere.

Rachel had to move.

She rose tentatively from her chair. There on the blue plastic seat was a smear of red. She felt her cheeks flush immediately, and panic flooded through her. Grabbing a scrap of tissue from her blazer pocket and as discreetly as she could, she wiped the smear away. Now she had to get to the toilet without anyone seeing her. She took her blazer and wrapped the arms around her waist to cover her rear and almost ran to the loos.

The vest strips had leaked down one side, the blood making their once white material all red and brown. What was she going to do? Is this normal? She readjusted the strips and added some toilet tissue, carefully hoisting her pants and arranging the makeshift pad to avoid any further leaks. Her school trousers were thankfully black, so it was difficult to see the blood, but there was no way she could carry on like this. Rachel headed to the library and breathed a sigh of relief when she saw that the research computer was free.

It didn't take her long to confirm she was having her first period, and so she avidly read up on the information her mother would have told her.

She needed a pad, but where was she going to get one from? Rachel hadn't any girl friends she'd trust in school, trust to not go and snigger behind her back and tell the rest of the class. The thought of everyone knowing mortified her. There was only one person she could turn to, Miss Mayhew.

Miss Mayhew was on duty in the playground when she eventually found her, and the bell for a return to classes was just ringing. Children were streaming into the school building, but Rachel stood firm against the human tide and waited for Miss Mayhew to be alone.

'Miss Mayhew?' she tentatively asked. The pain was one thing, but the agonising embarrassment of what she was about to say was worse. 'Can I ask you something please?'

Miss Mayhew looked at her and gave a perfunctory smile.

'Hello, Rachel, of course.'

There were still a few children sauntering past, too many ears to risk saying it aloud here.

'Somewhere private?' Rachel added.

Miss Mayhew looked at her watch.

'I've got English now so it will need to be quick, or do you want to catch me at lunch?'

'Now please,' Rachel meekly replied.

Miss Mayhew didn't look overly pleased. She looked at her watch again and pursed her lips, but she led her into the empty Arts classroom.

'What is it, Rachel, I don't have long?'

'I think I'm having my period.' Rachel almost whispered the last word, her cheeks burning hot.

'Oh, OK, that's perfectly natural you know, nothing to be worried or embarrassed about.' Miss Mayhew's voice had softened and when Rachel looked up her face had a veil of sympathy and a warm smile.

'But I don't have a pad or anything,' Rachel blurted out.

'Oh, you poor thing. That's not a problem, come with me and I'll get you one.'

Miss Mayhew led her to the teachers' staffroom. 'Are you feeling OK?' she chatted along the way. 'How is your dad? Is everything all right at home?'

'He's fine, thank you. I'm fine,' Rachel replied. She was grateful for Miss Mayhew's help on this occasion, but there was no way she would give her an opportunity to interfere at home.

The teacher went straight to a cupboard in the staffroom and pulled out a medical box from which she plucked a packet of sanitary towels. She took one out, hesitated, and then took another three, before handing them to Rachel.

'Here you go, we're only supposed to hand out one, but you'll need to change it every few hours depending on how heavy the flow is.'

Rachel quickly stuffed them away into her bag like an illicit contraband, fearful that someone would walk in and catch her.

'Thank you, Miss,' she replied.

'No problem. You know you can always come to me if you've got any issues, don't you?' Miss Mayhew said to her.

There goes that sympathy again. Rachel looked away.

'Yes. Thank you,' she replied before walking off quickly to the toilets.

It was a horrible day. Rachel cowered back into the shadows even more than she usually did, suffering from pain and embarrassment. By the time the bell went for home, she'd already soaked through two pads and had to use the third for the journey home. She found that walking heightened both the pain and the bleeding, but she knew that as soon as she'd got in, and got some money from her dad, she was going to have to go back out again to the shop.

As Rachel walked into the yard, she saw a van from the electricity company and two men at the front door talking to her father. His voice was raised, theirs calm and professional. The look on her dad's face was not a welcoming one.

Rachel didn't want them to see her, so she diverted round the back of the farmhouse to the kitchen door and then ran straight up to her bedroom. She changed out of her school clothes and went to the bathroom where she used the last pad. Walking somewhere was the last thing she felt like doing right now, but she had to get to the shop to get some more sanitary towels.

The front door slammed shut, rattling the sash windows in their frames. Rachel ran down to find her father.

He was standing in the kitchen, leaning on the table, head bent. His back was to her. The jumper he wore hung off him now, making him look scruffy with his beard and hair that hadn't seen the barber since before her mother died. She hesitated but needs must.

'Dad?'

She startled him.

'Rachel, you're back. I didn't see you come home.'

'Are you OK?'

'Yeah, yeah fine.'

Rachel crossed to the fridge to see what they had in. It was empty apart from some milk, brought in by Reg or George, a scraping of butter and a half-empty can of baked beans.

'I'm hungry can I go to the shop, get something for our tea?'

'I'm sorry love, I've literally got about two pounds. Here you can have it, but that's it until tomorrow.'

She thought he might be about to cry, but he didn't.

'What about the bank? They have money.'

Her dad gave a wry half smile.

'Yes, but it's not mine.'

'They could lend you some.'

'No, I don't think they will. You walk to the shops and get something. Don't worry about me, I'm not hungry. I need to think.'

Rachel took the £2.22 that he handed her in coins and traipsed to the door. The pain in her stomach was draining her, but she had to get to the shop and get some sanitary pads, and she was hungry, really hungry. She'd barely had anything for lunch.

The only way she could keep going was to imagine she was on an expedition and their lives depended on her succeeding. She had to battle through the pain and exhaustion to keep walking. Along the way she was encouraged on by her mother, who walked by her side, smiling reassuringly when the pain got worse. In her head she ran a commentary, a narrator recounting the highs and the lows of her trek.

'Rachel Hill bravely battles the elements, walking through desert dust storms to save her father.'

Her throat felt dry, and the dust she kicked up on the track had irritated her eyes. She was relieved when she reached the main road and could walk along the narrow pavement to the outskirts of the nearby village.

'Struggling on without food and water, Rachel's determination is the only thing keeping her going. This young heroine is battling against all the odds, climbing mountains and trekking across barren wastelands to get to her destination.'

When Rachel got to the shop, the enormity of her reality hit her.

£2.22 was only going to buy one or the other. A loaf of bread and can of baked beans would wipe it out, or she could choose the sanitary towels. There was no way she was going to be able to afford both, and yet she had to have them. She wandered around, looking at every item of food she could, checking prices. She needed to get something her dad could eat too. And what about their lunches tomorrow?

The smell from the bakery and delicatessen sections made her tummy clamour with hunger. A bowl of pasta salad was just inches from her, cheeses and hams sat protected by the glass counter, mocking her.

She moved away from them, standing in front of the magazines and newspapers, pretending to scan their front pages, while she thought. 'Hospitals get warnings on killer bug', 'Who will be the new James Bond?', 'An interview with Take That's Robbie Williams'. All of it meaningless, all of it irrelevant to the battle going on inside her head. Throughout it all, her stomach and back were in pain as she progressed to womanhood.

Rachel knew she had to make a decision. Once again, she did a sweep of all the food and as she was walking round, she spotted one of the shop assistants starting to reduce the boxes of eggs. 75p. Rachel jumped on them. Back to the breads and she saw a loaf for £1. They could do without butter. 47 pence left. The cheapest sanitary towels were £1.50.

It was as the song 'Everything Changes But You' was playing through the shop speakers, that Rachel committed her first crime. She didn't want to, she didn't want to steal, but the alternative for her was even worse. She picked up the packet of sanitary towels and discreetly slipped them into the pocket of her jacket before walking up to the till to pay for the food.

'Brave explorer Rachel Hill is left with a life and death decision. Foraging for food, she is forced to take desperate action to protect herself and her father. It is survival of the fittest out there.'

Rachel walked home with 47 pence in coins jangling in one pocket and the stolen pads like lead weights in the other.

43

CLAIRE

18TH OCTOBER 2016

The team was having a quick catch-up to go over the latest developments in the case. Claire was glad she wasn't involved in trying to track down Mike in Vietnam because Bob was getting mighty annoyed about the fact they couldn't find him. The young DS who had volunteered to take on the search would now have wished, more than a million times, that he hadn't opened his mouth. The search had become the bane of the poor guy's life. Claire was sure he'd developed a nervous tick in the last few days.

Sandra/Carly had been downgraded as a suspect with Rosa McKenna now under scrutiny. They were discussing next moves for the investigation when an email popped in from Mark Rodgers. Claire's heart gave a little skip—for more than one reason. She told herself it was because she's desperate to see if he'd found anything unusual with Todd Fuller. The email was brief: *Got something you are going to find very interesting. Your place or mine?*

She loved the flirtatious tone of the email, but she loved the promise of an interesting result even more.

Is it worth showing to DCI Walsh? she replied.

Definitely, was his response.

I'll book us one of the conference rooms here and get some coffees in. Let me know when you can come over.

Claire's adrenaline was pumping now. It must be something fairly conclusive for Mark to be so sure. She knew he wouldn't waste Bob's time otherwise.

Bob was reluctant to take time away from the Neil Parsons investigation, but she was insistent and within an hour they were all sitting round a table looking at a screen. Mark had a smug air about him and was enjoying the audience. Claire found the smugness attractive—it was more professional confidence than conceit.

'OK, so original autopsy report,' said Mark. 'Standard stuff. It wasn't negligent. All the routine tests were done and nothing unusual showed up. There was also nothing at the scene to suggest anything criminal had taken place. I've gone through the first responder reports and I spoke to the officer who dealt with this. Quite simply, Todd was found sitting in his armchair, dead. It happens.'

Bob and Claire were sitting upright, all ears.

'With Claire's suspicions that he might have been murdered, I ran some further tests, only this time I specifically looked for things which I know are hard to detect and which wouldn't be picked up in standard autopsies. And bingo.'

Mark flicked to the next slide which was a shot of a suicide victim. The man was also sitting in a chair, only he had a gas bottle next to him and a pipe running from that to a bag over his head, held tightly sealed by large elastic bands.

'It's a method that's suggested on many suicide sites and of course with suicides it's easy to detect because the victim will be found with the equipment used still on them.

It's apparently one of the nicer ways to go, non-violent, and if you do it right, it's quick. In Todd's case, the gas cylinder and bag must have been removed after death and thus there was no trace of a suicide or murder weapon. It would have looked like he'd just died.'

'What is it?' Claire asked.

'Helium. Asphyxiation is quick. For someone who was intoxicated, it would have been fairly easy for anyone to have put something over his head or face and pumped pure helium in. Helium contains no oxygen, so the brain is very quickly starved of it, making the victim unconscious fast. Death follows within minutes.'

'Blimey.' Is all Claire could say.

'So you found evidence of this in Todd's body?' Bob asked.

'Yes, we were lucky. Helium is an inert gas, there're no signs of it in usual toxicology testing. The body simply shows the results of sudden death, cerebral edema etc, but thankfully we still had an intact lung. It wasn't easy. Helium is obviously invisible and odourless, but I definitely found helium present. Now, you could argue Todd might have been playing silly games with balloons prior to his death, but to be detected it has to have been a significant amount. I would be 99 if not 100% certain in saying that Todd Fuller died through helium asphyxiation. The question now is whether this is an assisted suicide or murder.'

'No suicide note was found,' Claire confirmed.

'So, we could be looking at a series of silent murders with bloody balloon gas,' Bob said. 'Shit.'

Mark held his hands up.

'Sorry.'

'No, it's not aimed at you. I wasn't trying to shoot the messenger. That's good work, Mark. Good work both of you. So why weren't these deaths ever linked?'

'Because there was no link obvious. They happened in the victim's homes, unexplained natural causes. There would simply not have been anything to link them to the dating agency and so they were all completely separate cases. It's only when you look at them with the agency link that you realise what a massively high death rate there was,' Mark explained.

Bob shook his head.

'There's something else,' Mark added. 'From what I can tell from reading the coroners' reports, most of them didn't have family around either. There was no one to make a fuss over them. All except one, Robert Jones. A sister came out the woodwork after the inquest, started saying he'd been murdered. Nobody took her seriously, though. She had a history of alcohol abuse and no evidence. Maybe she was right after all.'

'Well, the pair of you have just massively scaled up this enquiry. I'm going to have to go and tell the DCS. Can you put all this in writing for me, Mark?'

'Sure. There're a couple of other things you should know, though,' Mark said, more gravely, 'First, it is going to be highly unlikely, if not impossible to tell if the other people were asphyxiated by helium. Several were cremated and the other one would be so badly decomposed by now we'd have no chance. You're going to have to focus on this one death I'm afraid, when it comes to prosecution. Second, I ran the test on Neil Parsons. No helium. I had wondered if his could have been a botched asphyxiation, but it wasn't.'

'Then we could still be looking at two completely different murderers,' Bob thought out loud, 'but there's one definite link: SoulMates dating agency.'

44

CLAIRE

18TH OCTOBER 2016

B ack in the incident room, the board now showcased photographs of Rachel's dug up rabbit. There had been a few jokes about bunny boilers and zombie rabbits, the usual grown-up professional emergency service humour.

Claire stood staring at the board.

'So far, the stalker hasn't shown himself to Rachel. There doesn't appear to have been any physical contact,' she said out loud.

'Yup, which could mean he's known to her,' Bob chipped in. 'That's the likeliest explanation. He doesn't want her knowing his identity because she'll be able to name him and tell us. Go and see her, you've got the best relationship with her, find out who else she has regular contact with, apart from those at SoulMates. Has she spurned someone's advances? While you're there, ask if any of those who died ever tried it on with her, or did she ever see them outside of work? In the meantime, I've got Lew working on the other agency deaths. He's tracking down family and friends to see if we can get any inkling as to what may have been going on before they died.'

WHEN CLAIRE GOT to Rachel's house, a red BMW was just pulling out of the drive. She took down the registration, just in case.

She found Rachel quiet and thoughtful, not surprising given the circumstances.

'It's an estate agent,' Rachel told her, rather ashamedly. 'I can't take this, all this abuse. The house doesn't feel like my home anymore.'

'You can't let them win,' Claire replied.

'It's easy for you to say that,' Rachel answered, not nastily, just matter-of-factly. 'I don't like coming home anymore. I don't want to invite people round in case something happens to them. I've never thought of myself as the victim type but he's making my life miserable, so what's the point?'

'We'll catch him. We will.'

'Look, I know your focus is on finding Neil's killer, and it should be. I've just got to look out for myself and with the agency in a mess, it's looking like a good time to be making a move. I can't help but keep thinking about what's happened to other women, Lily Allen and do you remember that Jackie Stiller case last year. He killed her, that was awful.'

Claire did remember the Jackie Stiller case only too well, but she wasn't about to admit that to Rachel and she couldn't disagree with her. It made her angry, though. She promised herself never to let that happen again. She was determined Rachel's stalker wouldn't go unpunished.

'Look, we've got to catch him. Find out who it is and bring them to justice.'

Rachel grimaced.

'Is there anyone else you might have had contact with? Someone who perhaps asked you out, and you said no, or who you went out with and then didn't want to see again?'

Rachel was thinking hard.

'In the last year or so? No, I really can't think of anyone. Work is where I focus my time and apart from inviting Neil around, and occasionally Gary, there's been nobody else.'

Claire nodded.

'How about clients? Did you ever see any clients outside of the office?'

'Well, when you say outside of the office, yes, I guess. I used to take some of them out for coffee, the ones who seemed to be struggling to find a partner. We'd go out to a café or something, and I'd coach them on date etiquette. You'd be amazed how many of them just have no idea how to talk to someone of the opposite sex.'

Claire consulted her notebook now.

'OK, would that have included, Todd Fuller, Robert Jones, Mark Baxter, or Steven Marshall?'

Rachel paused and thought again.

'Certainly, Todd and Robert. Oh yes, Mark we went for lunch, and Steven? That was some time ago, but I think so. There were others, too. Why?'

Claire's heart was skipping beats. It was all falling into place now.

'Who would have known about these coffees?'

'Just the guys at the agency: Eddie, Gary, Felicity, and Sandra, they'd have known. Anyone else? I don't think so, not unless… Not unless someone was watching me.'

'When did you become aware of the stalker?'

Claire could tell Rachel's mind was racing, too.

'A few months before Neil died. It was really low key to begin with.'

Claire jotted down in her notebook and was about to look up and ask another question when Rachel's mobile buzzed that a message had come through.

Rachel looked at her phone on the kitchen table, then at Claire.

Claire didn't need to ask who it was from. The dread was written across Rachel's face. Slowly, she lifted up her phone and read it. Her face hardened, and she shoved it away from her towards Claire.

She took the phone. *The police can't protect you. I'm coming for you.*

'We will protect you, Rachel, I promise,' she said to her.

Rachel had paled.

'I just wish I knew who it was, why they're doing it,' she said quietly.

'I know, but we must be getting closer now. Let me just phone this in and have a chat with the team.'

She went to leave the room and then thought of the question she was going to ask before.

'Rachel, have you ever seen Gary with a partner?'

'What do you mean?'

'I mean you say he's gay, but have you actually seen him with someone, seen photos, heard them calling, has he ever talked about anybody?'

Rachel thought for a few moments. 'Well, now you come to mention it, no. He's never talked about anyone specific.'

Claire nodded. 'OK, thanks, give me a few minutes.'

Bob was more than a little interested in her news, and he had some of his own.

'We spoke to Gary Foster's landlady. She was absolutely

certain he was out the night of Neil's murder because she distinctly remembers him coming back in after she'd watched *Married at First Sight* on Channel 4 and thinking about how he didn't have a partner and yet he worked at a dating agency.'

'He told us he was home all night.'

'Yup, and so we checked out the nearby CCTV, and she's right. She also mentioned that apparently he often comes back quite late. Late enough to be hanging around Rachel Hill's house!'

45

CLAIRE

18TH OCTOBER 2016

Bob was playing hardball. He had Gary Foster arrested for obstruction, and he was on his way to the station.

'I'm sick and tired of mucking about with this case,' Bob told Claire. 'We need to start ruling some people out or ruling them in properly. The only way we're going to get them talking is to put the wind up them. Neil was Gary's client. He's got no alibi, and he's being decidedly cagey. If he knows something, I want to know it.'

Claire finished her phone call to Bob and then apologised to Rachel.

'Something has come up so I've got to get back to the station. You've got the panic button. Keep it with you at all times.'

Rachel nodded.

'Are you coming back?' she asked.

Claire thought for a few moments, looking at the frightened woman in front of her.

'Do you want me to pop back this evening? I could get us a takeaway and perhaps if he sees my car parked up outside, he'll be scared off.' Claire found herself saying.

She'd never usually make an offer like this, but Rachel looked like she needed the company and it's not as if she'd got anyone to rush home for.

Rachel brightened.

'Thank you. I'd appreciate that.'

'OK. Chinese, Thai, or Indian?'

'Indian, please.'

Claire left with her conscience feeling slightly better and some hope that maybe they'd get to the bottom of Rachel's stalker before the day was out.

WHEN CLAIRE DROVE BACK to the station, there was a small huddle of people standing in the car park talking. It was Jack and Lara with two of his mates, Cal and Stewart. Instantly, she froze. It was hard seeing Jack with someone else. Especially as he looked so damned happy about it. Lara looked radiant, as though she'd been somehow filled with sunshine. They were holding hands. Claire momentarily indulged a fantasy of pressing her foot on the accelerator and knocking the smiling Lara and Jack over like pins at a bowling alley.

She parked as far away from them as she could. She hated this feeling and most of all she hated the intrusion on her working life. As she got out the car, Stewart said something to the group, and they laughed. Was it about her? What had he said? Were they laughing at her?

She never did like that Stewart. She was sure he thought she was too boring for Jack. Always encouraging him to do daft things. You could guarantee that he would be the one wearing the stupid hats and outfits at any party. A complete goon.

There was a small rage inside of her, fuelled by humiliation and by a growing feeling of loneliness. She saw

Jack surrounded by friends, happy with Lara. Then she saw her flat, her life, empty and quiet. No one but her to fill its void. Had she made a mistake? Had she thrown away a relationship which made her happy? Was it Jack who was the one having to put up with her social inadequacy? She quickly walked inside, ignoring them. She'd take it out on Gary Foster instead.

Claire could tell Bob was also in no mood for messing about. This case was irritating him. When Gary Foster sat down with the duty solicitor, Bob wasted no time.

'Mr Foster, could we start by asking you again, this time on the tape, where you were on the evening of October thirteenth?'

'I was at home.'

'All night?'

'Yes.'

'Well, unfortunately for you, your landlady has an excellent memory, and she's told us she heard you coming back around 11 p.m. We also have CCTV footage to confirm this. Now do you want to try again? Where were you on the evening of October thirteenth?'

'Um… Maybe I got the dates mixed up.' Gary looked to the solicitor. 'I'll have to check my diary again.'

'Mr Foster, you have had plenty of time to check your diary. You know which night we are referring to and it's not so long ago that you won't be able to think back. I ask again. Where were you on the night of October thirteenth?'

Gary's right leg started jiggling under the interview room table.

'I was working late.'

'Working late? Working until 11 p.m.? What were you doing?'

'I can't remember,' Gary mumbled and sniffed.

'Surely, Mr Foster, it must be unusual to have to work until around 11 p.m., so can you try hard and think back to that night? We can check CCTV around the office to corroborate.'

'I can't.'

'You can't because you won't, or you can't because you don't know yourself?'

'I just can't.'

'You have to understand, Gary, that this looks suspicious from our point of view. Neil was your client. In fact, Neil's phone records show that you spoke to him that afternoon, but you can't say where you were at the time of his death.'

Claire looked at Bob. She didn't know this about the phone call.

Gary now looked frightened.

'It was a standard client call. I was seeing if he liked any of the matches I'd sent through to him. There were a few women keen to meet him.'

'You didn't mention you'd talked to him that day when we last spoke.'

'No, I know, I'd forgotten. I can't always remember which days I speak to who. Honestly.'

'Not got a great memory, have you? Can't remember where you were, can't remember when you spoke to him.'

'I know how this looks, but it's nothing to do with Neil's murder, I promise you.'

'What about Eddie?'

Gary's face registered surprise.

'What do you mean, "what about Eddie"?'

'I mean, do you know if he might have any reason to want Neil dead?'

'No. No, absolutely not.'

'So you can be certain about some things.'

'Eddie's a good man. He set up that agency because he enjoys helping people. He wants them all to have happy ever after endings. Eddie wouldn't hurt anyone.'

'He's on the verge of filing for bankruptcy. The agency has been struggling financially for a long time. Did Neil know this?'

'I don't know. No. There was nothing for Eddie to hide. You're blowing it up out of all proportion.'

'What about the fake marriages he said were agency clients? What else did he lie about, Gary?'

'They were just pictures. Eddie isn't a murderer, I'm telling you, he isn't.'

'From where I'm sitting, he has the motive. Get rid of those who didn't look good for the agency image.'

'Don't be ridiculous.' Gary looked angry now.

'Did you help him then, Gary?'

'No. No, neither of us hurt anyone. Not like that…'

'What do you mean "not like that"?'

'I just mean, no.' Gary was starting to crumble again, and he looked at his solicitor who raised his eyebrow. 'No comment,' Gary replied, turning back to Bob with defiance.

'OK. Well, no comment isn't going to make your situation look any better, Mr Foster. Are you sure you don't want to tell us something? Something which might help you? Whoever it is you're protecting is not here protecting you, are they?'

'No comment.'

'OK, Mr Foster, you have been clearly lying to us about your whereabouts on October thirteenth, so perhaps you'd like to take the next hour or so to think about where you really were. We are now terminating this interview at fifteen thirty-five and Mr Foster will be returned to the cells.'

46

RACHEL

18TH OCTOBER 2016

R achel was sitting down writing names on a pad, dredging faces from her memory. She was trying to remember all the clients that DI Falle mentioned to her and any others that come to mind, including her colleagues. Of course, it could be someone from her past, but who? Who would know she's here? From the notes she'd been receiving, this wasn't some random stalker. One of the names on this list could be the culprit or at least a link to them.

Eddie, Gary, Felicity, Sandra, Rosa, could it be one of them? Could someone she knows so well be trying to harm her?

The panic button sat on the table next to her. It was reassuring, but Rachel tried not to think about the circumstances which might prompt her to use it. She liked DI Falle; it was obvious she really was trying to help her. She liked the professional way in which she dealt with things, rather than the sympathetic approach she'd had from others in the past. She wasn't keen on having people round the house, especially strangers, but she's actually looking forward to tonight and their takeaway.

She looked around her sitting room. The house was always tidy and clean, that's one thing her aunt drummed into her. She'd trained her up well after she'd taken her in. Rachel was a feral cat when she first came here, she'd roamed the house looking for answers and escape routes, biting the hand that fed her until she learnt to respect her aunt—even if she never really loved her.

Her aunt had been gone nearly four years now, eaten away by cancer and tormented by death's denial of dignity. Rachel had returned from her travelling to care for her in those last few weeks. She could still remember turning up at the house after more than a decade away. She was filled with a million new experiences and sights, alive with possibility and opportunity. The house was like an old woman itself, its breath reeking of death and decay as she opened the front door. She'd found her aunt shrivelled and wasted in her bed, waiting for release.

For five long weeks Rachel sat by her bedside and listened to the hushed ramblings of her aunt's regrets. She had held her hand, her bony, claw-like hand, which was cold and unforgiving. She had taken down her instructions for arrangements and contacted those who needed to know. Then she had watched as her aunt's soul slipped from between her lips and left the body which had given her so much pain.

Rachel had never intended to stay, but somehow she did. She'd found a way to carry on the work she enjoyed at the SoulMates agency and she'd felt needed. Now this shadow was driving her away, threatening her. She knew it was time to move on again.

47

RACHEL

LATE MAY 1994

It was a Friday when she arrived. Rachel was walking up the lane just as some fighter jets from the American airbase flew over. The roar of their engines made the cows look up and stop their chewing and momentarily quietened the birds in the trees. Rachel loved to see the jets, breathing in the sight of them as though she could catch just a tiny scrap of their excitement and freedom when they flew by.

She was still scanning the sky, hoping to catch another glimpse, when she saw the car. It was silver and sporty, and it looked expensive. Rachel didn't recognise it.

When Rachel walked into the kitchen, she was there with her dad. He'd been crying, and she looked more like a mother to him than a sister. Rachel's Aunt Alice had come to visit.

'Rachel!' her aunt said as though she hadn't been expecting to see her. 'How are you?' She looked her up and down.

'Hello,' is all Rachel replied, she'd got out of the habit of being civil.

There was no hug or kiss, no warmth. Aunt Alice was

all edges and corners. She was thin and high-cheeked, a woman born out of her time. She would have made an excellent stern governess in Queen Victoria's day.

Whether as an antidote to her hardness, or because she had taken away the responsibility, her father seemed to have suddenly become more demonstrative.

'Rachel, come here,' he said, opening his arms.

She was almost too surprised to go to him, a dog so long ignored by its master she wasn't sure what this affection meant. She hesitated, feeling the power shift in the room, and then walked over, melting into his arms. The hug and love she had longed for.

'Aunt Alice is visiting us for a few days, isn't that nice?'

Rachel turned and looked at Aunt Alice, not sure if it was a nice turn of events or not. Her aunt, sensing the defiance, was quick to assert her authority and claim top status.

'You go on up to your room, Rachel, and get changed. Bring those school clothes down for the wash. I assume you do have a washing machine?'

Her dad shook his head.

'Then we have some shopping to do tomorrow, Rachel. We've a busy weekend ahead of us.'

Rachel felt the tension and stress pour out of her father's body. It took her a couple more hours before she too rolled over for Aunt Alice, but the prospect of good meals and clean clothes were irresistible incentives.

What Aunt Alice lacked in warmth, she made up for in organisation and efficiency. She also made up for it with the fish and chips they went to get, after Aunt Alice had looked in the cupboards and seen the two pans they possessed and the lack of food to go in them.

Her zero local knowledge meant she needed her

brother with her to navigate, and that in turn resulted in Rachel also going along.

It had been a long time since Rachel had been in a car and she'd never been in a car as nice as this one. Its shiny silver paintwork was perfect, clean except for a thin film of dust from the drive up. Inside was cream leather with a walnut dash and dark grey carpeting. The seat squeaked at her as Rachel got in and she ran her hands over the soft leather. It was a Jaguar, sleek and racy like its namesake, and Rachel settled into its backseat, a new experience starting to shape her.

They drove into Holt and Rachel waited in the car while Aunt Alice and her dad queued at the Holt Fish Bar for cod and chips. The smell of food reached her nostrils even though she was sealed inside, and her mouth physically salivated. The reaction was made worse as soon as her dad returned with a bag full of wrapped-in-paper dinners.

She didn't think she had ever tasted anything so good. Rachel devoured her portion and she and her father shared the chips which Aunt Alice, who turned out to be a bird-like eater, didn't want. Her aunt moved right to the top of Rachel's appreciation list, and so when she told her to go to bed, she complied without complaint. Rachel had been used to setting her own bedtimes since her mother's death, but a full belly and an organised adult in the house were enough to make her look forward to sleep and to getting up the next day.

Saturday morning and Aunt Alice was up early. She stayed at a local bed and breakfast, which Rachel suspected was because she didn't like the look of the guest bedroom. They'd had mice in there, and the smell of damp and mould made Rachel's nose wrinkle.

Her aunt arrived at the farmhouse around 9 a.m.,

having already been to the supermarket. She got Rachel and her dad to help unload the car, which was full of bags of cleaning products, a mop, bucket, and lots of food.

Rachel had a proper breakfast for the first time in months and sat in a kitchen that smelled of cleaning fluids. The floor was no longer sticky underfoot from months of yard dirt and spillages. The cobwebs Rachel had stared at every mealtime, the ones which hung from the ceiling to the central light fitting, were gone along with all the others around the walls and ceiling.

Her aunt was a fresh breeze wafting through their house and their lives.

After breakfast, Aunt Alice gave her brother a list of things to do, then she told Rachel to get in the car. They drove into Holt, and Rachel hoped someone from school would see her in her aunt's Jaguar.

She took her to Bakers and Larners where she bought Rachel dresses, skirts, tops, and new shoes. The smell of clean, new fabrics massaged Rachel's nostrils. They bought some new clothes for her father, some mugs, crockery, and cutlery for the kitchen. They got a kettle, so they didn't have to keep heating up a saucepan of water for tea, and a big box full of pots and pans. Finally, they got a new Henry hoover to replace the broken one in the under-stair cupboard.

Once she was home, Rachel took the bags of clothes up to her bedroom. The shop assistant had given her the hangers too, so she carefully took each purchase out and hung them up, pulling the old clothes, the ones that were far too small for her, out and tossing them onto her bed.

She couldn't resist trying some of her new clothes on again. Her favourite was a pleated white skirt with a band of black around the waist and hem. She loved the contrast, the pure whiteness of the crisp fabric. Rachel didn't think she'd ever seen anything so white. She wasn't sure when she'd wear it, if she dared wear it, for fear of sullying its pristine state. She went to her parents' bedroom and looked in the old full-length mirror in the corner near her mum's dressing table. For a little while, she felt good.

When she headed back downstairs, she could hear the sound of raised voices. Her aunt sounded like she was telling her dad off.

'You've got to pull yourself together and stop this moping, it's getting you nowhere.'

'That's easy for you to say.'

She could hear the misery in his voice.

'She's gone. Get over it and get on with looking after that child. She's like a feral cat. You've got to sort yourselves out. This house is a pigsty. I can't keep picking up the pieces—and the bills!'

'Then don't. Go back to London if you want. We're fine without your help.'

'You're going to lose the farm and you're not doing anything about it. Get a grip and stop the drinking.'

Rachel was sitting on the stairs. She wondered what her aunt meant by 'feral cat'. What even is 'feral'? Did that mean she didn't like her? And were they really going to lose the farm? What would they do? Where would they go?

She heard her dad stomp out through the kitchen, no doubt off on one of his wanders around the farm. She stood up and returned to her bedroom. If her aunt thought her 'feral' perhaps she'd better keep out of her way. Her heart felt heavy again. She was silly to think her aunt might actually like her.

She didn't get to hide in her bedroom for long, Aunt Alice called her down.

'Right, young lady,' she said to her. 'I'm going to show you how you need to help your dad keep this house clean.

There's a washing machine arriving this afternoon and we are going to be using it.'

For the rest of Saturday and for most of Sunday, the three of them worked together to get the house in order. Hoovering, dusting, scrubbing, and cleaning. Her dad still drank, but less than usual. Having his sister there was clearly good for him. Rachel started to see some of her old dad back again. He joked with her, pretended to scare her with cobwebs and spiders, or sucked at her clothes with the hoover whenever she walked past. They smiled, and they laughed. It felt so good.

On Sunday her aunt cooked one last meal, lasagne with peas. She got Rachel to watch her make it and gave her a cookery book as a leaving gift. She also gave her £50, which was more money than she'd ever had, to spend on herself.

There were hushed words between her aunt and father, scowls from both of them and a shake of the head from her aunt. Then she was gone. They watched as the silver Jaguar slipped out of sight and the blanket of silence fell on their house again.

Out of respect, Rachel went to bed at the same time as her aunt had told her the two nights previous, and in the morning she was grateful to wake to a proper breakfast and a fridge and cupboards stocked with food. She headed into school wearing the new uniform she'd been bought and with a decent packed lunch for the day ahead. She felt different, lighter. Perhaps her new clothes would help her be accepted.

She wanted to tell someone about her aunt, her car, the fish and chips; share details of her new wardrobe. At lunchtime, she sat with her soft sandwich and waited for someone to sit next to her.

When Elaine Bunting and Sharon White sat down

beside her, her heart thumped. She could feel their eyes on her. Could this be her moment when she became accepted again?

'What you got?' Elaine asked first.

Rachel's heart thumped harder, and she became conscious of every muscle in her body, the slow churning of her jaw, the way she sat.

'Ham,' she replied.

'I've got ham too,' Elaine pronounced in camaraderie. 'Sharon's got fish paste, eugh!'

'It's nice, I like it,' Sharon wailed at her.

'You like fish paste?' Elaine asked Rachel.

She shook her head. She wanted the words to tumble out of her, busting to tell them about her weekend. She'd never had fish paste sandwiches, but she liked fish and chips. But she said nothing, frightened to say something that would ruin this moment, afraid that they'd think her even more of a freak if she talked.

'I don't like fish paste,' Elaine pronounced, just to make sure they both realised. 'My favourite sandwiches are BLT.'

'My favourite is smoked salmon,' Sharon chipped in.

Rachel said nothing. She didn't know what BLT meant, and she'd never tasted smoked salmon. If she told them her favourite sandwich was the egg mayonnaise ones her mother used to make, then they'd think she was a saddo. So she just smiled weakly at them.

'How can you like smoked salmon?' Elaine asked Sharon.

'I've always liked it.' Sharon beamed back at her. 'Have you tried it?'

'Yeah, at Christmas, it's horrible.'

'You done the history homework? I haven't.' Sharon

suddenly changed tack and threw a curve ball to the pair of them.

Elaine shook her head, and they both looked to Rachel.

She'd done the homework the same day they were given it, the same way she does all her homework: at lunchtime in the library. If she said yes, then they might think she's some goody swot that doesn't have a life. She wanted to say no and be like them.

'No,' she answered, but she was ashamed of lying, and so she looked down quickly and concentrated on finishing her sandwich, taking tiny bites to make it last.

'Did you hear Mrs McCloud is leaving?' Elaine said to them.

'Good, she's a bitch. She's given me two detentions already this term,' said Sharon, picking out the last crumbs of crisps from her packet and licking her fingers.

'Yeah, she's always shouting at everyone. Can't wait to see who they get instead. Anyone will be better than her,' Elaine added.

Rachel felt their eyes on her again, but she didn't look up. Mrs McCloud was all right. She left her alone.

'Come on then, let's go and see if the hut is free,' Elaine said, rising from her chair.

Rachel didn't move, and the two girls hovered for a moment, waiting.

Rachel was itching to stand up and go with them.

'See you,' she said, the torment of wanting to go and the fear of being found out for the feral weirdo she was, battling inside her chest, which felt tight.

The two girls shrugged and walked off chatting.

The dining room was loud, filled with children and chatter. Rachel sat in a bubble of isolation, unable to connect. She was a freak, the weird girl, different to everyone else with their happy homes and normal lives. She tried to finish her sandwich, but she was filled with emptiness. Her aunt had reminded her what life was once like, what life should be.

DEPRESSION HUNG weights on either side of Rachel's mouth, so even if people laughed and joked around her, she couldn't curl her lips and join in. It filled her whole body with heaviness, dragging it into tiredness. Everything was too much effort. Depression was her companion, but it made her lonely and allowed no room for enthusiasm.

Depression made her hang her head and wish she were some place else. Someplace, anywhere, but in her own body.

Depression wrapped its heavy blanket of lead around her and whispered that it was best to lie in bed and sleep. Sleep brought release—sometimes.

Depression made her forget about tomorrow, next week, next year. It smothered her with its thick couldn't care less attitude until she had no fight left in her to defy it.

TUESDAY, Rachel couldn't face school. She left home with her schoolbag and packed lunch and walked to the bus stop as she did every day. This time, when she saw the school bus coming, she felt overcome by a suffocating sensation. An invisible hand was over her mouth and nose, and she couldn't breathe or scream. The bile rose in her stomach and she felt sick. Her heart banged inside of her.

She couldn't face another day of alienation, another day of looking in from the outside. Life seemed to be going on around her without her taking part. She was an invisible bystander, a movie goer watching the action, standing still while all around her life went on. When she saw the school bus round the corner, she hid. Darting into the bushes at the side of the road, she crouched down. The bus pulled into her stop, the driver peered through the windows to see if he could see her. When she didn't appear, he indicated and pulled out again.

She was free.

Rachel took off her school blazer and stuffed it into her bag. Without it, she was just a girl in black trousers and a white shirt. A girl who could catch the next bus and see where life took her.

The first bus headed towards the coast and so she rumbled along through Salthouse and Cley, past Wiveton and through Blakeney, Morston, and Stiffkey and onto Wells. Looking out the windows at big skies and flat fields, sand dunes and stone houses, wild birds and wetland. A big pub garden with wooden benches and seating, empty and closed. A group of hikers in boots and with backpacks, walking along the road chatting and laughing.

When they pulled into Wells, she got off and headed to the harbour and to the sea. The urge for fresh salty air and open space drove her away from the tourist shops and seaside gaming arcades. Little boats were moored up in rows along the harbour side or lying beached on the brown mud and sand banks: white whales on cocktail sticks, their bare masts rising barren into the wind. Rachel walked past them and took the walk down along the harbour to where the sea opened up.

A row of brightly coloured beach huts, trimmed the big golden sandy beach, marred only by the dark strips of wood which rose up out of the sand and towards the sea. Rachel remembered their names, groynes. They had learnt that in geography last year during their coastal erosion lessons. They'd also seen photographs of houses falling into the sea from cliff tops and heard about the big flood of 1953. Jack Lewis said his grandfather had died in the flood and everyone in the class had listened intently to his family story. Rachel hadn't lost her mother then. She couldn't imagine what it must feel like to lose someone close.

It was low tide and there were just a few people on the beach today: dog walkers and tourists. It was still just that bit too cold for sitting and swimming. She found a spot by the side of one of the beach huts and sat herself down. It was out of the wind and in the glow of the weak spring sun. Rachel took her shoes and socks off to feel the sand between her toes.

The beach huts were on stilts, wooden stairs leading to their doors. She imagined living in one, having a tiny bed in the gloom of the single room. A little sunlight seeping in through gaps between the wooden planks and under the wooden shutter. The pounding of the sea in winter while you slept, the baking heat of the sun and muffled sounds of families talking and playing in the summer. She liked the thought of being cocooned inside, hiding away from the world, hiding from people, from the possibility of pain and loss.

THE FIRST THING her dad said to her when she got back home was, 'Where have you been? School called, said you hadn't turned up.'

He was angry. Rachel hadn't seen him angry for a long time, but she could see it was driven by fear.

'Sorry, Dad. I couldn't face going in today. I didn't feel so good, and I thought that if I came home, you'd get into trouble.'

'I was worried, Rachel. I had no idea where you'd

gone. If you were OK. If someone had taken you. Don't ever do that again, do you hear?'

She nodded vigorously and then watched as his anger crumbled into his whisky glass.

Rachel changed and made dinner. Sausages, lumpy mash, and baked beans.

Her dad seemed to have become needier since her aunt left. As though her presence had awakened in him a lost urge for company and order in his life. Did she make him feel shame, open his eyes to the life he was living and making his daughter live? If she did, it had only served to make him withdraw further from the world.

After dinner Elvis filled the house, and her father tried to drown his ineffective life with whisky. Rachel found him mumbling to himself in his chair. An imaginary conversation with someone.

'Good night, Dad,' she said to him, making him jump from his self-induced coma.

'Rachel!' he exclaimed. 'Rachel, you're back. Come here.'

She walked over to him, his eyes filling with tears.

'Please promise me you're never going to leave me. You won't leave me, will you?'

At that moment Rachel realised the selfish driver of his earlier anger. She looked at him: drunk, saliva on his stubbly chin, greasy hair, and dirty clothes. What she saw was a stranger, a broken human being.

'No, Dad,' she simply replied, the image of her beach hut refuge in her head.

He nodded, settled back into his chair, and poured himself another whisky. Rachel stayed a few moments longer, long enough to know he was content with his bottle companion, and then she went to bed.

. . .

A FEW DAYS LATER, Rachel awoke to the sound of hooves. It wasn't the clip clop of hooves on cobbles. Instead, she heard the clomping clop of the herd going up wooden ramps into large transporter lorries. For a few seconds she panicked that they were being stolen, and then she saw her father. He was standing, arms folded, watching the scene in front of him, Reg and George and two other men herding the cattle up the ramps. Once the last one was in and the doors closed, the lorries drove away. Her father stood watching them disappear up the drive until she could no longer hear their moo-ing or see the trucks. Then he turned and walked back inside.

The stillness of the house now fell on the yard.

48

CLAIRE

18TH OCTOBER 2016

Claire shouldn't really be spending time with Rachel like this, but Jackie Stiller was on her mind. The same place she'd been ever since she'd found her battered body.

Besides, she justified to herself, Bob had told her to find out about as many men and potential suspects as she could. This would give her the chance to get to know Rachel better, work with her to come up with a list. It's amazing how you can be so familiar with something or somebody, that they don't register as a threat.

She texted Rachel to let her know she was on the way and stopped off at the Delhi Star to pick up the curry. The rich spices filled her car as she drove over, and she found herself wishing she could have a couple of glasses of wine with it, too. The aroma reminded her of the flat, of lying in bed with Jack in the summer and giggling about the spice-laden scent wafting into their room from the Indian restaurant outside. They had fun in the early days, talking about a trip to India, imagining holding hands and kissing at the Taj Mahal.

After a while the smells in the flat became an irritant and the fun evaporated. She's not sure how or why that happened, but it did.

When she got to Rachel's house, the kitchen table was all ready to receive the takeaway. Rachel was more relaxed than she'd ever seen her, which Claire guessed to be down to the prospect of company.

'Have you ever been to India?' Rachel asked her as she set out the tubs of curry and rice.

'No. Most exotic place I've been to is France,' she replied. 'My parents weren't ever much into travelling. You?'

'Yeah, I lived there for a few years, loved the country and the people.'

'What took you there?' Claire asked.

'I went travelling, you know how it is, wanted to see the world. I'd spent most of my childhood hidden away on a farm in Norfolk, and then it was boarding school. When I'd done my A levels, I decided it was time to explore the world a bit.' She smiled now, remembering. 'Were you brought up in London?' she asked Claire.

'No, Jersey. My dad's family has lived there for generations. Mum was an import from the UK.'

'Ah, Jersey's exotic, isn't it? No wonder you didn't need to travel so much.'

'I've never thought of it as exotic, it's very small, but yeah, it's a nice place to grow up.'

'Was it just you? Are you an only child?' Rachel questioned.

'I am, but I wasn't always. I did have a brother. He was killed when I was about ten.'

'I'm sorry,' Rachel replied, genuine sympathy on her face. 'My mother died when I was eleven so I had to deal with grief when I was young too. Then my dad died not long after. He never came to terms with Mum's death. Became an alcoholic and then… It's why I do my job you know. I had to watch loneliness and heartbreak destroying the person I loved, both physically and emotionally.'

Claire nodded.

'I saw the effects on my parents. It must have been hard for them to lose one of their children. I don't think either of them were ever the same again.'

There was silence for a few moments as each of them considered their memories. Claire looked out into the garden.

'This pasanda is good,' Rachel said, taking another spoonful of the rich, golden brown sauce. 'Have you found yourself a new boyfriend yet?'

Claire was a little surprised by the question, but considering Rachel's job, she realised she probably shouldn't be.

'No. Too busy at work, to be honest, and it's too soon.'

'You missing him?'

'In some ways, yes, of course. I keep seeing him at the station. We were living together for over three years.' Claire surprised herself by realising she did actually feel quite sad about it and then became aware of Rachel watching her. 'But I've been quite enjoying the peace and quiet,' she jauntily replied back, breaking the downcast expression on her face.

Rachel smiled.

'Yes there's a lot to be said for it.'

'Are you a romantic?' Claire asked her. 'Working at a dating agency I'm surprised you're not hooked up.'

Rachel considered this a moment.

'I'm quite happy with my own company. Being in love can make you vulnerable. Opens you up to the possibility of being hurt.'

This honesty surprised Claire and Rachel looked as though she'd just realised how open she'd been too, because she clammed up and studied her nearly empty plate. What hurt had she suffered in the past that could make her this nervous to commit?

Claire felt her discomfort and changed the subject.

'What sort of time do you see the stalker, if they come?'

'To be honest, it can be anytime, but if they're in the back, it's usually when it's completely dark and everyone is inside. Anytime from now onward, but they may not come with your car parked in the drive.'

'Have you given any more thought as to who it could be? An ex-boyfriend maybe, or disgruntled client?'

'I wrote a list earlier of everyone I could think of from now and the past. I honestly cannot think of anyone other than those you know, and I can't believe someone from the agency is doing this.'

'You'd be surprised how people can live double lives. The worst sociopaths are the most charming people on the surface, but underneath…'

Rachel looked upset.

'Sorry, I didn't mean to frighten you.'

'It's OK,' Rachel replied more quietly now. 'I know you're doing your best, and I really appreciate you being here. The worst part isn't the threats, it's the not knowing who it is. You know, could I be talking to them, or be standing next to them in a shop? Is it the man who walks towards me on the street, or one of my neighbours?'

'We will find out. They'll make a mistake and when they do, we'll be on them.'

Jackie Stiller's broken body flashed through Claire's mind on permanent video loop. That will not happen again.

At just gone 10 p.m. Claire started yawning to the point where she knew she had to get home. She made her apologies to Rachel.

'It's been nice having you here,' she replied. 'I really do appreciate it.'

'And don't you forget to keep that panic button with you at all times and if you're not sure of something call me or 999.'

'I will.'

As Claire left and Rachel closed the front door, she wondered whether her earlier good mood would now disappear. Would the realisation she had the rest of the dark night to get through alone, keep her up tonight? Claire looked around her, straining to see past the dark shapes of the bushes. Were there eyes watching her leave?

CLAIRE

19TH OCTOBER 2016

The whole team had gathered, and it was rumoured the DCS was going to be making an appearance to chivvy on the troops.

'I've got the press office on my back,' Bob growled. 'Getting it from every angle right now. We need a result or at least some progress.'

Everyone shuffled and looked away, grateful that it was him and not them having to deal with all the pressure.

'If we don't find something, we're going to have to let Gary Foster go in the next few hours. We don't have enough to hold him and he's sticking to his no comment routine. It means that we have him, Eddie Scott, and Rosa McKenna all without alibis on the night Neil was killed. Not to mention, our invisible man of a stalker and the incredibly elusive Michael Stratton—who appears to have completely disappeared into the wilds of Vietnam. Felicity Baxter and Carly Watson are both accounted for. But we do have a connection between Rosa and Michael Stratton.' Bob paused and looked around the room. 'I want to know everything on those two. I also want the list of every single one of the women Neil dated from the agency, all cross-referenced.'

'We've started interviewing them, sir,' Lew interrupted. 'We've got about another half-dozen to get through. He was a prolific bugger.'

'Well, get to it. Pull in more support if you need to.'

'There's something else, sir, concerning Rosa McKenna. She was involved in a domestic violence charge about two years ago.'

'Huh, I'd be surprised that anyone would have the gall to try to hit her.'

'That's the thing, sir. It wasn't her being hit. Her former partner brought the charge initially, said she'd regularly hit him, that there was both physical and verbal abuse.'

'Why didn't we spot this before?'

'It never went any further, sir. He withdrew the claim, apparently after a nice settlement from Ms McKenna, and refused to cooperate.'

'OK, so we know she's capable of low-level violence, but is she capable of murder?'

Lew shrugged. 'You've met her, sir.'

'Don't forget she also engineered it so that she could get a date with Neil,' Claire joined in. 'She met him through Michael, liked him, and persuaded him to join the agency, whereupon she promptly applied for a date with him. Only he didn't like her.'

Bob was nodding thoughtfully. 'OK, Lew, she's your priority today. I want you to get to know everything about Rosa McKenna. Talk to neighbours, friends, colleagues. What makes her tick? Is there something in her past that has prompted her to behave like this? Any other complaints about her? Did anyone at the agency go out with her for more than one date? If they did, let's talk to them. She's well-off, there's no reason why she couldn't have hired someone to kill Neil after he snubbed her. And find out if she dated the other unexplained deaths at the agency, particularly Todd Fuller. Get to it.'

Claire was gasping for a coffee, but she didn't feel up to running into Jack this morning. She was hormonal and could feel her emotions were on the edge. The last thing she wanted was to lose it with either Jack or Lara. So, she broke her rules and used the incident room kettle and local supermarket's best instant coffee. The whole set up just made her nose wrinkle. Used teaspoons and a tray with various spillages stained into its surface. She could at least find a clean mug, but the supermarket brand coffee smelled disgusting. There's something chemical about instant coffee. It was nothing like the rich aroma of fresh beans. Still, needs must, so she poured in some milk, making a grey/brown liquid that looked nothing like her usual latte, and headed back to her desk. She managed about half of the mug before she really couldn't take anymore.

'Slumming it?' Lew quipped as he walked past. 'Thought you hate instant?'

'I do I...' She realised that she was just about to tell him she hadn't wanted to go to the canteen in case she ran into Jack and so quickly shut up. 'Just didn't have time to go to the canteen,' she said instead.

Just across from them, Bob slammed down the phone on his desk. He wasn't angry for once, his face alive.

'Edward Scott has just walked up to the front desk and said he's got something to tell us,' Bob announced. 'Maybe we'll get things moving along now.'

.   .   .

EDWARD SCOTT WAS SITTING bolt upright in interview room two. Claire immediately sensed there was something that had changed about him. His pasty stressed-out face had been replaced by something altogether more determined. He was dressed smartly, as though off for Sunday service in a striped, blue shirt and new black cords.

'I've filed for bankruptcy. You've finished off my business,' he announced to them as soon as they walked into the room.

'I'm sorry, Mr Scott. We have been discreet. We haven't mentioned anything to the media. This really isn't the responsibility of the police force.'

Eddie Scott scrunched up his mouth as though battling to keep something in.

'I'm glad you're here though,' continued Bob. 'Because we need to ask you about Sandra Jennings – or should I say, Carly Watson. You knew she had given you a false name, but you did nothing about it.'

Eddie raised his chin and got back some of his defiance.

'Yes. That's right. She told me her history. I thought she and her daughter deserved a second chance. I just chose to ignore it.'

'That's illegal, Mr Scott,' Bob replied, eyebrows raised.

'Yeah well… I decided that a mother and daughter's lives were more important than worrying about what they called themselves.'

'It's also perverting the course of justice. Why didn't you tell us she was living under a false name when we came to the agency and told you she'd disappeared? You wasted our time.'

That seemed to register with Eddie.

'Sorry. I knew I'd be in trouble if I told you, and besides, I didn't know her real name. I'd told her not to tell me so that I could never make a mistake and risk blowing her cover.'

'I will have to report this. You realise that.' Bob tested Eddie's resolve.

Eddie just shrugged.

'It's all over, as far as I'm concerned. I've had enough of the lies. You need to release Gary Foster, he's done absolutely nothing wrong,' he declared, looking defiantly at Claire and Bob.

'I think that's for us to determine, Mr Scott,' Bob calmly replied.

'He is innocent. There is absolutely no way he could have killed Neil Parsons.'

'How do you know this, Mr Scott?'

'Because he was with me.'

Bob looked to Claire. 'I thought you told us you were at home with your wife?'

'I did. I lied. She knows about it. We kept up appearances for the business. Ask her.'

'Knows about what, Mr Scott?'

Eddie hesitated, his features wrestling as though he were trying to bring up a giant fur ball.

'Gary and I are partners. We've been in a relationship for years. He was with me on the night of the thirteenth.'

Bob didn't miss a beat, although it took Claire by surprise.

'How do we know this is true, Mr Scott? You've both lied about where you were already.'

Eddie had the air of somebody who now didn't care about anything. 'I can find you plenty of people who will corroborate that we're partners. We were at the office that evening. Like we are most nights. I'm sure there will be some CCTV cameras that caught us on the street outside.'

'Why have you been lying about your relationship? This isn't the 1900s,' Claire asked him.

Eddie turned and looked at her in the eyes.

'I run... I ran a dating agency. My wife runs a wedding events company. People wanted *us* to be a happy couple. I've been shoring up the facade of a successful business and marriage for years now. Times have changed, but we hadn't. I should have let the agency go years back.'

Bob sighed as they stood in the corridor outside interview room two.

'We need to see what we can get to corroborate what he's just said about their relationship,' he told Claire.

'I can interview Gary again if you like?' Claire volunteered. 'We've only got Eddie's word for it about the relationship. Maybe he's covering his own arse after seeing Gary arrested?'

'Maybe, but we've got nothing on either of them over Neil's murder, especially not if their alibis stand up.'

'Still doesn't mean they didn't knock off agency clients to try to help the business,' Claire said.

'No. No, it doesn't and if Eddie Scott has been prepared to live a lie all these years to keep the business, then what else has he done? Perhaps that's the tactic, fess up to the gay affair and prove you couldn't have killed Neil, to distract us from looking at the other deaths. Keep digging, but in the meantime, we'll probably have to cut Gary Foster loose.'

With that, Bob disappeared into the Gents.

50

CLAIRE

OCTOBER 19TH 2016

C laire was sitting staring at her screen for inspiration, when the call came through from the front desk.

'There's a Tanya Morgan here, says she needs to speak to the SIO in the Neil Parsons case urgently.'

Bob was on tenterhooks; he'd been expecting a phone call from Vietnam at any time. He'd got the DCS on his back about the extra budget and resources he was now using and yet they'd nothing to show for it—apart from Neil Parsons in the morgue and a suspicion that there had been several potentially dodgy deaths at the dating agency he went to.

'Can you take it for me?' he said to Claire.

She nodded.

Tanya Morgan turned out to be dripping in jewellery that looked remarkably real, as though she'd turned out for a bling competition. She was also very nervous and jittery. An attractive woman underneath the thick make-up, with long dark hair and a petite frame in a floaty long-sleeved coat. She reminded Claire of a trapped bird fluttering around the interview room, unable to sit down.

'Would you like to take a seat?' Claire suggested.

Tanya sat down, but it was obvious she was uncomfortable.

'How can I help?' Claire asked. 'I understand you have some information about the murder of Neil Parsons?'

Tanya nodded vigorously.

'I need to know first that you'll protect me, like. You know… put me on the witness protection programme.'

'We can certainly look into that, but we would have to make an application and it's obviously going to depend on the strength of your case.'

'I can't go back home.' Tanya jumped up again. 'He'll kill me, don't you understand?'

She pulled back the sleeves of her coat and revealed thin bruised arms.

'I got cuts and bruises all over me. He never puts 'em on the face, only places where they can be hidden.'

'Who is he?'

'My husband, Darren Morgan. Drug squad will know 'im. I can give them stuff too.'

Claire wasn't sure if this was a woman trying to find a way to seek help from a violent husband or if it could be genuine information relating to Neil. She didn't have to wait long to find out.

'He killed the wrong bloke. It wasn't him I was having the affair with, but as usual he went ballistic after that bastard Charlie Higgins gave him wrong information.'

'Sorry, are you saying that your husband has killed someone?'

'Yeah, Neil. Poor bugger.'

Claire sat up alert.

Tanya continued, 'He don't know, but I kept some

evidence. He had blood all over 'im like, wanted to show me see. He destroyed everything except I kept one glove. Dropped it after he'd come back pumped up and raped me. It's in my bag.'

Tanya reached into her handbag; Claire could see her hands were shaking. She was a woman who had obviously been through a lot and was surviving on her nerves. Coming here must have taken a lot of courage.

Tanya pulled out a plastic bag with a black glove. Dried blood spatters were easily visible.

'He says he's going to kill me next. I haven't told him he murdered the wrong bloke. They were always out together you see and Charlie's a thick shit. Too many years in the boxing ring. He just made assumptions coz Neil was the handsome one. It's not about looks though, is it? I told Mikey to get out the country, but we're gonna be together again once this is all over.'

Two hours after Tanya Morgan walked into the police station, Darren Morgan was in custody. In the next-door cell was the caretaker from Neil's block of flats, who'd not only sorted the CCTV but had let Darren in and helped him get out, in exchange for a nice hefty sum towards paying off his gambling debts. Tanya, meanwhile, was now less trapped bird and more singing canary, sitting chatting with the Specialist Crime Division about all her husband's 'business' affairs.

A message had been sent to Michael Stratton via the mobile number he gave to Tanya, and the incident room was celebrating the end of the long days and weekend work—for now. They had Neil's murderer.

The relief on Bob's face was palpable, and the exclusion zone around his desk had lifted.

'Knew it was a crime of passion.' He beamed at Claire.

'But what about Rachel Hill and her stalker, or the deaths at the agency?'

Claire felt cheated somehow, that it could all be so easily solved by one woman standing up to her husband.

'We now know they're unrelated, we might need to pass those on to another team.'

'But what about Rachel's stalker?'

'I'll make sure that doesn't get ignored, but it is outside our remit. Whoever is bothering Rachel Hill is not the killer of Neil Parsons. That is our case, DI Falle. We can't solve all the crime in London, and we have to stick to what we've been told to do. I'll make sure it's picked up, don't worry, and we'll finalise the initial enquiries into the agency deaths so we can hand it all over, send it upstairs, and see what's next.'

Claire went to open her mouth to protest. Bob stopped her and drew her aside.

'Listen, I know what happened with Jackie Stiller. I of all people know what you went through with that case, but you need to step back a bit here. We are professionals. You are a professional, Claire. You're letting yourself get personally involved in this because you feel like you let Jackie down. You didn't. Jackie's death was not your fault. There were a whole host of failures in the system that should have protected her.'

Bob stopped a moment and studied Claire's face. She was trying hard not to let her emotions leak onto her features, but she knew he'd see through the mask.

'Rachel deserves to be properly protected, and her stalker brought to justice. I'll make damned sure he is, I promise you. It's just that it might not be you who does it. I also promise that I'll make sure the deaths at the agency are thoroughly investigated. I'll even ask for you to be on that team if it's not given to me. They might decide it's better with a fresh SIO used to cold cases.'

'So you're saying you don't think I should be investigating Rachel's stalker?'

Bob chose his words carefully.

'I'm saying that I don't think it's in your best interests, and possibly not even in Rachel's best interests, that you continue with that case. It was different when it could have been part of our murder investigation, but now... There's a danger here that you could lose sight of the procedures and methods needed because you're emotional about it. I'm not being sexist here. I'd say the same thing to a bloke if he'd had a recent bad outing with a similar case to one he's investigating. I'm saying this to you as a friend as well as a senior officer.'

Claire clenched her jaw and chewed her lip, but she nodded. She wanted to say lots of things, like it was unfair, that she should be given the chance to redeem herself, but deep down she knew Bob was right.

Bob took her silence to be acquiescence.

'The agency deaths are going to be expensive and difficult to investigate, and that's even if they're all suspicious deaths in the first place. From what Mark Rodgers was saying, we may find it impossible to prove that any of them, apart from Todd Fuller, were not natural—let alone find a murderer. We don't have crime scenes to investigate and it's unlikely anything can be proven. This is specialist work.'

Claire appreciated Bob wasn't dumping the case. His report would be thorough. She also knew that what he was saying about proving murders was also true. The same thoughts had been running through her mind ever since Mark showed them the results from Todd.

'What do I say to Rachel?' she queried.

'Go and tell her that Neil's killer has been charged. Her stalker needs to be looked at with fresh eyes. We were viewing him as being connected to Neil Parsons, but that's highly unlikely now. We need to look again at all areas of her life. Maybe it's not even connected to the agency. She'll benefit from it being looked at from a different angle. Also, now we know it's not connected to Neil's killer, there's less likely to be immediate danger to her. The stalker has never approached her or physically threatened her, we can downgrade the threat level.'

'But, sir…' Claire tried to reason with him.

Bob was already walking away and held up his hand to hush her.

'We've had a result, DI Falle, don't complicate issues. Leave the panic alarm with her if you're concerned, but step back and get a sense of perspective on this.'

She should be happy, they'd solved their case, but instead she was fuming. All the work she'd put into the SoulMates killer investigation and they might take the case off her. Even more upsetting was the fact Rachel Hill was going to end up being handed on to some other investigative team. How did she know Rachel wouldn't be treated like Jackie? She'd promised her she'd be safe.

She could see Bob's point of view. They'd assumed Rachel might be in imminent danger from the same person who killed Neil. But what if the stalker was connected to the agency deaths and once word got out that they'd arrested Darren Morgan, whoever had been picking off the agency clients was going to think they'd got away with it? What if they then go after Rachel?

Who could it be? Eddie and Gary had given each other alibis, but did that mean they're both out of the frame? If they're lovers, they could easily be lying to protect each other. Or what about Rosa McKenna? Was she bitter and angry enough to kill?

CLAIRE GOT into the car and sat for a few moments. She felt tired, her body heavy. It had been a hell of a week with work, Jack, Rachel. Someone walked past her, headphones on, marching purposefully forward in bright orange trainers. She wished she could feel like that. She sighed, turned the key in the ignition, and drove off.

Claire was halfway to Rachel's when a call came in from Bob.

'We are on a roll today. Looks like we may have found Rachel's stalker.'

'Really?' Claire was incredulous.

'Lew has just called up. He'd gone round to Bethan Jones's house, the sister of one of the agency deaths, Robert. She wasn't in, so he took the liberty of peering in through her windows. There's an entire room filled with photographs of Rachel, surveillance-type images. Obviously, we're getting a warrant right now to get in there, but I think it's safe to let Rachel know and ask her a few questions.'

'Her stalker is a woman? Have you got her?'

'Nope, not yet, but we will. Neighbour says she's at work, so Lew has gone to find her.'

'That is good news, thanks Bob. Can you ask Lew to let me know what's going on will you? I'll feel a whole lot happier once he's got her and it's all confirmed.'

51

RACHEL
19TH OCTOBER 2016

Sometimes, when life was stressful, Rachel dreamt about her mother. She always came to her, soothing and reassuring. Ever present. Rachel may live on her own, but she was never alone. Each morning she woke up to the sight of her mother's photograph, now in a beautiful silver frame. It was bookended by the little ceramic cow and the small bottle of Angel perfume—its contents long since evaporated.

This morning the alarm jolted her awake, and she was grateful to be ripped from the dark, swirling pits of her nightmare. Hands were grabbing at her from the earth, arms rising from makeshift graves, trying to drag her down. She'd been sweating and her head was throbbing. This intrusion in her life was taking its toll. The constant fear of somebody trying to invade her space, watching her, toying with her. The feeling that eyes were everywhere. Trapped in a jam jar. Nowhere to hide.

She had taken to constantly checking the curtains were fully closed, adjusting the corners, smoothing down the edges, ensuring there was no possibility that any part of the window opening could be left uncovered. She dressed in the near dark, fearing the shadows that might be created, and the thought of her actions being silhouetted for all to see on the curtains.

With no job to go to, Rachel had become a prisoner in her own home, her days only broken by the odd phone call from the estate agent. Allowing strangers into her home had been so hard. The fear that her stalker could arrange a viewing meant she'd kept the sale private, no *For Sale* boards and no advertising.

When the first clients came round with the agent, Rachel sat in her car across the road, watching who went in and ensuring they all came out. She took photographs of the young couple and checked every inch of the house after they'd left to ensure nothing was disturbed.

When they made an offer, cash buyers, she accepted immediately, grateful she wouldn't have to suffer any more visits and on the proviso the sale was quick. She knew it was time to move on. It didn't matter that she had nowhere to go yet, she just had to get away from here.

Her relief that Reg was inside the house and she didn't have to venture out into the back garden was tempered only by his malaise. Separated from his mate, he too had taken up the hunched in a corner pose of Amber that alerted Rachel to her condition. Reg wasn't ill. He was broken-hearted and while Rachel was glad she could focus her time on him and not on her own predicament; she was struggling to draw him out of his depression. It broke her heart to see him like that.

When DI Falle arrived, she was cradling Reg, stroking him and talking to him, hoping that company would ease his loss. She peered around the curtain to see the auburn-haired police detective standing on her doorstep. She looked apprehensive. Rachel wondered what she'd come to tell her this time.

'Rachel,' she greeted her. 'I have some news. Could I come in?'

'Yes, of course.' Rachel smiled. She did like the woman, reminded her of herself in many ways. Completely comfortable in her own skin.

'How is he?' DI Falle nodded at Reg.

'Not good,' Rachel answered. 'He's missing Amber terribly and is off his food. I can't seem to cheer him up.'

They went through to the sitting room and Claire positioned herself in the armchair to the left of the fireplace, opposite Rachel.

'OK, so we have some good news,' Claire began. 'First, we have made an arrest in connection with the murder of Neil Parsons.'

'Great, that *is* really good news. Is it anyone I know?' Rachel asked.

'There doesn't appear to be any connection between the suspect and the dating agency and neither does there appear to be any connection between him and your stalker.'

'Well, I'm glad you've got him.'

'There's more. It's not definite, but I had a phone call on the way here to say that an officer has been to the house of a,' Claire consulted her notes, 'Bethan Jones, and found a room covered with surveillance photographs of you. I'd say that's a pretty big clue to suggest she, or someone who lives with her, is your stalker.'

Rachel's face didn't show any emotion, but inside her heart had lurched.

'Have you arrested her?' she asked.

'Not yet, but we will, they're going round to her workplace now. Do you know her?' Claire questioned.

Rachel thought carefully. How should she answer this? They hadn't spoken to Bethan yet, but it was just a matter of time. That could change things, change how they viewed her and if they believed Bethan, then that could spell real trouble for her. They wouldn't understand the importance of her work. The police detective took her thinking to mean she was wracking her brains to remember.

'We will bring her in for questioning. Get to the bottom of it so don't worry now. The great news is that your ordeal should hopefully soon be over. That's not to say you shouldn't still take precautions until everything is confirmed, as she's not in custody yet, but I'm really hopeful that this is it.' DI Falle continued. 'I can wait with you until we get some further confirmation if that helps put your mind at rest? Do you have any questions?'

'No, it's fine, thank you,' Rachel replied. 'It's a lot to take in, but I'm relieved.'

'It is, take your time.'

'Would you like a hot chocolate?' Rachel asked her. 'I was just about to make myself one.'

'Thanks, I would. Could do with the sugar hit,' Claire smiled back.

Rachel placed Reg down in front of Claire and left them both.

It was such a shame that it was going to end like this. She really had liked her.

52

CLAIRE

19TH OCTOBER 2016

They'd had a really successful day, by any standards, but Claire was annoyed and something didn't feel right. Neil's murder was straightforward, poor sod, mistaken identity. No wonder Michael Stratton was AWOL and making sure nobody could find him. But who was this Bethan Jones, and why was she stalking Rachel? That didn't make sense. They were missing a big piece of the jigsaw somewhere and she was worried that it was going to implode on them. The euphoria of closing the Neil Parsons case and the pressure to save budget might leave stones unturned, and Rachel was still a potential victim.

When she got to Rachel's house, she had opened her front door like a woman under siege, peering out first to see who was invading her territory. There was clear relief on Rachel's face when she saw it was her.

Rachel had sat listening to Claire share the news, stroking Reg the rabbit for comfort. She'd seemed to welcome news of Neil's murderer's arrest, but there didn't seem to be quite so much enthusiasm for the identification of a suspect as her stalker. Maybe she wasn't going to feel safe until they were under arrest, or perhaps she was trying to work out how she knew her.

'Would you like a hot chocolate?' Rachel asked her. 'I was just about to make myself one.'

'Thanks, I would. Could do with the sugar hit.'

While Rachel went off to make the hot chocolates, she put Reg on the floor in front of Claire. The rabbit barely moved, he just sat there, nose wiggling and ears forward. Claire could see why Rachel thought he was depressed.

'Did you ever have any pets when you were little?' Rachel asked her as she came back into the room with their drinks.

'No. My dad wasn't really into animals in the house - or garden for that matter. I always wanted a guinea-pig.'

Rachel bent down and picked up the rabbit which was still sitting grumpily at Claire's feet.

'Oh Reg, what are we going to do with you? Poor broken hearted bunny,' she said to him, kissing his head.

'I can see what you mean about him,' Claire replied and took a sip of her hot chocolate.

'He's missing her so much. I got them both from a rescue centre, they'd always been together. Rabbits need other rabbits, you know, just like most people need somebody. Some people just can't exist without someone special. My dad was like that after my mother died.'

'I don't think my dad's like that,' Claire said. 'If my poor mum died, he'd just buy in a home help and carry on. Lovely hot chocolate by the way. Thank you.'

Rachel smiled weakly at her.

'So have you had the chance to think about why Bethan Jones could be stalking you?'

'I remember Robert, her brother' Rachel began. 'He

was one of those who couldn't live without someone. He was always so sad and lost. I know it's not the sort of thing you'd do—join a dating agency—but for some people, it's a lifeline. Robert was miserable and he just couldn't find anyone. We honestly did our best to help him. Such a shame. He was a sweet man. He and his sister Bethan hadn't seen each other for years. He talked about her but she'd never been there for him. She was his only family, he had nobody.'

'So do you think it was suicide, then? His death?' Claire asked, as she finished her hot chocolate. Its warm sweetness had tricked down her throat and seemed to relax her. It was a nice feeling and she settled back into the armchair.

'He was very lonely, but there are lots of people who aren't able to take their own lives, not brave enough, even if they wanted to. His sister confronted me once, said it was all my fault. I had no idea she'd taken it quite so badly.'

'Hhmm,' Claire replied. Her eyelids were feeling heavy and she'd started yawning. Surely she couldn't be so exhausted that a hot chocolate could make her this sleepy? She tried to rouse herself, shifting in her chair, but her limbs felt heavy and her head started to nod.

'It's OK Claire,' she heard Rachel say, 'You don't need my help. You're not like them, you're strong. It's just you don't know it. Always trying to achieve. You've got nothing to prove to your dad you know. He's the one with issues, not you.'

'What?' Claire tried to stay awake. The room kept disappearing into darkness as she battled to keep her eyes open. She was vaguely aware of a buzzing in her pocket - her mobile phone - but she couldn't seem to lift her arm to answer it.

The last thing she saw before her eyes closed fully, was Rachel's rabbit Reg. He was still lying on Rachel's lap in front of her, and she was still stroking him, but his eyes stared open. Glassy. His head hung loose. Neck broken. Dead.

53

RACHEL

JULY 1994

In one sense, Rachel was glad it was the school summer holidays. She now had weeks without having to go into school, without needing to avoid Stella Wainwright and the rest of her gang. The downside was she had weeks in which to rattle around their farmhouse, watching her father slowly kill himself with alcohol.

The farm had become a wasteland, frozen in time from that day when the cows mounted the wooden ramps and were driven away. Her father had touched nothing. Reg and George never returned. To walk around the farm was like visiting the scene of some strange apocalyptic event. The cow barns remained uncleaned, rats shuffling in the hay and scratching in the feed troughs. The tyre tracks were gone. No vehicles entered their yard unless it was from a utility company come to chase up a bill. In their farmhouse garden the pots her mother used to lovingly tend to were full of dried and withered plants—ghostly skeletons of the beautiful flowers they once were.

Rachel asked if Aunt Alice would be coming to visit them again, but her dad just scowled at her, muttering under his breath. She wasn't sure if her aunt had abandoned them, or her father ostracised her.

Rachel had taken to long walks or to lying in the fields with a book, keen to seek the sunlight. She joined the Holt library and, when she had enough money, caught the bus in, filling her bag with novels that promised a life of colour and excitement beyond their pages. Today she had lain in one of the fields, reading *The Bridges of Madison County* and her mind was in Iowa with Francesca Johnson and Robert Kincaid.

Sometimes she would stay on the bus and not get off at her stop. There would always be somebody who would come and sit next to her and ask her what she was reading, or chat about the weather and their latest ailment. The topic of conversation didn't matter to Rachel. Sometimes she just felt the need to talk to another human being who wasn't inebriated.

Today as she walked home past the barns, she was pulled back from Madison County to Norfolk by the waft from the slurry tanks. The rotten egg smell of the hydrogen sulphide burnt her nostrils and made her feel slightly heady. Her father always forbade her from going into the barn where they'd stored and mixed the slurry, but today she felt emboldened with boredom and slowed down, peering inside.

It had been months since anyone attended to the slurry pit, and with the summer heat its noxious gases were slowly leaching out. She could see a couple of dead rats around the doors to the main tank, even they'd become overcome by its fumes. Rachel knew not to venture in further. She understood the danger of opening the doors and breathing in the gas.

In the kitchen her father had clearly been attempting to make something to eat because he'd discarded a small pan in the sink, something burnt and dried in its bottom. It wasn't the first time he'd put something on to cook and forgotten about it.

She found him in the sitting room searching through a cupboard: books, photographs, and paperwork strewn behind him as he burrowed in hunting.

'Dad, what are you looking for?' Rachel asked.

He was startled, but only in a drunk way, sitting up and trying to focus on her face, swaying slightly as he did so.

'Hello, love. You seen my binoculars?'

'Dad, they got sold ages ago. They were never in that cupboard, anyway.'

'Sold?'

'Yes. Not long after the cows went.'

Rachel sat down on the sofa, choosing the seat on the right so she could play with the threads on the arm where the piping had come unstitched.

'Really?' he slurred.

Her father collapsed back onto his haunches and put his face in his hands. It was only 3 p.m., he hadn't been this drunk this early for a while.

'I've got nothing, nothing. What's the point?'

'You've got me, Dad,' Rachel replied.

'I miss your mum so much.' He started to sob now, shoulders shaking. 'There's no point without her. Why did she have to leave me? There's no purpose left in my life.'

'Dad, we have each other. We'll get through this,' Rachel said, but she knew he wasn't listening to her, not in that state. If she was honest, she's not even sure she believed it herself.

'No.' He stopped swaying for a moment and looked at her hard. 'No. You have to find your own purpose.' Then he swayed again. 'I can't bear this,' he gesticulated around him, 'I can't bear any of this anymore.'

Rachel looked at her father, really looked at him. The man he was. Her dad died that day her mother was killed. She had been sharing her home with a walking corpse for months. He had no hope left in him, no desire for life. Living had become hell. Each morning waking up and knowing that the one you love is no longer with you.

Her father would never be happy again. Life for him had become one long torment.

It was in those next few minutes that Rachel's purpose in life became clear to her.

HE WAS SO drunk it was easy to encourage her father to stumble outside with her. He leant heavily on her shoulder, breathing alcoholic fumes as he lurched from side to side or tripped over a non-existent rock.

'Come on, Dad,' Rachel said gently. 'Let's take you to Mum.'

ON HER WAY back into their farmhouse a few minutes later, Rachel paused to draw a smiley face in the dust on the door. It was over. No more pain. She'd done the right thing, she knew that, but he'd surprised her. He'd surprised her because he'd fought. When she closed the slurry tank door, she'd heard his muffled cry and the scratching and banging on the door. She hadn't expected that, hadn't expected him to fight back. She thought he'd welcome death with open arms, surrendering to the inevitable peace, grasping its release and the opportunity to be with her mum again.

Life was full of surprises.

54

RACHEL

JULY 1994

The hours after her father's death were a blur. At first, she sat in the house for a bit on her own, waiting for her father to talk to her like her mother did, to thank her for reuniting them. She didn't hear him, but maybe it was too early. Maybe he was overwhelmed by meeting her mother again. She worried that she'd lost her mother's company too—that now her dad was with her they'd be happy together and abandon her.

She gathered a few things, sorting through what she wanted and what could stay. She knew she wouldn't be allowed to remain in the farmhouse on her own and she was eager to escape, to explore the world. See what other homes were like, try life outside their farm.

Rachel took her new skirt, the white one her aunt had bought her with the black hem and waistband, and she put it on. She brushed her hair until it was silky and smooth. Then for an hour or so she wandered around the house, touching familiar things, saying goodbye. She wrapped herself in her mother's dressing gown for one last time, but her scent had faded, and it now held only the aroma of dust and a tinge of mould. She didn't find her mother there anymore.

In the sitting room she sat staring at the bottles of spent whisky by his chair. She tried to remember the dad who used to sit there, the man who worked seven days a week and would never have worn his dirty boots and overalls into the house. It was hard to see him, he'd been blotted out by the depressed drunk that took his place, but maybe he'd come back.

Then she walked outside to the yard. It was quiet, and the sun was just beginning to set. The sky had turned a fiery red. The relief of knowing her dad was finally out of pain, at peace, eventually brought the tears and she stood looking out over the fields and watching the birds fly home to their roosts. The tears poured down her face, dripping onto the dry dusty earth below.

By the time she'd walked to the shop to ask for help, her eyes were puffy with the emotion.

THE GROWN-UPS ARRIVED en masse to help her: police, paramedics, social workers. Flashing lights and uniforms filled the yard. Unfamiliar faces peered at her. A blanket was put around her shoulders and she was led to a car. Her aunt was called and that evening she was able to finish reading *The Bridges of Madison County* at the home of a nice foster carer, Lucy, whose eyes clouded over with sympathy each time she looked at her.

They were all so apologetic, as though it was their fault her father was dead. Their fault he'd stumbled into the slurry pit while intoxicated.

· · ·

HER AUNT ARRIVED the next day in her silver Jaguar. She displayed little emotion, and like everything she attended to in life, she dealt with the arrangements with precision and efficiency. Rachel was taken back to the farmhouse to pick up her things.

'Take what you need. I'm getting a clearance company in,' her aunt informed her. 'But I don't want loads of rubbish, you can fill one suitcase.'

Rachel looked at the clothes in her wardrobe and put in just the new things her aunt had bought. She took with her the mementoes and memories she had gathered from around the house yesterday, but the case was still only half-filled. She left space for her new life.

'What about school?' she asked her aunt.

'You'll be going to boarding school,' she replied, as though there weren't any other possibility.

The thought of having to share space with other girls made her go cold, but she would survive. Her father had given her a purpose in life.

THE FUNERAL WASN'T the closure she'd hoped it would be. Deprived of going to her mother's, she had thought it would be a great sense of occasion, but she didn't relate to the coffin in front of her. Her father wasn't in it—he had gone already.

Her aunt refused to allow him to be buried in the out of the way church in Norfolk where her mother lay. Instead, his body was taken to the cemetery where their parents were and he was interred in the family grave. There was no big service, just a brief reading from the vicar, and then Rachel and her aunt stood and watched as they lowered his coffin into the ground.

It was a hot day. Rachel wore the new dress and shoes

her aunt had bought her. It was good to have comfortable feet again and not have her toes being pinched and squashed each time she took a step. She closed her eyes by the grave, imagining herself tipping forwards and into the pit with her father. She didn't. Rachel opened her eyes to the bright white glare of sunshine that warmed her face.

She was blinded for a few seconds, but she saw her. At the other side of the graveyard, watching, was her mother. Rachel blinked, and she was gone. Melted into the blue sky and sunshine.

She looked at her aunt. Her face was set. She could be one of the alabaster busts on top of the big family tombs. There was only a flicker of something in her eyes as she watched her brother's last descent.

At the graveside, there were just the three of them: herself, her aunt, and the vicar. Standing under a tree were two men, the gravediggers, waiting for them to leave so they could finish their day's work.

Rachel liked the peace and quiet of the graveyard, and she allowed it to envelop her. Life was just starting.

She had found her purpose.

55

CLAIRE

19TH OCTOBER 2016

C laire was vaguely aware of Bob speaking to her and of the sounds of emergency radios barking instructions. She felt fresh air on her skin as she was transferred to the ambulance. Then there was an antiseptic smell as they placed an oxygen mask over her face, but nothing more.

Nothing more until she woke up groggy in a hospital bed, dry mouthed and a cannula out the back of her hand. Its sharp needle restricting her movement and a corner of the tape holding it in place, catching on the hospital blanket. Then she became aware of the throbbing and confusion in her head.

As her eyes focused, she saw Lew sitting by the bed reading something on his phone. He smiled at her as she woke.

'Afternoon, DI Falle. Nice of you to wake up and join us.'

A thousand questions were running around her mind, all tripping up over each other and jumbling together. She remembered being with Rachel in her sitting room…

Hot chocolate.

The rabbit

Feeling drowsy.

'What happened?' she asked.

'We're not entirely sure. You were drugged by somebody, but we're not sure if it was Rachel or Bethan Jones. Bethan had been tipped off by a neighbour that we were looking for her and when she wasn't at her work and we couldn't contact you, we went round to Rachel's house and found she'd broken in and was ransacking the place. There was no sign of Rachel and you were out cold in the sitting room. Bethan claims that Rachel hadn't been there when she arrived and that she had nothing to do with what happened to you.'

'Do you think Bethan attacked Rachel?'

'There's no evidence of that and a neighbour saw her leave. Bethan claims that Rachel is your serial killer. Been trying to gather evidence on her for months. She believes Rachel not only killed her brother, but also several other agency clients.'

'No way!'

'Well, we are investigating, but it's a bloody mess. Rachel has totally disappeared. We found her car abandoned at a service station. No idea if she is on the run from us or from Bethan. We were kind of hoping you might be able to help us by filling in what happened. What kind of emotional state was Rachel in? We found a dead rabbit which we presume Bethan killed.'

Claire scrubbed at her forehead with the palm of her hand. At the moment pictures were swirling in a grey mist in her head. She vaguely remembered the rabbit sitting on Rachel's lap but that was it.

'Bethan said she's been following Rachel for months,' Lew continued, 'Trying to scare her into not killing anyone. Reckons that Rachel kills people who are lonely and broken-hearted. But she has no hard evidence at all. For somebody who has been stalking her, she hasn't done a good job of collecting evidence if Rachel really was up to no good.'

'You think Bethan's lying?'

'I think Bethan is a bereaved alcoholic who hasn't got a good grasp on reality. However, what I don't get is why Rachel has disappeared. Did she drug you and go on the run? If so, then that suggests she does have something to hide.'

In her mind, Claire saw a picture of Rachel's scared face peering round the door when she first arrived.

'She was scared, absolutely petrified. She talked to me about moving on.'

'Scared of what though? Us or Bethan?'

'I don't know, I just can't remember any of it…' Claire trailed off. 'I remember getting to the house, talking to Rachel in the sitting room, but after that, nothing.'

Lew shook his head.

'At the moment, there's not a shred of evidence to support what Bethan is saying, and my bet is Bethan's going to plead diminished responsibility, anyway. She was raging and screeching when we took her into custody. Her lawyer is going to argue that Bethan was beside herself over her brother's death, possibly feeling guilty, and then did exactly what you did, saw several deaths and thought it was a high number, so she's looked for somebody to blame. The big question is who drugged you?'

The sound of footsteps interrupted their conversation and a cheery Mark Rodgers appeared carrying three drink cups.

'Hello, sleeping beauty,' he said to her, eyes shining

with warmth and concern. 'I'm glad you're in bed and not on my table.'

'Yeah, thanks, Mark. Funnily enough, so am I.' Claire smiled back. She might be only half conscious, but he could still make her heart leap.

'Thought you might need a nice cup of tea.'

Mark handed Lew one and put the other cup by the side of Claire's bed.

'So,' he said, sitting in the empty chair opposite Lew. 'You always take a nap like that on the job?'

56

CLAIRE

20TH/21ST OCTOBER 2016

L ew dropped her off at home after the doctor gave her the all-clear and discharged her from hospital. He gave Claire his mobile number, said to call if she needed anything. He was being nice. Maybe he was feeling guilty about what happened with Jack.

She wasn't quite sure what to do with herself. The shock of what had happened was still sinking in. She lay on the sofa, forcing her brain to try to see through the fog and remember every detail of her conversation with Rachel. She wrote notes, hoping something would prompt her memory, but it was still just a swirl of confusion and she couldn't quite see those last few minutes before she passed out.

She vaguely remembered Rachel worrying about the rabbit. It was on her lap. Did Bethan kill Reg to get at Rachel? The woman really was insane. Rachel had loved that rabbit. Why did Rachel just disappear without calling the police? She left Claire there. So many questions and no answers. Was Rachel a victim or a killer?

When Lew dropped her off, he asked if she was going

to go for a drink tomorrow with the team to celebrate their success.

'I'm not sure,' she'd replied. It didn't feel like a complete success to her, not until they'd found Rachel and got to the bottom of the agency deaths.

Lew had become thoughtful then—unusual for him.

'Claire, you'll get on better with people if you chill a bit, you know.'

'What do you mean?' she'd asked, surprised by his candour.

'I mean, half the team is scared of you. They're in awe of your determination and drive. It's cool, but sometimes it helps if you show a bit of a human side too.'

She'd felt a bit embarrassed by Lew's honesty. Did she really come across as that driven? That black and white? The old discomfort she used to feel around Jack's easy sociability was re-awakened. She'd go for the drink. She dreaded the thought of it, but she'd go.

She knew she should call her parents, but she wasn't up to it right now. She'd wait and see if they managed to find Rachel Hill in the next twenty-four hours. Her dad would only ask questions she wouldn't be able to answer.

Later, as Claire lay in bed, her mind wandered to what could have happened. She could be dead. No more. A police funeral to be arranged. The thought scared her. It could all have been so different.

In the morning Bob was delighted to see her, in his own inimitable, understated Bob way.

'You gave me a fright yesterday.' He smiled. 'Walked in and saw you out for the count. Thought you'd been on the balloon gas.'

'You don't get rid of me that easily you know.' Claire joked back, but she saw the real concern in his eyes.

'The Neil Parsons case is wrapping up nicely. I suspect you'll want to work on gathering what we have on the agency deaths?' Bob teased. 'Still no sign of Rachel Hill. She's gone to ground. We need to find out all we can on her. I think you'll find Bethan Jones's dossier interesting reading, but it's still looking like a work of fantasy not fact. We're trying to ascertain what was used to drug you and if we can tie it to either woman. In the meantime, Bethan Jones is going nowhere, we've got her on a whole list of charges.'

Before she settled down at her desk to go through it all, Claire headed to the canteen for a coffee and a pastry. Her head was pounding, and she'd had to take some painkillers again this morning. Now she needed some caffeine and something to eat.

She saw them as soon as she walked into the canteen— Jack and Lara sitting together. They looked great as a couple. He was definitely a lot happier with her than he ever was with Claire. She knew in her heart that she hadn't been happy either, she'd known that for a while, but it had been him who was brave enough to make the move for both of them.

The realisation that their relationship had come to its natural end dawned on her and she saw him in a different light. As she paid for her coffee and pain aux raisins, she smiled a hello at them both. They looked surprised, then smiled back. She'd make the peace with them both later.

57

CLAIRE

24TH OCTOBER 2016

Claire spent the next few days sifting through Rachel's life. The school reports told of a normal child before she became bereft with grief following her mother's death, abandoned to her own devices by her father. Her dad's passing was the first question mark in Bethan's evidence trail. Only there wasn't any evidence, just the police reports of a grief-stricken child and an alcoholic father. Once her dad had gone, Rachel's aunt picked up the pieces and put her back together again. There are years when Bethan had been unable to find out anything on what Rachel was doing, where she was living, but there were also many other years where she claimed that a trail of death followed her. A slippery, glistening slug's trail, hard to get hold of, but visible if you looked in a particular light—or had a particular viewpoint to see it with. Bethan had been obsessed.

Claire watched the interview tapes with Bob and Lew questioning Bethan after her arrest. The life she'd led was written on her face. Once a well-respected journalist, she'd fallen victim to the lure of alcohol. For twenty years she'd allowed it to ravage her body and mind, and wreck her relationship with her brother, Robert.

'I tried to reconnect with him,' she told them, tears in her eyes. 'But I had hurt him too many times, let him down so often, that he could barely bring himself to see me.'

She stopped a few moments and Bob offered her a tissue, but she refused to end the interview.

'I spoke to him the day he died. I was trying to get myself back together, and I wanted to tell him. He said that he couldn't see me, that Rachel Hill was coming round for dinner. He sounded happy, excited. Said she had some new ideas for how she was going to be able to help him. Then they told me he'd died. When I asked Rachel about that evening, asked her what he'd talked about, what had happened, she denied ever going round. That's when I first became suspicious. Of course, no one listened to me. I was drunk when I'd spoken to my brother, and I was drunk when I reported it to the police. But I knew, I saw it in her eyes. So I stopped drinking, and I started watching her. I saw her go to Todd Fuller's house. I saw her go in and I saw her come out. She was carrying a suitcase both times. I'd no idea what was in it, what she told Todd was in it. But afterwards, I found out he was dead.'

'Why didn't you report what you'd seen then?' Bob asked her.

Bethan shook her head.

'I asked Todd's neighbour what had happened. They said that he'd just died of natural causes. I couldn't work out what was happening. I doubted myself. You have to understand where I've been in the last twenty years. How could I expect anyone to respect what I said when I have no respect for myself? I admit I was angry at her, I wanted her to suffer. It became an obsession. At first it was fuelled by my own anger at myself, but then I realised I was onto something. Then, I wanted to avenge my brother's death.'

Claire could tell that Bethan was convinced, but she didn't have a scrap of evidence and the Rachel that she'd known bore no resemblance to the cold-blooded killer she was describing. Bob said the same to her in the interview.

'In her eyes she's not killing. She's helping them,' said Bethan. 'She thinks that if people are lonely, they're in pain and she wants to put them out of their misery.'

'But she enjoyed working at the dating agency, helping clients find a partner.' Bob put to her.

Bethan shrugged. 'Yeah, and she got Robert lots of dates, but none of them worked.'

As she watched the interview, something sparked a memory in Claire's head. That last day when she'd been talking to Rachel, she'd said to her about people being broken-hearted and lonely, and there had been something else, but Claire couldn't quite put her finger on it.

SEVERAL DAYS after Rachel's disappearance there were no leads, no sightings, nothing to go on in the hunt for Rachel Hill. She appeared to have vanished into thin air.

'I'm arranging a press conference,' Bob told the team. 'And DI Falle is going to be leading it.'

Claire looked up, shocked. She hated going in front of the cameras.

'You're the last one to see Rachel,' Bob explained. 'You have the best connection with her. Put out a call for her to come in and help us with our enquiries and ask the public for information if they see her. We'll sit down with the press office later to agree on a script. I want to flush her out. We are legitimately concerned for her welfare, as far as we are aware, she is the victim in all this, and we need to be sure she is safe.'

'Do I have to, can't you do it?' Claire asked Bob once the rest of the team had disbanded.

'Yes. You're good at this. You've got a gift, you can talk to anyone, including the media, and come across as professional and friendly. I've put my foot in it too many times before.'

'The team call me Telly Tart as it is.'

'The team respect you. Stop worrying about what everyone else thinks and get on with being a good cop. This is your case.'

Claire was so nervous; she knew that the story had got a lot of media interest. A crazed female stalker convinced that there was a serial killer on the loose who had potentially drugged a police officer and left her victim to flee for her life. There'd be national as well as local TV and papers there, and they'd all be looking at her.

Claire put on a little extra make-up and practised her statement in the changing room mirror when nobody else was around. Then she went out in front of the lights and cameras and asked Rachel to please get in touch to help them with their enquiries. 'I'm concerned for your safety,' Claire said, looking directly into the camera lenses.

It was true. Claire was concerned for her. The doubts and the confusion over what happened in that last hour she was at her house didn't take away the fact she felt responsible for her safety after all the promises she had made her. Yet Bethan had got to her. Something was creeping under her skin and bothering her, and she didn't know what it was. A seed of doubt, perhaps a hint of a memory? Bethan's assertions that she hadn't been responsible for drugging her? The one thing she knew was that the only way to resolve it was to speak to Rachel herself.

By 6 p.m. it was all over, and they were watching it go out on the news. A team was ready assembled to answer the phone calls they hoped would follow and in Jersey, her mum and dad were recording the news on both channels so they could watch her.

Claire watched the news report and her clip of the press conference. She didn't do too badly in the end, although she hated her voice, it sounded so girly. She wanted to sound bold and authoritative, like the DCI when he talked to the media.

Considering how long she talked for and how many minutes of video they shot, they used very little of the press conference. Claire saw images of Rachel's house and the closed door that once led into the SoulMates dating agency, sandwiched between the hair salon and French café.

The big question was, would Rachel get in touch? Or would someone call in with any vital information? Claire sat at her desk, catching up on paperwork, and waited for the phones to ring.

Most of the calls that came in were sightings of women who looked like Rachel. There were, of course, the usual nutters who just rung up for a chat.

Around an hour after the evening news programmes had been broadcast, the calls dropped off and Claire started thinking about going home.

She shut down her computer and was about to stand up to leave when she heard her name being called.

'DI Falle, we have a woman on the line who wants to speak to you, and only you, about Rachel Hill,' one of the civilian support workers shouted across to her.

'Did she give a name?'

'Sally Rochester.'

'OK, don't think I know her. But put her through anyway, you never know.'

Claire took a big sip of her coffee and answered the phone.

'Mrs Rochester?'

'Yes, that's right, is this DI Falle?'

'It is. You wanted to talk about Rachel Hill?'

'Yes,' the voice replied. Claire could hear the nerves.

'How do you know Miss Hill?' Claire asked, fiddling with her coffee cup.

'I'm her mother. My name was Sally Hill and twenty-two years ago I walked out on my husband and daughter. Now I want to help her.'

Claire caught her breath. Was this for real?

'Rachel's mother died.'

'I know that's what she thinks. He told her I'd been killed in a car crash. I left because I could no longer stand being married, but I knew he loved Rachel and I thought he was the better parent. He said I would be dead to them both if I walked out. But I'm not dead. Afterwards, I stayed away because I thought it would mess with her head and because his sister threatened to poison her against me. It hasn't been easy.'

Claire's heart was thumping in her chest.

'Mrs Rochester, are you able to come into the station to have a chat, or would you prefer if I came round to you?'

'I don't mind. I'm just glad I can come clean about this. It's felt like I've been living a lie all these years. I hope she can forgive me.'

Claire had no idea how Rachel was going to react if Sally Hill was for real. She knew that her mother's death and eventually her father's had a huge impact on her life.

So if this was true then it had all been a lie. He'd deceived her, made her think her mother was dead.

Claire now had the bait to lure Rachel out of hiding and ask her the questions which were gathering in her mind.

I HOPE YOU ENJOYED LONELY HEARTS

I hope you've enjoyed reading **Lonely Hearts** and meeting Claire, Rachel and the other characters, in the first of the DI Claire Falle series. Thank you so much for your support.

I would be very grateful if you could spare the time to leave a review on the Lonely Hearts' Amazon page. Reviews are extremely important to authors, not only do they guide other readers, but I write for you and so hearing about your reading experience is a huge part of my motivation to keep writing.

I've written a short novella about Rachel's mother Sally Hill. **Sally's Story** looks at her life before Lonely Hearts begins and explains why she made the decision to leave. It is available FREE and exclusive to members of my readers' club. The club itself is also free to join, you can find out information at: www.gwynbennett.com

Finally, thank you again for choosing to read Lonely Hearts, I really do appreciate your support. Next in the series is ***Home Help***, and you can read the first two chapters on the following pages.

Many thanks and happy reading

Gwyn

HOME HELP

BOOK 2 IN THE DI CLAIRE FALLE SERIES

Some families need more help than others...

When a man is murdered in a London street by a Cobra bite, not surprisingly, the media are very interested. DI Claire Falle is still struggling to deal with the consequences of her last case. When a clue comes up linking the man's murder to her birth island of Jersey, she is sent over to investigate. She thinks returning home will be easy–Claire's in for a few surprises

HOME HELP: CHAPTER ONE

CLAIRE, LONDON: SATURDAY 4TH NOVEMBER 2017

'I can't believe it's happened here, it's a nice neighbourhood.' Trails of cigarette smoke escaped from the woman's mouth as she spoke. She paused to take another drag. DI Claire Falle stepped back slightly, finding it hard to take her eyes away from the woman's black tooth and gash of red lipstick—hastily applied before coming out to share the gossip. No-one ever believed it could happen on their doorstep, but they always wanted to know what went on.

'You didn't see anything? Hear anything unusual? Anyone shouting maybe?'

The woman shook her head. She'd dyed her hair a vivid pink, all the rage in 2017 Britain. Claire thought it was a pleasant colour, but it didn't do a woman in her sixties, with red lipstick and a green lounge suit, many favours.

'Strictly was on. Had it up loud so Felix couldn't hear the fireworks. Bloody things, scare him witless. That JLS lad, Aston something, got voted off —he was the bookies' favourite. Caused a right rumpus. Not my favourite though, Anton and Ruth did a great Pasodoble. That Craig Revel-Horwood called them a drag act, he can be such a bitch sometimes. I think…'

They were distracted from their conversation by a loud screech as a woman rushed from a side road towards the police cordon. Claire was quick to react. She was across the road and had grabbed both of the woman's arms before she reached the car.

'David!' the woman screamed at the top of her voice before collapsing onto her knees, nearly pulling Claire down on top of her. 'My David.'

In front of them the forensic team were working quickly to cover over the scene inside the parked car but, from this angle, David's red, swollen face was still visible. Contorted. Mouth open. His head hung at a strange angle. Circling his shoulders and the headrests and agitated by the movement outside the windows, were two black and yellow snakes which had kept the car doors closed and the emergency services outside. It was obvious the paramedics didn't need to risk a bite.

The white forensic tent encircled the car just as a specialist team arrived to deal with the reptiles. It was just after 9 pm. Right now Claire wasn't sure if this was an accident or murder, but she did know it was going to be a long night.

The paramedics seemed relieved to at least be able to help the hyper-ventilating wife of the snake-bitten corpse. It was bad enough discovering your husband dead, but the sight of him had sent her into immediate shock.

'He hates snakes,' she kept saying over and over. Claire gently tried to coax some information out of her. Where was he going? Was he transporting the snakes for someone? Could this in any way be an accident?

It didn't take long to surmise that two poisonous snakes

being carried in the car of a reptile-hating accountant were highly unlikely. Added to this, the fact that once an attempt was made to open the doors of the car, it became clear they'd been sealed shut, and DCI Robert Walsh's arrival on the scene marked the launch of a murder investigation.

The whole of Pennyfoot Road became a crime scene. Police swarmed through the neighbourhood, knocking on doors, searching for clues. The pink-haired, green lounge suit was in her element, telling anyone who would listen about the gruesome discovery and the grief-stricken wife. Her gossip was lapped up by the row of reporters confined behind the crime scene tape and watched over sentry-like by Special Constables.

Claire escorted the grieving widow, Mrs Alice Lyle, back to her home a couple of roads away, leaving forensics, and her boss, to gather as much as they could.

'Why would anyone do that to him?' Alice asked repeatedly. 'He's just an accountant, why would anyone want to kill him?'

Claire resisted the urge to quote a few famous cases where accountants, ideally placed to have their fingers on the money pulse, have either brought down criminal empires or used their knowledge to make themselves rich.

'That's what we need to find out, Mrs Lyle. Would you mind if myself and a couple of colleagues look through your husband's things? See if we can find any clues? These first few hours are critical.'

Alice Lyle shook her head and whispered a barely audible, 'That's fine.' She stumbled, and Claire caught her elbow to support her.

'Mrs Lyle, can I ask you how you knew your husband had been attacked?'

'Twitter. I recognised his car. Someone had posted a video. They thought he was drunk or something.'

Claire discreetly sent a text to DCI Walsh. They'd want to find that video quickly in case they took it down, as it might show something useful.

Alice Lyle led Claire along a row of neat brick houses. The neighbourhood wasn't affluent, but it wasn't working class poor either. One of the London streets that had seen a 'gentrification' as they called it. In other words, an influx of city workers that had spent money doing up the properties and caused such big hikes in house prices that only the well paid could now afford to buy there.

Halfway along, Alice stopped in her tracks and caught her breath.

Claire followed her stare. In front of them, the door to a house was ajar, light shafted from the hallway into the night. Her heart sank for Alice. Hadn't the woman suffered enough tonight without her house being burgled too?

Alice patted her pockets.

'I didn't take my keys. I think I just ran out.'

'Let me go in first. You wait here.'

Claire left her leaning against the gatepost and gently pushed open the door with her shoe, careful not to contaminate any potential evidence.

The hallway was empty, but she could hear a TV on in the sitting room. Men's voices shouted. She recognised the last episode in the Gunpowder Plot on BBC One. She'd got it on record at home. It was difficult to hear anything else with the TV on so she edged into the house, muscles tensed for action, scanning with her eyes and keeping her back to the wall where possible.

She relaxed slightly when she got into the sitting room. Alice's handbag was in plain sight, her mobile phone on the sofa and a quick check found her purse still inside the bag. If a burglar had entered, they would have gone for the easy pickings first.

Still, she was cautious. After a quick check through the window to see if Alice was still OK, Claire carried on through the rest of the house, all senses on high alert. In the hallway, the movement of her reflection in a mirror startled her. She gulped and then gave the auburn-haired woman staring back at her a hard, "man-up" glare.

It's hard to know what instinct tells you something is wrong, despite what you see and what your head reasons. The kitchen was also seemingly untouched, but something still didn't feel right. Perhaps it was the shift in the air or a disturbance in the balance of the energy of the house, but when Claire opened the study door and found its contents tossed and scattered, she wasn't surprised.

HOME HELP: CHAPTER TWO

The diamond was another beauty, she absolutely loved it. Flawless, ageless and priceless. How ironic. Today's event was regrettable but necessary. The perfect rock in her hand made it all worthwhile. She almost purred as she looked at it. The only sound seeping through the large double-glazed windows was the whisper of waves crashing on rocks. Outside it was nearly dark, but she hadn't bothered pulling the curtains—there was no chance of prying neighbours in this room.

Her mind wandered back to the phone call she'd received just a few minutes earlier. The cobras had been an extra expense. The guy who she'd employed hadn't been keen on her methodology, but thanks to the rapid rise in her Bitcoin values, he'd been persuaded without her feeling out of pocket. Everything had gone to plan. If only *he* knew just how clever she'd been.

The accountant had been foolish, greedy. Pity, she'd quite liked him. His death would be sure to make all the headlines, and that was the intention. The others would be quaking in their beds tonight, and she should have no more trouble.

The gem shone in the lamplight as she held it, caressing its smooth surface. From somewhere down below, a front door banged. Her knuckles turned white, and she took one last look at the diamond before putting it safely away, ready to add to her growing collection.

She knew it wouldn't be much longer now. The accountant's action had triggered her final hand. It was a shame, she'd been enjoying the power trip and the deception. Still, the best was yet to come.

You can buy Home Help on Amazon NOW:
  https://geni.us/HomeHelp

ALSO BY GWYN BENNETT

THE DR HARRISON LANE CRIME MYSTERIES
by GWYN BENNETT

To catch a killer you have to think like one...

Book 1 BROKEN ANGELS

A breath of sky broke through the canopy of trees in the small clearing. A wooden cross had been pushed into the earth, and four candles surrounded the boy. He looked as if he was sleeping, but the rotting leaves upon which he lay were his grave.

In the early hours, Head of the Ritualistic Behavioural Crime unit, **Dr Harrison Lane**, is called to a woodland to find the lifeless body of a young boy. Scrawled across his chest is a Latin satanic exorcism prayer and scraps of paper covered in quotes from the Old Testament are stuffed in his mouth. Who would want this innocent child dead?

Harrison is certain the killer has links with a religious group, and the clue lies in the twisted individual's childhood.

As he delves further, Harrison visits a cemetery and realises he's been there before, dredging up a chilling memory from his past. When he was a little boy, his mother, dressed in a black cloak, had brought him there just before she died.

While Harrison tries to make sense of his traumatic flashback and how it might be linked to the case, a child goes missing while on his way to a leisure centre on a busy Saturday morning.

Can Harrison battle the demons of his own past and find the killer before the life of another innocent child is taken?

This book was previously published under the title **Preacher Boy** *by Gwyn GB.*

READ BROKEN ANGELS ON AMAZON

Also available on audio, and with iBooks, Google, and Barnes & Noble

ABOUT GWYN BENNETT

Gwyn is a writer living in Jersey, Channel Islands. Born in the UK, she moved there with her Jersey-born husband and their children. Gwyn has spent most of her career as a journalist, but is now a full time writer.

You can connect with Gwyn online:
Website: https://www.gwynbennett.com

BRITISH SPELLING GLOSSARY AND POLICE TERMINOLOGY

British spellings have been used throughout this book. Despite sharing a common language, there are clear differences between British and US English including using an 's' instead of a 'z' and 'ou' instead of 'o'.

For example:

analyse vs analyze

Colour vs color

Centre vs center

Grey vs gray

Theatre vs theater

Traveller vs traveler

etc

For American readers, I hope this hasn't reduced your enjoyment of Lonely Hearts.

Ballistic 'he went ballistic' = he was crazy/furious

Bedsit = Small one room apartment with bed/kitchen/living areas as one

Bloke = Guy/man

Boob job = Breast enhancement

Cadaver = Corpse

CCTV = Closed-circuit television or security cameras

Chit chat = Small talk/chatting

Chivvy = Keep saying something repeatedly, can be encouragingly or harassingly

CID = Criminal Investigation Department – plain clothed detectives investigating major crimes

Copper = Police officer

Coronation Street = Longest running British soap opera

DCI = Detective Chief Inspector

DI = Detective Inspector

DS = Detective Sergeant

Duty Solicitor = The lawyer assigned to be on call to help someone who has been arrested with their legal defence

Estate agency = Real estate agents

Feral = Wild, untamed, often formerly domestic animals gone wild

Fess up = Confess

Flat = Apartment or condo

Fork out = Pay for something

Footy = Soccer/football

Gawping = Staring stupidly or rudely

Georgian = Period of British history, 1714-1830 when George I to George IV ruled

Gutted = Really upset

Hedgehog = Small, spine covered creature that lives wild in Europe

HOLMES = The IT/computer system used by police in major investigations

Intel = Intelligence/information

Jager Bomb = Short cocktail shot, usually Jagermeister and Red Bull.

Jots = Notes down

Lads/laddish = Young guy/young guy behaviour

M & S = Marks & Spencer UK retailer – sells food/clothes/homeware etc

Major Incident Room = Office/room used by police team put together to investigate big crimes like murder

Mare 'Having a mare' = is having a nightmare/terrible time

Mate = Good friend

MO = Modus Operandi – a particular method of doing something

Niggling = Annoying

Noses put out of joint = Upset or irritate someone

Nutter = Crazy person

Pathologist = Medical Examiner – trained to investigate deaths and carry out autopsies or post-mortems

PC = Police Constable

Puked = Threw up/sick/vomited

Reccy = Reconnaissance

Scraggy = Scruffy/untidy

SIO = Senior Investigating Officer

Slob = Lazy, scruffy and often unclean person

SOCO/Scenes of Crime Officers = CSI/Crime Scene Investigators

Sod it = Expression of anger/annoyance or couldn't care less attitude

Social Services/Social workers = UK social support service for vulnerable adults and children

Squeaky clean = No police record or signs of past trouble

Stroppy = Bad tempered/grumpy

Takeaway = Takeout food

Tanked up = Drunk/inebriated with alcohol

Tod/On his tod = On his own

Truncheon = Short thick stick or baton carried as a weapon by police

Uniforms = Uniformed police officers, not Criminal Investigation Department (CID) detectives (who don't wear uniforms on a daily basis)

Weasel = Small, slender wild animal – similar to a polecat

Whack 'cost a whack' = Cost a lot of money

Zero hours contracts = Work contract where neither employer or employee is obliged to offer/work a minimum number of hours

Made in United States
Orlando, FL
26 January 2024

42896884R00182